BLOOD TRAIL

DAVID J. GATWARD

WEIRDSTONE PUBLISHING

Blood Trail
by
David J. Gatward

Copyright © 2022 by David J. Gatward
All rights reserved.

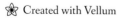 Created with Vellum

To Elijah and Gabriel

Grimm: nickname for a dour and forbidding individual, from Old High German grim [meaning] 'stern', 'severe'. From a Germanic personal name, Grima, [meaning] 'mask'. (*www.ancestory.co.uk*)

"On Pen Hill Crags, he tore his rags.
Hunters Thorn he blew his horn.
Cappelbank Stee happened a misfortune
and brak' his knee.
Grassgill Beck he brak' his neck.
Wadhams End he couldn't fend.
Grassgil End we'll mak' his end.
Shout lads, shout!"

PROLOGUE

Two years ago ...

AS BREAK-INS WENT, this one had been a breeze, and he laughed to himself as he rolled the quad bike quietly away from the farm and down the track. At the end of the track, he pushed the quad bike up onto a rickety trailer attached to a red pick-up truck, which was now more rust than metalwork. It did the job, though, which was all that mattered.

There was easy money and then there was this, and he wondered why he hadn't done it before. Because farmers, he decided, were idiots. Every single one of them. And it was a whole lot easier to nick stuff from a place in the middle of nowhere, surrounded by fields and fells, than it was to break into a house on a street.

Any house in a town or village worth breaking into had security alarms and cameras and pets. Dogs weren't always the worst, either. Cats, though? He hated cats. They'd appear out of nowhere, meow, trip you up, fall on you and scratch your eyes out, then vanish like little furry ninjas. As far as he was concerned, a good cat was a dead cat.

Then there was always the risk that someone was going to see you, not just at a property either, but on a street, a bus stop, at a road junction in another car. Eyes were everywhere because people were everywhere. The police only added to the problem. Not just because there seemed to be so many of them, but because of all that CCTV stuff he'd seen going up over the years. Cameras in every shop, even on some street corners he'd noticed, everyone spying on everyone else, Big Brother watching you. He hated the police more than he hated cats. Not that he'd ever kill a police officer. Unless he had to, of course. At least, that's what he told himself.

Here though, out of town and deep in the countryside, nicking stuff was so stress-free he simply couldn't understand why more people didn't do it. If part of his skill set was to be a proper nosy bastard, then that's what had landed him where he was tonight. He always kept his ears and eyes open, looking for little bits of information that might lead to easy pickings. A loose word here, an open gate there, was all he needed. If only people knew.

He laughed.

It was almost as though the countryside was a huge all-you-can-eat buffet. All you had to do was pick any isolated house, watch it for a few days, then dive in and take whatever and as much as you wanted. Add in the fact that for one night every year people would be out for the night to celebrate that weird local tradition, the Burning of the Bartle, and having a few drinks, too, and it was a winner all round.

Just to make sure everything would go well, he'd done a bit of a recce a few days before, driving around posing as a lost delivery driver. He'd even made up a few fake parcels to carry with him as part of his disguise. Cut his hair, too. In the end he'd decided to hit three places at once. It had meant a busy night, but he'd be well in pocket now for a good long time, that was for sure.

The barn he'd just been rummaging around in was far enough away from the main farmhouse that even if anyone was home, there was no way they would hear anything. The lock on the door had been a joke, the chain giving way to the bolt-cutter like cheese. Inside, he'd been spoiled for choice. The quad bike he'd known about, which was why he had the trailer. What he hadn't been expecting, though, was to be able to bag a chainsaw, a small generator, and an old air rifle, which had been resting in a rack on the wall of a small office inside the barn.

He filled the back of the pick-up with the smaller items first, then once the quad bike was strapped down onto the trailer, he would be on his way. He could already taste the celebratory beer he'd be having when he got back. So what if it was going to be in the early hours of the morning? That beer was going to taste like the best beer in the world. He might even have two. And there was some leftover takeaway in the fridge from that place round the corner. A well-deserved feast, for sure.

A few minutes later, and with the quad bike nice and secure, he shuffled down the side of the pick-up and jumped up into the driver's seat. Lights drifting slowly up the valley caught his eye. He watched them disappear again into the dark, leaving it a few minutes before easing off the hand-brake. They were nowhere near him, but there was no point doing a nice little job like this then being caught out by some late-night passer-by. At last, he rolled the vehicle and trailer silently down the lane to the road.

Ahead of him, dark vales sat waiting. Wensleydale was fast asleep now with the brightest moon he'd seen in a long time perched high overhead. He'd always wondered why anyone would choose to live here, how they coped with the monotony of the place, the boredom. He'd certainly never been able to.

Even though the town was small, he preferred living there. He could leave the house and, within a few minutes, buy everything from a pasty to a car to a couple of pints. Hell, even some antiques and a few stuffed animals if he wanted to. Out here, though? Everything was miles away. Why anyone would want to live in a place where you had to get in your car to buy a pint of milk, he hadn't the faintest idea.

Rolling through the gate at the end of the lane, he turned on the ignition and the engine rumbled to life. Lights off, and in first gear, he eased out onto the main road. He drove just far enough away to see the farm disappear in his mirror behind a small woodland, then turned on his head-lights. A bright arc of white light splashed out across the road.

A figure walked straight out in front of him.

He hammered his foot down on the brakes. He felt the rear of the pick-up twist and turn as the trailer reacted to the sudden drop in speed, snaking left and right, threatening to jack-knife. Pumping the brakes, he managed to get just enough control back and prevent catastrophe, bringing the pick-up and trailer to a stop.

Heart racing, his arms ached from gripping the steering wheel so hard. He was angry, too. What kind of lunatic walks around the lanes at night jumping out in front of vehicles? He looked up, but the figure was gone. Lucky for them, he thought, because he was well up for having words and punctuating them with fists.

A knock at his window plucked at his already tightly strung nerves. He turned to see ... nothing.

Seconds passed, filled with the sound of his own heartbeat, almost deafening in the silence.

Another knock, this time at the passenger window.

He snapped around, stared into the dark, saw it yawn back at him, like it was trying to suck him in.

Something was off about this. It didn't feel like a prank, like someone just messing about. He felt threatened. What if it was the owner of some of the stuff in the back of the pick-up, he thought?

Sod this ...

The engine was still running. All he had to do was get out of there and get home. They'd never catch him, would they? Time to shift it.

He stamped on the accelerator pedal, but a bright flash of light off to his left startled him, followed by the sharp, deafening crack of a gunshot. The night broke in two and the pick-up's engine stalled.

Not just shaking now, but crying, because this was all so wrong, and he just wanted to get out, get going, get home, he turned the ignition and sparked the engine to life.

Another flash, another gunshot, this time to his right.

The pick-up juddered forward, and he knew his front tyres were dead. He'd get nowhere trying to drive on them.

He wiped his eyes, angry at himself for losing control so easily. He punched the roof of the pick-up, roared, swore.

They'd shot out his tyres and, by the sound of it, had used a shotgun to do it. But he was still alive, so that was something. Maybe they didn't want him dead. Maybe they just wanted to scare him then grab him before they called the police, he thought.

He had nothing to use to protect himself, no weapon at all other than a half-empty can of Coke, the crusts from a very unappetising cheese and onion sandwich he'd bought from a garage earlier in the day, and a pocketknife. The knife had a locking blade and had a seriously mean edge. Good for a quick stab in a pub or a dark alley, but it would be no match for someone wielding a shotgun. The air rifle might have been useful, if only as a threatening silhouette, but that was in the back and not exactly to hand. His choices were limited. Either stay in the pick-up and wait it out, or make a run for it.

Time turned to treacle as he stared into the dark, searching for the courage to escape. Where he'd go wasn't an issue right now. He'd lose the haul from the night, but there would be other farms, other houses to turn over. He'd worry about the pick-up later. All that mattered right now was getting the hell away and staying alive.

The night was silent, the darkness all around him pulsing in time with his racing heart. He took a deep breath, had another quick look around, then opened his door and jumped out.

A fragment of the surrounding night broke away and stepped out of the gloom. He saw a figure built of shadow.

He turned, he ran, his lungs heaving in the cold night air, legs and arms pumping. Then something crashed into him and all his strength disappeared, his legs gave way, and he was on the ground, face in the grit, in the dirt, rolling and tumbling. A split second later, he heard a boom from the shotgun, the sound of the shot that had just smashed into him.

Pain then, a dull ache, and a coldness stretching through him as though a bottle of iced water had been emptied down his back.

He moved slowly, edging into deeper darkness, seeking some haven in the long grass and bushes and broken sticks from whispering trees, pulling himself along with his elbows, the tips of his fingers.

He saw a face in the moonlight, didn't move, didn't breath, not for the longest time.

No choice now, no choice at all.

He reached into the back pocket of his jeans, clenching his teeth as white-hot pain coursed through him, and found his phone. By the time his call was answered, the world was already fading, a grey blanket dragging itself over his heavy eyes.

CHAPTER ONE

PRESENT DAY ...

'SO, you ready, or am I going on my own?'

Detective Chief Inspector Harry Grimm was sitting in his flat in Hawes. Grace had just walked through from the bedroom all dressed and ready for an event she was taking him to down dale. She smiled as she asked the question, warmth in the small creases at the corners of her mouth.

'You're not asking that because I'm supposed to change into something posh, are you?' Harry asked, already baffled by what lay ahead that evening. Whatever it was, he was certainly hoping it didn't involve dressing up.

Grace's laugh was as bright and happy as the sound of a stream burbling over pebbles.

'No, I'm not,' she said.

'That's a relief. I don't really have anything posh, or smart if I'm honest. Haven't had since I left the Paras.'

'But you're in the police,' Grace said. 'Surely you had things to dress up for?'

Harry shrugged. 'That doesn't mean I actually did.'

Harry was a man whose wardrobe had always served but one purpose: to be practical. Fashion had nothing to do with it. So, he bought clothes based on three things alone, all of which he viewed as vital: cost; washability, and wearability. It was an approach which had certainly done him well over the years. Though he was realising now, with Grace around, he might have to change things a little. Not too much, or too soon, though. These things took time to consider.

Harry stood up.

'Well, that's a relief,' he said, checking his watch. 'We're off now then, are we?'

'West Witton isn't that far, but we'll need to find somewhere to park,' Grace said. 'The Burning of the Bartle is pretty popular.'

Harry knew West Witton as well as he knew any of the villages in Wensleydale now, though less well than Hawes, which had become home. Situated down the Dale, towards Leyburn, it was a place that lined either side of the main road, and whose main purpose seemed to be to bottleneck traffic and make people swear at each other from behind their windscreens.

When Grace had told him about the Burning of the Bartle, he hadn't really been sure how to react. It sounded like a weird version of Bonfire Night, just more brutal and disturbing. Taking place on the Saturday closest to St Bartholomew's Day in August, it was something the locals looked forward to and had kept going as a tradition for decades, which only added to the strangeness.

'And this happens every year, does it?' Harry asked, grabbing his jacket. Smudge, the black Labrador puppy he'd somehow acquired during an investigation a while ago, did her level best to trip him up as he made his way through to the hallway. 'You all gather round, follow a stuffed dummy, then burn it?'

Smudge was certainly growing, he thought, her enormous paws no longer looking so out of whack with the rest of her. Though this increased size only added to her clumsiness, the puppy enthusiasm for life throwing her into furniture and walls and gates and anything else in her way on an almost hourly basis.

'It happens every year, yes,' said Grace, 'but there's a bit more to it than that. And it's more of a down-the-dale thing really, so it's fairly localised. I don't think many folk from Hawes head over. Which is probably why you didn't hear anything about it last year.'

'So, you're to blame, then?'

Grace laughed.

'I Reckon most think it's a bit odd. Which it is, but oddness adds flavour to a place, doesn't it?'

Like the locals' quite astonishing dedication to cheese and cake, Harry thought. Though that was a taste he'd somehow not only become used to but found himself enjoying. The Dales were, it seemed, getting under his skin.

'Can't say I blame them,' he said. 'It sounds bloody weird to me, if I'm honest.'

'And you always are.'

Harry's younger brother came through to the hall to squeeze past.

'It's a little bit cosy, this place, isn't it?' Ben said as he reached for a jacket, his elbow brushing against Harry's nose.

'You're off, then?' Harry asked.

'Heading out to the same thing as you,' Ben said. 'Liz is picking me up on her bike.'

'Going well, is it?' Grace asked. 'You and Liz?'

'It is,' said Ben, and Harry warmed at the smile on his brother's face. There had been times he'd wondered if he'd ever see something like it in their lives. 'Rides like a nutter, though.'

'Not the kind of thing you should be telling your older brother, who also happens to be her senior officer,' Harry said, referring to one of the two Police Community Support Officers on his team, who also happened to be dating his brother. 'Especially not right before you jump back on that thing.'

Ben laughed and rested a hand on Harry's shoulder.

'You worry too much.'

'And you don't seem to worry at all. Also, it's my job. Comes under the Older Brother job description.'

'Perfect!' Ben said, then pushed his way out into the evening air. 'See you later.'

'He's got a point though,' said Harry, glancing at Grace as he hauled on his own jacket, his hands scraping the walls as they pushed through the sleeves.

'About what?'

'The size of the place. It's been good here, I know, but it'll be sensible to get something else.'

'You're still looking to move, then?'

'It would be good to buy something,' Harry said. 'I can just about afford to, I think. Though I may just keep on renting. Just have to see, really.'

'Got anything lined up?'

'Not yet. I'll pop into the estate agents, see what's what, start the ball rolling.'

'Places go quickly round here,' said Grace. 'Not enough houses for the number of people who live in the area for a start, and those that do come up are usually too expensive for most people.'

'Oh, I've realised that.' Harry had already been having a look at a few places on the Internet, and that had almost put him off.

'Outside buyers flounce in and pay stupid money for their own little slice of the James Herriot way of life. I don't blame them for it, but it's no help to those who live and work here.'

'You'll remember then that I'm an outside buyer,' said Harry. 'Though, I don't think I do much flouncing. Not sure I'd know how to.'

'And I think I speak for everyone when I say, I'd prefer it if you didn't try.' Grace laughed. 'Anyway, you're not. You live here, you work here. You're not buying a cottage for half a million just so you've got somewhere to bolt to at the weekend, are you? That's the difference.'

Harry wasn't so sure but said no more. Hawes was home now. He'd made that decision by turning down the offer of a job back in Bristol. He was here to stay.

Climbing into Grace's vehicle, Harry asked again about the oddly named Burning of the Bartle.

'So, how long has this been going on then?'

'No one really knows for sure,' Grace said, starting the engine. 'It's completely unique to West Witton as well. Most reckon a couple hundred years at least. Hard to say, mind.'

'You mean there aren't dozens of villages up and down the country burning a Bartle? You do surprise me.'

'And stabbing him,' Grace said. 'Don't forget the stabbing. That's very important.'

'How could anyone?' Harry said. 'And no one knows who this Bartle is, then?'

Grace eased her vehicle off down the road, the thrum of the tyres soft and gentle.

'Probably some sheep rustler who was chased around Pen Hill by the locals before they caught him and finished him off. A bit of local vigilante justice.'

'It's a little worrying that something like that's celebrated,' said Harry.

'It's nothing more than a bit of fun,' said Grace. 'And a place needs its weird traditions, doesn't it? It's no different to Bonfire Night, really, if you think about it.'

Harry wasn't so sure. He'd had run-ins with vigilante justice before. Not much, but enough to know it was never a good idea and that it invariably got out of control.

'So, are you going to tell me what it involves or is it all a delightful surprise?' Harry asked.

'Better for you to experience it as it happens, I think,' said Grace. 'We'll park in the playing fields and walk up. You'll have a chance to grab a pint afterwards as well if you want. The ones who carry the Bartle end up half-cut thanks to all the drinks they're given.'

Harry found himself thinking back to an event that had crashed into his and Ben's lives with such force the ripples had yet to fade.

Arriving home on leave from the Paras, he had come home to find the lifeless body of their mother on the floor, and Ben battered, bruised, and sobbing in the dark. Intent on seeking out his own form of justice on the one responsible – their own father – he had tracked him down, only to have his own actions unintentionally help the man escape not only from him, but the police. By taking the law into his own hands, he had ultimately ended up in its way. He would never make that mistake again, or allow someone else to, either.

The August evening was balmy, the air rich with the scents of high summer and a land steeped in agriculture. Harry noticed notes of dry grass and pollen wafting in through his open window. Behind that was the occasional thin scent of sheep, and maybe, if he concentrated, he could just catch the peat of the moors and the heather burning up under the hot, early evening sun.

Arriving in West Witton, Grace parked up and led Harry back into the village. A bellowing voice called out and Harry saw Matt waving to them. With him, in her wheel-chair, was Joan, and in her arms, their new-born daughter, sound asleep.

'Look like a proper little happy family, don't they?' Grace said, waving back.

'They do that,' agreed Harry. 'Though, I wonder some-times if that's Matt's default setting, being happy, or at least generally positive, no matter what the day's been like.'

'World's most content man?'

'Something like that.'

'Now then,' Matt said, as Harry and Grace arrived. 'Ready for this?'

'As ready as I can be, I think,' said Harry, then he looked down at Matt's wife. 'How are you, Joan? And the wee one?'

'We're all doing fine,' Joan said. 'Seems I love this little bugger more and more each day, even though that seems impossible.'

Harry could see the tiredness in her eyes, her lids half-closed, though her smile was enough to keep the weariness at bay.

'Pleased to hear it,' he said. 'I'm assuming Matt's doing his fair share and looking after you both.'

'Always,' Joan said.

'Come on, we'd better get on,' said Matt. 'It'll be starting soon.'

Harry fell into step behind Matt as he pushed Joan along, his pace swift and steady. Once in the village, they made their way along to where a crowd was gathering. Harry could make out in the centre two men holding a dummy between them, like a Bonfire Night guy, holding him up as though he was a little the worse for wear. Then, after gathering everyone together, the older of the two men shouted out in rhyme:

'On Pen Hill Crags, he tore his rags. Hunters Thorn he blew his horn. Cappelbank Stee happened a misfortune and brak' his knee. Grassgill Beck he brak' his neck. Wadhams End he couldn't fend. Grassgil End we'll mak' his end. Shout lads, shout!'

The crowd cheered.

'I'll be honest,' Harry said, shaking his head, confusion screwing up his face a little, 'I've not the faintest idea what it was he was saying or what any of it even meant.'

The two men were then presented with a couple of glasses of whisky from a nearby house. These were sunk swiftly and then they moved on.

'What it is, you see,' explained Matt as they followed on, 'is a rhyme about the chasing of Bartle. There's even a little trail you can walk around if you want. It's quite popular. You can see all the places mentioned on a nice little afternoon stroll. Grace'll take you one day, I'm sure.'

'Does anyone think this actually happened, though?'

Harry asked. 'That some poor sod was chased down by the locals, stabbed, then burned?'

Matt went to answer but was interrupted by a voice from behind Harry that he didn't recognise.

'If you ask me, we could do with a little more of it around here.'

'Too bloody right,' agreed another, and then a general murmur of agreement rippled through the crowd, chilling Harry's blood just enough to stop him dead.

CHAPTER TWO

HARRY TURNED SLOWLY ENOUGH FOR EVERYONE TO notice. Which was the point, really, because sometimes his presence was enough. He found himself under the steely gaze of a short man with a round face and narrowed eyes. He was staring through a pair of thin-rimmed glasses as though he didn't approve of wearing them, but knew he had to. He looked, Harry thought, like a mole with a bad temper. Various others were standing around and about in the crowd, some looking at Harry, others pretending to look elsewhere, but clearly more interested in what he might now say in response to what he'd just heard.

'Don't know what you're looking at me for,' the man said.

'Let's just say my police sense gets a little bit twitchy when I hear something like that,' said Harry. 'Though I'm assuming you're just talking rather than being serious.'

Harry held the man's eyes for just a little too long, making his point nice and clear.

'Oh, I know who you are,' the man continued, pushing his glasses deeper into his face, leaning in closer. 'We all do.

Grimm, isn't it? That new detective fellow up at Hawes. I'm Andrew, in case you're wondering. Andrew Greenwood.'

'I'm Detective Chief Inspector Grimm, yes,' said Harry. 'And I've been here a while now. It's good to hear that people know who we are.'

'You're not exactly easy to forget,' Andrew said.

'Then it's probably best that I remind you that's what the police are for,' said Harry, immediately wishing he'd just kept quiet. And this was a night off, wasn't it? Just a bit of fun, nothing to worry about. People were allowed to air their views about whatever they wanted, after all. But then again, so was he, and he'd never been one for zipping it.

'Like I said, it wasn't me that said anything,' Andrew said. 'But I find myself agreeing with it, which is what you heard.'

Harry looked around to see who had spoken first. No one stood out and no one was putting their hand up to admit it, either. A sea of eyes stared back at him.

'And we all know what's been happening, don't we?' Andrew continued.

This comment baffled Harry.

'Do you?' he asked. 'What's been happening? How do you mean?'

Another man leaned in, pushing past the other as though he wasn't even there, his face thick and meaty, eyes mean and narrow. When he spoke his voice was quiet, conspiratorial, dark, as though there was menace hiding behind it, afraid to come out and show itself.

'One officer strung up, another in a hit and run. We've all heard about it, so don't go thinking we haven't. Something needs to be done.'

'That's what I'm trying to say, Steve,' Andrew said.

'Well, you're not saying it well enough, are you? And we talk about it every year, some of us, don't we? Every time we do this Bartle thing we think, you know what? They had balls back then, didn't they? Chasing down a criminal, sorting it all out themselves.'

'Some of us are worried,' Andrew said, looking at Harry. 'A lot of us, actually. Properly concerned, if you must know. It's not right. None of it. Not here. Not in the Dale.'

'Freak events,' Harry said. 'Bad things happen beyond our control. I can't see that there's anything for you to be worried about. That's my job, and the job of the rest of the team.' He eyed Matt. 'Isn't that right, Detective Sergeant?'

'It is,' Matt said, but Harry could see from the look in their eyes they weren't about to shift their position.

'With regards to those incidents you've just mentioned, all of those responsible were caught and dealt with accordingly,' Harry added. 'So, like I said, there's nothing for anyone to be worrying about, I assure you. And certainly no reason to be taking any unnecessary action, if you know what I mean.'

'I reckon there's a few of us around here thinks you could all do with a helping hand,' said the man Harry had heard Andrew call Steve. As he spoke, Harry thought how he looked like he was chewing gristle. He moved closer then, resting a hand on Harry's arm as though trying to comfort him. Which was the last thing Harry needed. And even when he did, touching him was never a good idea. But there was no comfort here, because the grip was more than a little condescending.

Harry moved away just far enough to allow Steve's hand to fall.

'It's not that we don't think you do a good job,' he said. 'You do, a great one, actually. You've a cracking little team and we respect you all. But there's nothing wrong with the locals getting more involved in things, now, is there? We're all in this together, aren't we? Look after our own and all that, you know?'

Harry frowned, clenched and unclenched his hands, took a long, slow breath in through his nose, and then out again, working to keep himself calm.

'I'm not sure that chasing people across the moors to stab them and set them on fire, all while reciting poetry, is the help we need,' he said, pretty sure that this wasn't what the man was suggesting. At least he hoped it wasn't.

A woman stepped into the conversation. Her hair was pulled up in a bun so tight that Harry wondered if it had been permanently glued in place. There was a healthy air to her, he noticed. This was someone who spent a good amount of time outside. Though there was stress in the corners of her eyes and lying deep in the shadows beneath them.

'Something needs to be done about all that dog shit for a start,' she said. 'It's everywhere! Not good for Martha, or any of the others. I know who's responsible, too, not that anything is ever done about it. And we've had a few things go missing. We all have, haven't we?'

Nods and murmurs of acknowledgement bristled through the crowd.

'I think there are more important things to worry about than dogs doing their business in your fields, Agnes, if you don't mind me saying so,' Steve said.

'We had some fencing go missing,' said a voice from somewhere in the crowd.

'My old trailer disappeared last year,' said another.

Harry, though, was looking at Agnes.

'Martha?'

'I own goats,' Agnes said, as though that explained everything. 'Martha's our oldest. We've a herd of them. Dog shit doesn't do them any good at all. And I can't lose any of them, not just because of the cost of it, but for Danny's sake.'

'Danny?'

'My son.'

Harry was beginning to feel as though he was getting sucked into a whirlpool. He didn't quite know what to say, so he suggested that if she suspected anyone of fouling a public place, or of taking anything, then she should report it.

'We've a footpath that runs right through the farm,' Agnes said. 'There's folk walk along there with their dogs just shitting all over the place. Wherever I go, there it is, massive stinking piles of the stuff. And do they clean it up? No, of course they don't. They just leave all that awful dog shit behind for me to clear up. It's disgusting. But it's not just them, is it? It's my neighbour, him and his dogs. They're the worst. Not that he cares.'

'Have you reported it?'

'There's no bloody point, is there?' said Agnes. 'What can you do about it? Really?'

'I'm sure we can do something,' Harry said. 'Police, remember?'

'There's always Neighbourhood Watch, as well,' another voice said, though Harry couldn't see where it had come from in the crowd.

The comment garnered a few laughs.

'Neighbourhood bollocks, more like,' said Steve, and to Harry it seemed like he had taken over proceedings. 'Anyway, you're just one man, Keith. You do your best, right enough, but I'd have thought after all you've been through, you'd agree with what I'm saying. So pipe down, eh?'

Whoever Keith was, he said nothing more, put in his place.

'Anyway, I can't go blocking off public rights of way, can I?' Agnes continued. 'We've all got the same problem. Folk can just walk on our land, look at what we've got, see if any of it's worth anything, then come back and help themselves.'

'I can see that security is an issue,' said Harry.

Agnes, though, was on a roll, and back to the dog issue.

'And why is it that even if they use a poop bag, they seem to think it's fine to just hang it from a tree or leave it at the side of the path? It doesn't make any sense!'

Voices from around them chirped in with their agreement.

'I'd like to pick all of that shit up and shove it through their front door, that's what I'd like to do!' Agnes said.

'You could set it on fire, too,' someone suggested. 'That'd show them.'

Harry noticed then that more and more faces were leaning in with interest and general murmurs of approval were bouncing around with abandon. He gave Matt a wide-eyed look to say *Help*.

Matt took the hint.

'Well everyone, it looks like the Bartle is at the next house,' the detective sergeant said, stepping forward to push Joan towards what was happening. 'Best we get along, now, hadn't we?'

With the gathering crowd distracted just enough, Harry was able to make a break for it and move on. But no sooner had they stopped than Agnes, Andrew, and Steve were with them again, along with a few new faces for support.

'We only want to help, you see,' said Andrew. 'You can't be doing everything. Not fair to expect you to, either. We're a community in the Dale, you know that. Like to do things ourselves whenever we can. We look after our own.'

'Too right we do,' said Steve, stepping forward again. 'We've sorted things out before, you know, and we'll sort 'em out again, that's for sure.'

He punched a fist into an empty hand. The sound of it was the thick slap of a steak on a chopping block.

'Look,' Harry said, locking each of them in turn with his stare, forcing them to come under the shadow of his scarred face, 'I understand where you're coming from. I really do. You can trust me on that.'

'Well, that's good, then, isn't it?' Steve said. 'You agree with us, that we should help.'

'That's not what I'm saying,' Harry said. 'At all. You see, the thing is, what you're talking about, it really is best left to us, to the police. It's our job to enforce the law. That's what we do. What the public pays for.'

'Oh, we know that,' agreed Steve. He looked like he was about to say something else when Andrew stepped forward.

'Look, we're not talking about doing anything daft, are we? Just that maybe we should all be keeping an eye out a bit more, that's all. That seems to make sense to me.'

'And me,' said Agnes.

Another voice quietly added from somewhere in the crowd something about *finding the buggers who keep nicking my hay* and what they would do to them with a drench gun.

'But people are people and good intentions don't always lead to good outcomes,' Harry said. 'As for doing anything daft, giving out your own form of local justice, for example, is best avoided for exactly that reason. And we—the police, that is—would only end up having to do more to sort it all out. So, my advice? It's best avoided by everyone, I think.'

'We could fix up a trailer like a little prisoner van,' a voice said to Harry's right, a new member of the Wensleydale Justice League, he noted.

'That's not quite what I mean,' said Andrew, a frown on his face. 'What I'm talking about is more of a sort of sharing of information, maybe a deterrent by presence or something. That kind of thing.'

'Well, it makes a lot of sense, I reckon,' said another voice.

'No, it doesn't, and you won't be doing so either,' Harry said, working hard to keep from raising his voice. He kept it firm, though, the edges hardening to make sure everyone who heard him understood. But it wasn't easy, and the members of this small, impromptu crowd were clearly not interested in listening.

'Andrew's onto something,' added another. 'We're all of us out and about plenty often enough, aren't we? If we had like flashing lights or something, then folk would know we were around, what we were up to.'

Cheers of approval for that, the idea of flashing lights clearly exciting them.

'And we've all got an empty barn or two,' said another. 'Make a nice place to put someone to have them think on what they've been doing, if you know what I mean.'

Cheers and a bit of laughter at this ripple through the crowd.

'Bit of chicken wire across the windows, stop the buggers getting out,' added another voice, which followed by more cheers.

'Throw a tup in there, too,' said someone else. 'That'd definitely have the sods reassessing their life choices.'

Laughter joined in then, and Harry hoped it meant that perhaps those around him weren't as serious as he'd first thought. Though as the laughter continued, it clearly wasn't as jovial as he had hoped. And he knew full well that sometimes people do stupid things with very little encouragement, and the smallest of seeds could easily grow into the biggest of mistakes.

A few steps away from where they stood, one of the men carrying the Bartle started his rhyme again. The crowd cheered. Harry was pleased with the distraction, but it still wasn't enough.

'We just want to help,' said a man with the most enormous sideburns Harry had ever seen. 'And this is where we live, isn't it? It's our home. We should do something, surely, to help look after it. Things go missing, and we can't report everything, can we? What's the point?'

'The point is that you should always tell the police,' Matt said. 'That's always the best way. Just keep us informed, and we'll do the best we can.'

'You're not going to be fussed if a feeding trough goes missing though, are you?' said another member of the crowd. 'Stuff like that ends up in some vintage store down south, sold to some daft sod who thinks it'll look nice in their garden.'

'Yeah, you've plenty to be worrying about, as it is,' said someone else.

'You all know where we are and who we are,' Matt said, this time his voice firmer. 'And I don't need to say it, but I will ...' Harry saw him turn his eyes firmly on the woman. 'I know all of you, too. Don't I, Mrs Hodgson? And you, Andrew. And the rest of you, too.'

The bustle and bluster of those closest to them visibly died. Harry watched as the crowd seemed to deflate a little, though not enough to make him think that they were rethinking the opinions they had so enthusiastically voiced.

'So, if anything untoward happens,' Matt continued, 'or if I see someone dressed up like the caped crusader, or maybe a tractor comes trundling along with some poor sod locked in a trailer, then I'll know where to come looking, won't I?'

For a moment, no one said anything, Matt's words slowly sinking in.

Agnes broke the silence.

'So, are you going to do anything about the dog shit in my fields or not?' she asked. 'You'll have a word with my neighbour, at least, yes? Chris Black, he is. Not that he'll listen. That's not his strong point really, the great big arrogant bastard that he is.'

'We will do everything we can to help,' Harry said. Then wanting to kill this conversation and get back to enjoying the evening, he added, 'Perhaps I could pop out to see you next week sometime?'

'Perhaps I'll see you first,' Agnes said. 'If I can spare the time, I'll be over.'

'Great, we'll look forward to it, Agnes,' Matt said, a huge disarming smile on his face.

Agnes and the others who had spoken faded into the crowd.

'Well, they were a blood-thirsty bunch, weren't they?' Grace laughed.

'You may laugh, but I've seen where it can lead,' said

Harry. 'It doesn't take much for things to get very *Deliverance*, if you know what I mean.'

'They're just trying to help,' Matt said. 'Good film reference there, though. I'm impressed.'

'Maybe they are,' Harry said, 'but it's the kind of help we really don't want and we aren't about to encourage, either.'

A while later, the crowd gathered around as the Bartle was thrown with more than a little force up against a stone wall. Then the man who had recited the poem all evening did so again, stabbing the Bartle as he did so. And finally, just to make absolutely sure, he poured fuel on it from an oily container and set the poor thing on fire.

The crowd cheered as the flames gobbled up the straw-filled torso. Harry wondered just how chilling a sound that must've been back in the days of a public execution.

'I feel like I've walked onto the set of The Wicker Man,' he said, as the warmth of the flames whumped out and across the crowd.

'Two great film references in the same night,' said Matt. 'Ten points for that, I think. You're on fire!'

'So is that Bartle bloke,' Harry said. 'And I didn't know it was a competition.'

'It is now.'

The Bartle burned. It was a sad-looking thing, Harry thought, as the body slumped forward and the head rolled off, which garnered a very enthusiastic cheer from the crowd, particularly a small group of children laughing and pointing at the flames and the gradually collapsing body against the wall. He thought about what Agnes Hodgson and Andrew and all the others had said, the general sound of approval for prison trailers and locking people in barns.

Yes, it had been tough for the team this past while, they

were right. But as he stared at the smouldering remains of the Bartle and watched the silhouettes of children dance with chilling glee in the flickering shadows, Harry was as sure as he'd ever been of anything that this wasn't the kind of help that he and the team needed. Not at all.

CHAPTER THREE

LATER THAT EVENING, WHEN THE HUBBUB OF THE
Burning of the Bartle had abated and everyone had headed
home or to the pub, Andrew Greenwood was at the bar of the
Fox and Hounds in West Witton. There was no point
heading home yet, and if he had a few too many, he could
always walk home, seeing as it wasn't far, not across the fields
anyway. And sometimes an evening's walk in the soft darkness of the Dales was a thing of joy, so why not use beer as
the excuse? He would open the shop as always at eight am
sharp, and a little beery fug would make no difference to that.

He was already onto his third pint and had been mulling
over what he'd said to that southern police officer he'd
bumped into, the one with the scars all over his face. He'd
heard the rumours about the man being an ex-soldier, and he
could believe it from just looking at him. He didn't exactly
come across as someone you wanted to get on the wrong side
of, he was sure of that.

Maybe he'd have been better keeping his mouth shut, he
thought, but that had never really been his way, had it? And

anyway, it wasn't him who'd started it, was it? Someone had shouted something out. He'd agreed with it, and then that detective's eyes had been on him. And that had been a red rag to a bull.

Small he may be, but he had always made up for it by saying what he meant, and usually both loudly and obviously enough for everyone to take note. Gobby, some had called him. So much so that it had become a nickname at school. And he certainly didn't miss hearing, 'Aye up, here comes Gobby Greenwood!' being shouted at him wherever he went. Sometimes, he hadn't just been Gobby either, with fists playing their part. Not so much now, mind, because no one wanted to see a man on the wrong side of fifty throwing punches around. Still, the temptation was there.

Sinking his pint, Andrew ordered another and headed to a dark corner to steep himself in his thoughts. He sat down, took a sip, and thought how the walk home would do him good. Which was when a shadow loomed over his table and interrupted them.

'How do, Andrew.'

Andrew looked up into the stubbly face of Chris Black. It was quite a distance away on account of the man being so tall. But he wasn't thin with it, thought Andrew. Chris was powerfully built, a little scary even. And the weight he had, well, everyone knew he liked to throw it around a bit to get his way.

'Chris.' Andrew acknowledged him with a raising of his pint, then added a not very convincing, 'Good to see you.'

'Want another?'

'Just bought this one.'

'So, that's a yes, then, is it?'

'If you're offering.'

Chris left Andrew for a moment to return from the bar with another pint, a whisky for himself, and some crisps.

'Much appreciated,' Andrew said, doing his best to add in some warmth to his voice, which was then ruined by him saying, 'but I'm assuming there's an ulterior motive,' because there always was with Chris. Always.

'Never been the most trusting, have you?'

'Not generally.'

And not with you, Andrew thought.

'None of us have changed much, have we, not even since we were kids?'

Chris smiled and Andrew did not like it one bit. Never had. It was the kind of smile worn by dictators, people who got what they wanted by fair means or foul. He had no proof of anything ever being done that was foul, but they all talked about it. Those playground rumours had followed Chris his whole life, not that he'd ever tried to shake them off. Embraced them, he had, Andrew thought. Wore them like a protective cloak. And up at the auction mart in Hawes, the talk and the rumours were as ripe as the shite that covered the ground on market day. Though this past year or two, he'd seemed quieter, more cautious; maybe age was catching up with him.

'Well, after what you said earlier, I thought I'd come over and have a chat with you about it. If that's okay?'

Here we go, Andrew thought.

'Wasn't me that started it,' he said. 'I was just agreeing, that's all. Then everyone else threw in their penny's worth. Didn't see you there. Or hear you.'

'You know me, I like to hang back a bit, observe. Many agreed with you, and I do, to a point. It's dangerous talk, though.'

Andrew was a little taken aback. Surely Chris had heard what Agnes had said about his dogs? Maybe he was taking the piss. It was the kind of thing he would do; support you with one side of his face while laughing at you with the other.

'Not sure that police officer agreed.'

'I didn't say he had to. Things can get out of hand. Like I said, it's dangerous talk, and that leads to dangerous action. So, best to be careful, I think.'

'I wasn't suggesting anything daft or dangerous,' Andrew said, hoping to make his point clear enough for Chris to get the message. 'Others did, though, but that's not my business, is it? We've all had stuff go missing, haven't we? And there's only so much the police can do.'

'True.'

'I run a shop,' Andrew continued, 'and I can't be looking at every bugger who comes in and swipes a chocolate bar.'

'Vigilante action, though? That's more than getting a bit carried away.'

'It worked in Bartle's time. And, like I've just said, Chris, that's not what I was suggesting, as you well know if you were there and heard what I was saying.'

'You've security cameras at the shop.'

'I have. But I'll be honest with you, they're mainly for show. They worked when I had them put in, but it's too complicated for the likes of me, so I never switch them on. More of a hopeful deterrent now.'

'He's not local either, is he?' Chris said. 'That police officer, the one with the face on him, I mean.'

'So?'

'He doesn't understand us the way we do, those of us

who are born and bred. Not sure he ever will, either. He can't.'

Not sure that includes you either, if I'm honest, Andrew thought, but kept that to himself.

'Look, I wasn't suggesting we should start stringing people up. I made that pretty bloody clear, like, because that would be idiotic, wouldn't it? Like that police officer bloke said.'

'Things can get out of hand very quickly though,' Chris said, his eyes widening briefly but just enough to make Andrew wonder what he meant by that. Was he advocating such action, or not? Whatever it was, Andrew didn't like it.

He was beginning to wonder why they were still talking. Why he was somehow maintaining a conversation with a man he'd never liked and never would, for numerous reasons, when an angry, gruff voice interrupted them.

'Well, if you ask me, they do need stringing up, the whole bloody lot of them!' it said, spittle flaring at the end of each word, a rattlesnake's warning caught in a throat. 'And I'd be first in line to fetch the rope, that's for sure. Doesn't bother me one bit. I'd have them all, the bastards.'

Andrew turned to look at the owner of the voice, who was now clearly a part of the conversation, whether he'd been invited or not. Much like what had happened earlier. It was a farmer he knew by name, though his reputation was enough, what with his tups winning prizes all over the place and that fancy new Land Rover he owned and insisted on driving around in like he was royalty. Never seen a field in its life, Andrew was sure, which struck him as a bit of a waste. The man's face was a solid lump of grizzled meanness, as though it had been constructed from gristle cut from the oldest and chewiest of steaks.

'Best you keep that kind of view on the quiet side of things, I reckon, don't you?' Andrew said.

'You know each other, then, do you?' Chris asked.

Oh, we know each other, Andrew thought. But then everyone does round here, don't they? And Steve had been happy to jump in earlier with his own loudly voiced thoughts, hadn't he?

'Steve Hill, of Hill Farm,' Steve said, raising his glass. 'Been in the family for generations. We've seen each other about, not really ever talked, I don't think. But I had to say something earlier, like, at the Bartle. Thought what you were saying made a lot of sense. And I'm not one for keeping my gob shut.'

'Good to see you,' Andrew said, lying through his teeth and raising his glass just a little, pretty sure the coldness in his eyes was enough to have a film of frost cover them.

Chris then said, 'You think something needs to be done as well, then, do you, Steve?'

Andrew was about to say, *and so does Agnes* when a man came over to stand between Steve and Chris. He was dwarfed by both, not just in terms of height either, but wideness. He was slim, like winter grass, and pale, too, as though he'd never once in his life been anything other than just a little below par.

Andrew wanted to leave right then and quickly sunk his pint before reaching for the one Chris had bought him, though he didn't drink any yet.

'Now then, Keith,' he said, probably a little too loudly, but he wanted to shut Steve up before he put his foot in it. Though he doubted it would make any difference. Few things ever did. But talking about this in front of Keith, well, it just didn't make sense.

For a moment, Keith was quiet. He just stood there, holding his pint, rubbing his chin.

'Away then, Sunter,' Steve said at last, staring at the man. 'If you've got something to say, best you just come out and say it. Though I can guess what it is, can't I? I heard what you said earlier. We all did.'

When Keith spoke, his voice was soft and calm, though Andrew noticed it was him he was looking at, not the other two. And for a moment, it seemed to him that the man was doing so as a way of maintaining control. 'I heard what you were all talking about at the Bartle earlier. Thought it best I mention what I did, about Neighbourhood Watch.'

'I'm surprised you were there,' said Steve.

'Why?'

'Those white roses of yours back home and up at Hawes. Seems to me they take up most of your time now.' Steve leaned in a little too close to Keith. 'You try too hard to be all Yorkshire, you know that, don't you?'

Andrew wondered if Steve ever knew when to just shut the hell up. It was as though everything he said was designed to piss off whoever was listening.

Keith ignored Steve and said, 'I just thought I'd come over and have a word, if that's okay.'

'And what word's that, then?' asked Chris.

At last Keith turned from Andrew to stare up at Chris. Andrew saw a flash of steel in his eyes for the briefest moment.

'Taking the law into your own hands is never a good idea, Chris. You know that, don't you? Bad things happen.'

No one said anything. Andrew was desperate to leave.

Keith was still talking.

'We've the Neighbourhood Watch, Rural Watch, plenty

of things going on to help keep the Dale safe. But what folk were talking about, and what you're talking about now? You have no idea where it will lead. The repercussions.'

Andrew saw the briefest flash of awkwardness in Chris' eyes, as though what Keith had just said had somehow disturbed something. Though what exactly, he hadn't the faintest idea.

'God, you talk some bollocks, Keith,' sneered Steve.

Keith turned from Chris to level his eyes at Steve.

'Please,' he said. 'Trust me on this. If people start meting out justice, others will get hurt. And what if someone gets killed? Then what? That's all I'm saying.'

Steve dropped a hefty hand onto Keith's shoulder. It landed with the sound of a thick, wet steak landing on a slab of oak.

'How is that lad of yours, by the way?' he asked. 'And his mate?'

At this, Keith bristled, the steel sharpened.

'I've not seen him in two years,' he said. 'You know that as well as everyone else. And I miss him like you wouldn't believe. That's all there is to say on the matter.'

'Well, you're the only one who does,' Steve muttered. 'Just because his mum's gone, that was no excuse for what he got up to.'

'It hit him something terrible,' Keith said. 'We both suffered.'

'Like that would ever hold up in court. Sorry, m'Lord, but I did it because my mum died.'

Keith sucked in a breath so deep, Andrew wondered if there would be any oxygen left in the pub when he finished.

'I've said my piece,' said Keith. 'That detective, he's right. And like I said, there's plenty out there going on. But, you know what, maybe you should do something? Maybe that's the only way you'll realise that when you do things on your own, people get hurt.'

Andrew, like the others around him, had nothing to say to that.

With a nod, Keith turned and left.

Andrew was thinking it might be a good idea to leave himself when another figure arrived.

'Just thought I'd come over and say that I agreed with everything you said earlier, Andrew. And I'll be talking to that detective chap this week about you-know-who's dogs, that's for damned sure.'

'It wasn't me who started it, Agnes,' Andrew said. 'I was just agreeing, that was all. Don't lay all this on me.'

'My dogs causing you a problem, are they?' said Chris, and Andrew saw Agnes' eyes widen as she realised who she was standing next to.

She bristled. Andrew watched as she considered leaving, then decided on staying instead. He immediately wished she hadn't.

She turned to face Chris. 'I've asked you a dozen times, but your dogs, they're always out, aren't they? Running wild, bothering my goats. I've every right to shoot them. You know that, don't you?'

'It's probably best that you don't,' said Chris. 'I do try, Agnes, but they're buggers sometimes.'

Andrew was sure that the shadows skulking around the pub crept over to skulk behind Chris like a cloak.

'Is that a threat?' Agnes asked, reaching up to prod Chris in the chest.

Chris shook his head.

'I won't be threatened,' said Agnes. 'I won't! I'm going to

report it when it happens again, that's for sure. Take photos, collect evidence. Then we'll see what's what, won't we? And you mark my words, I'll not be messed with. Not anymore, I won't.'

'You should worry more about the walkers on the footpaths,' Chris suggested. 'Not my dogs.'

'Too right,' said Steve. 'A bit of local justice would make them think twice, that's for sure. Make an example of one or two of them, scare the living shite out of the others, you mark my words. And if I get my hands on Keith's lad, there'll be hell to pay, that's for sure.'

Agnes shook her head.

'I've not seen him around in months. Anyway, we all know the trouble they've been through.'

'He's a bloody waste of space, he is, right enough,' said Steve. 'Just because of what happened with his mum, that's no excuse to go wandering about and helping himself to other people's stuff, now is it?'

Steve, Andrew realised, was about to go off on one, so he jumped in quickly, hoping to calm things down a little. 'Look, maybe Keith's got a point. We should all join in more with what he does, the Neighbourhood Watch, that kind of thing. It can't do any harm, can it? We don't want anyone doing anything daft, now do we?'

At this, Steve turned on Andrew.

'You calling me daft, now, is that it? Say it to my face then, come on.'

Andrew stared for a moment at Steve, impassive, then looked at Chris. The man was standing there, impossible to read, just listening, observing, maybe looking for ammunition in the words of others. Steve, though, was clearly spoiling for a fight. But he'd picked the wrong person to wind up.

'All I'm saying,' said Andrew, deciding then to try one last time at bringing the conversation back to something not so high frequency, 'is that I think we need the community to be more involved in looking out for each other, that's all. Keith is maybe right. I'm not talking about vigilante justice or anything like that. We can all help the police with what they're on with, can't we? There aren't enough of them, and that's the problem. We can't expect them to be everywhere. That's all.'

'Neighbourhood Watch.' Steve laughed. 'Just nosy neighbours, most of whom are only ever here for the weekend with the kids. No, we need something more serious, like you said, Andrew.'

'No, that's not what I said, remember? Not at all.'

Andrew rubbed his temples. A headache was starting to scratch behind his eyes.

'Right now, all I'm bothered about is those dogs, their filth, and my goats,' said Agnes.

Steve wasn't listening.

'Pieces of equipment disappearing from our yards, our farms,' he said. 'Fencing, posts, troughs, yes, but generators, chainsaws, all kinds of stuff. What's next? They'll be in our homes next, I promise you, taking whatever they see fit. And the police can't do much about it except make a few notes and hope that something comes up. And it never does. We all know that. No, we need something more.'

'What are you thinking, then?' Chris asked.

Andrew finished his pint and was looking for an excuse to leave.

'Right now, I'm not sure,' Steve said. 'But I think we should maybe get a few folk together, have a chat, that kind of thing.'

'How does Monday evening sound?' Agnes suggested. 'Strike while the iron's hot and all that. Get the word round, plenty of folk will turn up. We can get the keys for the Temperance Hall over in Askrigg, so we'll gather there.

'Maybe pop upstairs afterwards for a game of snooker,' said Steve. 'Good idea.'

'The tables still there, are they?' Andrew said. 'Not been up there since I was a lad.'

As he thought back to days standing on tiptoe to even have a chance of hitting the balls, he remembered something he'd seen on television, goodness knew when. And before he knew what he was thinking, he said, 'We could maybe do something like the Guardian Angels in New York, couldn't we?'

'And who are they when they're at home?' Steve asked.

'The Guardian Angels, they're a patrol of civilians,' Andrew explained. 'Just everyday people trying to help everyone else.'

'I like the sound of that,' said Steve.

'So do I,' Agnes agreed.

'They've a uniform and they walk around the subway, that kind of thing, I think,' Andrew continued. 'Helps to make people feel safe, spot pickpockets, muggers.'

'Can they make an arrest?' Steve asked.

'That I don't know,' said Andrew. 'Probably a citizen's arrest or whatever they would call it in America.'

'They probably have guns as well, don't they, the lucky sods?' Steve said. 'That's what we need, you know? More guns. I've one myself, we all have. But can we use them to protect ourselves? Can we bollocks, like.'

'We absolutely do not need guns,' said Andrew. 'Maybe it's a bad idea. Sorry, ignore me.'

Agnes finished her drink.

'Well, I think we should do it,' she said, 'and I'll be mentioning your bloody dogs, Chris. You mark my words.'

She gave a nod to Andrew, a cold stare to Steve and Chris, and then left.

'Who gives a damn about dogs and her sodding goats?' said Steve. 'Not even real farming, is it? Bloody hobby, more like. But then what do you expect from townies? Coming here, thinking they can just do what they want.'

'Her points are as valid as anything you've said,' said Andrew. 'You need to focus, Steve. And keep your thoughts away from guns and violence or whatever else it is you're considering, which is why I'm trying to help you focus here. We want less trouble, not more.'

Steve stared at Andrew.

'I'm not a fan of being ordered about and told what to do by anyone,' he said.

'And I'm not best enamoured of the kind of person who thinks his problems are always more important than everyone else's,' Andrew replied, standing up.

More than anything he wanted to thump the man in the middle of his rough, badly shaven, meaty face. But he didn't. Instead, he just gave the man a hard stare and then pushed himself out from where he had been sitting to head home.

'You've not drunk the pint I bought you,' Chris said.

'Something's made it taste off,' said Andrew, his eyes on Steve.

Steve reached over for the glass. 'I'll be having that, then,' he said. 'Waste not want not, as my old dad always said.'

Andrew got there first, his hand brushing Steve's as he picked up the pint and necked it, never once taking his eyes off Chris.

'See you Monday, then,' he said, placing the glass back on the table and heading to the door.

Steve's voice caught him up.

'Let's say seven-thirty,' he said. 'And we'll see what everyone thinks of that idea of yours, the Guardian Angels, but with a Wensleydale twist? I reckon folk will love it.'

Andrew gave a nod, took his silence with him out into the welcome embrace of the cool night, and allowed the darkness to swallow him whole.

CHAPTER FOUR

Detective Inspector Gordanian Haig was on the night shift and was at that moment sitting in the office in Hawes, having a brew. There were worse things she could be doing, and better things, too, that was for sure.

This was Wensleydale, so it wasn't exactly a hotbed of crime and debauchery. She'd worked in places that excelled at both and seemed to wear them like badges of honour. The memories from some of them still had enough power to slam into her at random moments of the day and night and stop her dead. Anna had noticed it enough times to show concern, and the thought of her brought a smile to Gordy's face.

Love was a many-splendored thing, and strange. If someone had told her years ago, she would end up in a relationship with the local vicar, she'd have laughed. But then, here she was. In love, not that she was out there professing it from the rooftops. That just wasn't her style, and also probably wasn't the most sensitive of approaches. The Dales had welcomed Anna with open arms, that was true, her sexuality was never a concern, but Gordy didn't want to rock the boat. Well, not too much, anyway. Not yet.

So far, her night had consisted of a drive to a campsite to deal with a few drunk teenagers, helping someone change a tyre, and making yet another mug of tea. Unfortunately, the one she'd just poured hadn't really hit the spot. She'd left the teabag in just a wee bit too long and her first mouthful had made her wince. The sweetness of a Custard Cream biscuit had helped, but biscuits helped with most things, if not with others.

Gordy checked her watch. She had a few hours to go before Detective Constable Jenny Blades would be arriving to take over. And then she'd be heading over to Anna's to enjoy a lovely early morning breakfast with her. It was a Sunday, too, so she'd have communion to shoot off to, and Gordy thought that she might even head along with her. Church wasn't really her thing, but sometimes the peace of the place did her good; the smell of the cool air and damp stone pillars, the scent of candles, and the softly spoken prayers of the woman she loved mingling with those of the people she cared for, heads bowed in the pews.

A call on the office phone interrupted these happy thoughts drifting through her mind like swirls of the sweetest pipe smoke. Gordy reached out and answered it. And moments later, was out of the door.

The world outside the office was still, the marketplace asleep. Windows reflected each other in the moonlight and stars stared down through aeons.

Gordy climbed into her vehicle and headed off. No blues and twos needed, not with the roads empty. And it seemed wrong to disturb the Dale so. Best to leave it in slumber.

Soon, she was racing along, just quick enough to make

the journey interesting, but not so fast as to be out of control or unable to react should something leap out in front of her. Over the years she had dodged everything from rabbits and badgers, to hedgehogs, deer and, on one particularly memorable day, an emu.

The beautiful village of Bainbridge came and went in a swift blur of midnight green and Gordy sped out the other side, up the hill, and past the old Roman Fort.

Her destination was the village of Thoralby. She couldn't remember the last time she'd been over that way and could recall little about it other than it being yet another Dales village she could sometimes easily see herself living out her days in. Though such thoughts were always uncomfortable, because her soul, she knew, still hankered for the Highlands. And even thinking that was enough to bring to mind images of Glencoe, the road sweeping through that vast and epic valley, and the ghosts that still danced there.

The thoughts of her homeland seemed to compress time and Gordy found herself in Thoralby sooner than she expected. Through the village she rolled, past the triangle of the green and on, round a few bends, until she reached the address she'd been given. She wasn't first on the scene, a paramedic's vehicle was sitting out front next to a Land Rover Defender. It wasn't one of the new ones, but it was certainly capable. It was parked in front of a double garage. To the side of the garage was a lean-to greenhouse surrounded by various plant pots and a half-dozen demijohns.

Gordy came to a stop just in front of the Defender, climbed out, and walked to the front door. Finding it open, she called out and made her way inside.

'Through here,' came a voice, but Gordy was already trying to see a way through.

The place had been turned over. Pictures were lying smashed on the floor, the hooks which had held them sticking out of the wall like the empty hands of beggars. Smashed glass, scattered papers, a turned over table, the hall alone was a mess. Moving on, Gordy passed a door leading into a kitchen. It, too, had been ransacked. She didn't bother stopping, a glance was enough; drawers were open, cutlery scattered, a toaster on the floor surrounded by the blackened crumbs of its last task.

The next door led through to the lounge. Again, the room was a thumping reminder of how little people care about the belongings and homes of others when they're looking for something of value to steal. The space was a riot of destruction and in the middle of it, on a sofa, was a man bookended by two paramedics, both of whom Gordy thought looked young enough to still be at school. Which was more a sign as to her distance from those years than theirs.

'I don't think I need to ask what happened here,' Gordy said, and introduced herself.

'This is Mr Sunter,' one of the paramedics said, a woman with red hair in a neat ponytail, her face as pale as alabaster and dotted by numerous freckles.

'Disturbed an intruder,' said the other, a man with a shaved head and the whitest teeth Gordy had ever seen, to the point where she wondered if they might just glow in the dark.

She made her way through the detritus of whatever had gone on, scattered across the carpet like flotsam and jetsam on the sea, then crouched down in front of Mr Sunter.

'So, how are we doing, then?'

Mr Sunter looked battered and bruised but okay, all in all. There were a few plasters here and there, a graze or two still raw and seeping a little, and the man was rubbing his left leg, but whatever had happened, he wasn't in a critical state. So, that was something.

'Sore,' Mr Sunter said, smiling through the grimace as he spoke.

He rubbed his leg again.

'No sign of concussion,' said the freckled paramedic. 'He's got a twisted ankle, some cuts and bruises, but he'd already dealt with most of it by the time we arrived.'

'Really?'

The other paramedic gave a nod.

'First aid specialist for the mountain rescue, aren't you, Keith?'

Keith smiled and shrugged.

'Everyone has a hobby.'

'So, you'll be knowing a certain Detective Sergeant Matt Dinsdale, then?' said Gordy.

Keith gave a knowing nod.

'Everyone knows Matt. Not seen him for a while though, what with fatherhood taking over. How is he? Relishing it, I assume.'

'Oh, he's fine,' Gordy said. 'Bairn's keeping him and Joan busy.' She narrowed her eyes. 'Now, are you okay to tell me what happened here?'

'Yes,' Keith said.

Gordy took out her notebook.

'We'll stay just a while longer,' said the paramedic with freckles. 'But I think he'll be fine.'

'And the ankle?' Gordy asked.

'Oh, I've some crutches,' Keith said. 'Old ones from Mountain Rescue. I'll be fine, I'm sure.'

Gordy took Keith's details, then gave him a few moments to gather himself.

'And what is it that you do yourself?' Gordy asked.

'Oh, nothing too exciting,' said Keith. 'An architect. Work for myself, at home.'

'That must be nice.'

'It is and it isn't. Too much time on my own sometimes, I think. Particularly now.'

'In your own time,' she said. 'Just tell me what happened.'

'There's not much I can say, really,' Keith said. 'I arrived home after being over at the Burning of the Bartle. Poured myself a whisky before bed, then after a bit of a read, went upstairs and fell asleep.'

'Something woke you up, then?' she asked.

Keith shook his head, tapped his left ear.

'No,' he said. 'I sleep with earplugs. Always have. I'm a light sleeper, you see. If I don't have absolute silence, I'll just wake up for anything. A dark room, too. Blackout curtains, that kind of thing.'

'So, how did you find what had happened downstairs?'

Keith gave a shrug.

'Oh, you know how it is, the older you get, the more your nights are interrupted by the need to nip to the loo.'

'I do indeed.' Gordy smiled. 'Can't remember the last time I slept right through without having to attend to the call of nature.'

'Well,' said Keith, 'It was the middle of the night and I'd had to get up to visit the bathroom. It was while I was in there that I heard something downstairs. When I went to see what it was, I found things a little amiss.'

Looking around the ruination of the room they were sitting in, Gordy thought that Keith was the master of understatement.

'And you live alone?'

Gordy saw sadness in Keith's eyes at this as they fell to a photograph on the floor. She reached over and picked it up. In it, she saw Keith, though a good few years younger, with a woman and a boy, probably just heading into his teens. There were a couple of other photos scattered around, too, of the son, but older. He was wearing the scowl of a teenager, his dark hair growing longer, black hoody and jeans his uniform, like so many his age.

'I do now, yes,' Keith said. 'We lost Helen a few years ago. Car accident.'

'And your son?'

'Not here anymore,' Keith said.

A darkness had slipped over the man's eyes and Gordy was careful about questioning further, not wishing to pry too much.

'He moved out?'

'Fell in with the wrong type.'

'How do you mean?'

'The kind of people who do this, who make this their life,' Keith said, waving a hand to gesture at the disorder around them.

'I'm sorry to hear that.'

'It's not your fault. The loss of his mum, well, Anthony took it hard, you know? He was just a kid back then.'

A shrug.

'Where is he now?'

'In a happier place,' Keith said. 'I hope so, anyway. And that's all we have, really, isn't it? Hope?'

Keith stared into the middle distance, the pain in his eyes so deep that for a moment Gordy felt that if she looked into them for too long, she'd fall.

'So, you went to the toilet, heard something downstairs and came down to find you'd been broken into.'

'I didn't know what the noise was at first,' Keith said. 'I've had all kinds of animals break into the place, you know? Rats are the worst, but then this is the country, isn't it? Never too far from half a dozen of them. Funniest one though was a sheep. I was out in the garden and I came inside to find it just standing here, in the lounge. It had just wandered in through the front door, which I'd stupidly left open after popping out for a few things.'

'What did you do?'

'Nothing,' Keith said. 'It just looked at me and left.'

'I'm assuming it wasn't a sheep that did this, though.'

Keith shook his head.

'You're going to want a description,' he said, 'but I can't give you one.'

'You saw nothing?'

'No,' said Keith. 'Well, that's not strictly true, I saw them leave. Think I surprised them.'

'How many?'

'One, I think. They were wearing a dark top, with a hood pulled up over their head, I think. Jeans. That's about all I saw really.'

'They attacked you and you didn't see them?'

'No, they didn't attack me, I tried to stop them. Did a bit of a rugby tackle. Didn't really work out too well, did it, as you can see?'

Keith gestured at his face, the scratches and grazes.

'Serves me right, I suppose,' he said. 'You should never

take the law into your own hands, should you? Never ends up well. Ever. I know that.'

Gordy wasn't sure what to say, so said, 'You've every right to protect your property.'

'People get hurt though, don't they?' he said. 'And it's only stuff, at the end of the day, isn't it? All of this? It doesn't matter, not really. People are what's important.'

Keith shook his head.

'Anyway,' he said, 'I tried to tackle them, missed, and that was that. They were gone. I rang it in and these two rather lovely paramedics came out, seeing as I said I was injured. But I'm not really, I'm okay. I've had worse. Sorry to waste everyone's time, if I'm honest.'

Gordy closed her notebook.

'You've wasted no one's time,' she said. 'This is a break-in. You tackled an intruder. Do you know what was taken?'

Keith shook his head.

'Not had a chance to look. Anyway, I've nothing of value, really. Not anymore.'

Again, Gordy saw darkness in the man's eyes. Grief was there, raw and bleeding, and she had to resist the urge to just reach out and give him a hug. But she reached out and rested a hand on his arm, gave it the gentlest of squeezes.

The paramedics rose to their feet. Gordy saw them to the door, then came back to Keith.

'This place is quite the mess,' she said. 'I'll have a forensics team come out and do what they do. Hopefully, we'll find something.'

'You won't, though,' Keith said. 'It's just a break-in. I'm fine. Truly.'

'That you may be,' Gordy said, 'but I've procedures to

follow. And you'll need a forensics report anyway, for insurance purposes, that kind of thing.'

She stood up to make the call.

'Do you have anywhere you can go?' she asked. 'While we get on with sorting this out?'

'It's a bit late to be calling on my neighbours,' Keith said.

'You'd be amazed at how persuasive a police badge can be,' Gordy said. 'And anyway, I'm fairly sure they won't mind. Which house?'

'The one opposite, just over the road.'

'Come on, then,' Gordy said. 'Let's have you away so that we can get on with sorting this all out, shall we?'

Keith stood up. He was a small man, Gordy thought, and slight. That he'd attempted to rugby tackle anyone, never mind someone who'd broken into his house, was as hard to believe as it was impressive. She had nothing but respect for him, that was for sure. Sometimes, the meekest were the strongest. She smiled then, wondering if she'd heard that in one of Anna's sermons.

The neighbours took Keith in without a second thought, welcoming him into their home with open arms, as concerned for Keith as they were alarmed about what had happened.

'Get yourself some rest,' Gordy said, then leaving Keith in the care of concerned friends, pulled out her phone and made a few calls. By the time she had finished, she was already missing the breakfast she wouldn't be sharing with Anna in a few hours.

CHAPTER FIVE

'You didn't have to come. You know that, don't you?'

Harry stifled a yawn as DI Haig stared at him with little in the way of sympathy. He was standing outside the house waiting to go in, hoping the cool night air would wake him up. So far, it hadn't.

'You rang me, remember?'

'Because if I hadn't, you'd never have stopped going on about it when you found out. But as I said, everything was and is in hand.'

'I was awake anyway,' Harry said.

'No, you weren't.'

'Well, I was as soon as you rang.'

'You're impossible.'

'All part of being a DCI.' Harry's yawn threatened to come back, so he continued speaking to stave it off, his words coming out strained and stretched.

'Well, give my apologies to Grace. Last thing I wanted to do was drag you away from her.'

Harry laughed.

'She sleeps like the dead,' he said. 'Doubt she even knows that I've gone. So, what do we know?'

'Not much,' said Gordy. 'It's a break-in. We've a description that could basically be anyone on the planet. And as far as we can tell, nothing was taken.'

At this, Harry nearly did a double-take.

'Nothing at all?'

Gordy shook her head.

'He disturbed the intruder, tried to tackle them, too.'

'Forensics?'

'He's in there with the photographer.'

Harry huffed out a breath through his nose.

'There was a time when I never thought I'd say what I'm about to,' he said, 'but I wish Sowerby was here.'

Rebecca Sowerby, the pathologist they usually called in, had been injured during a previous investigation. She was still recovering. Not quickly enough, as far as Harry was concerned. Her absence had been filled a little too keenly by someone he liked about as much as being punched in the face. No, less than that, even; a punch to the face he could handle, but this stand-in pathologist made his skin crawl and his blood boil. It was a very odd and very disturbing sensation.

'But why's he here?' Harry asked. 'He's a pathologist. It's not like we have a body to deal with, is it?'

'Bit of a busybody if you ask me,' Gordy said.

'You mean a nosy little bastard.'

'He said he thought he'd take this one himself as he had nothing else to do. And he didn't want to ruin the weekend for any of his team.'

'He does know it's not actually *his* team, though, doesn't

he?' Harry said. 'He's just temporary while Sowerby recovers.'

'That's something he seems to be forgetting on purpose.'

Harry agreed.

'And I, for one, hope we don't have too long to wait till he's buggered off back to whatever hole he lives in and Sowerby is back on her feet. Maybe we could hurry her recovery along a bit.'

'How?'

'Not a clue,' Harry said. 'Can't see flowers or chocolates making much of a difference.'

He peered into the house.

'Where's the victim?'

'Mr Sunter is over the road with neighbours,' Gordy said. 'They took him in while we cracked on with all this. Nice bit of Yorkshire hospitality.'

'Is there any other kind?'

'They don't welcome just anyone,' Gordy said.

Harry stifled a yawn, gave a glance at the house, then nodded over the road.

'Best I go and have a chat with Mr Sunter, then,' he said.

Gordy laughed.

'You're avoiding him, aren't you?'

'Who?'

'The pathologist, Mr Bennett.'

'Of course I am,' Harry grumbled, and without another word, walked off. Behind him, he was sure he heard DI Haig mutter something not entirely polite under her breath.

The house opposite showed clear signs of life, warm yellow light squeezing itself out between pulled curtains. Harry gave a soft knock at the door.

A woman opened the door. She was small, but not tiny, and stared up at Harry, her jaw set firm.

'Now then,' she said. 'Can I help?'

Harry showed the woman his ID.

'Best you come in then,' she said. 'I've just poured a pot. Milk, sugar?'

'Just a spot of milk,' Harry said.

'You can have a bacon butty, too, if you want,' she added. 'I've made enough for the whole village, it seems. I always go overboard in a crisis. Once, when the chapel flooded, I made enough boiled eggs to feed the five thousand. Boiled eggs! I mean, who needs boiled eggs at the best of times, never mind hundreds of the buggers while you're trying to mop up gallons of rainwater!'

Inside, the house was warm, and Harry could smell the comforting, ageless aroma of well-seasoned, burning wood. Following it, and the woman's directing hand, he wandered through to a small lounge, the walls of which seemed dedicated to various displays of thimbles and teaspoons.

'This is Detective Grime,' the woman said.

'Grimm,' Harry corrected.

'Not sure that's any better, but if you insist,' she said.

'I didn't catch your name,' said Harry.

'I didn't give it,' the woman said. 'Clare Smith, without an i. In Clare, I mean, not Smith. You can't have Smith without an i, can you? You could have it with a Y, I suppose, if you were being posh. I've no idea why my name's spelled like that. There's bound to be a reason, but my parents are no longer around to ask, Lord bless them. And this is my husband, Paul.'

Harry nodded a hello to Paul, a bald man with a face

Harry suspected hadn't actually smiled in years and took a seat on a sofa and slipped his notebook out of a pocket.

'And you must be Mr Sunter,' Harry said, turning to the other figure in the room, a slight man almost swallowed whole by an armchair pushed up close to the fire. He was wearing an old, faded sweatshirt, the original colour of which could well have been anything from bright red to deep brown, jogging bottoms, and a pair of well-worn trainers, the shoes of a runner rather than just bought for fashion.

'I am, yes,' the man said, leaning forward a little. 'Keith.'

Harry thought he recognised the voice, though at that moment he wasn't really sure from where.

'Just popped over to ask you a few questions, that's all,' he explained.

'I've already spoken to that other nice officer,' Keith said. 'The one with the Scottish accent.'

'That you have,' said Harry, 'but I always like to have a little chat myself, if only to offer whatever support we can at difficult times like this.'

'Oh, it's not that difficult.'

'Your house was broken into,' Harry said. 'Some people find that very hard to come to terms with. The invasion of your home, your privacy.'

Keith leaned back in his chair to the point where Harry thought, if he went any further, he'd be in danger of slipping out of it and down onto the floor.

'What can you do?' he said.

'I understand you tackled the intruder.'

'You don't have to tell me, I know it's not the most sensible thing to do,' Keith said. 'And I always tell people that taking the law into your own hands, well, it's not the best of ideas, is it?'

Harry remembered then where he'd heard the voice.

'The Burning of the Bartle; you were there.'

'I was,' said Keith. 'And I agreed with what you said, not what the others were suggesting.'

'So, it was you who mentioned Neighbourhood Watch.'

Keith nodded.

'I try and run things across the Dale, but it's not that easy, really. People don't take it all that seriously.' He glanced then to his left as though staring for a moment at his own house through the wall. 'And it doesn't stop bad things happening.'

'It helps, though,' Harry said. 'I can promise you that.'

'Twice in three years, though,' said Clare. 'That's the worst of luck, isn't it? And on top of everything else, too, what with Helen gone and then Anthony.'

Harry looked up at Clare.

'You mean this has happened before?'

Keith held up a hand as though to hush a fuss being made over nothing.

'Mr Sunter?' Harry said, looking at the man.

'Yes, I've been broken into before,' he said. 'But it wasn't the same.'

'It's like the devil himself has it in for you, Keith, you poor sod,' Clare said.

She leaned down and rested a comforting hand on his arm for a moment.

Harry noticed that Paul had yet to say a single word. Though his expression suggested he had plenty of them to say and that his mouth was barely holding them back.

'When was the last break-in?' Harry asked.

'This time two years ago,' said Clare.

'Before my time here, then,' Harry said.

'To the day, actually,' Clare added. 'I remember because

we'd all been to the Burning of the Bartle, hadn't we? Go every year. Love a little bit of tradition.'

'I came back to find the place a mess,' Keith said. 'I'm sure it'll be in your records. A young female officer dealt with it for me.'

'Was that Detective Constable Blades?' asked Harry.

'That sounds about right, yes.'

Harry made a note to chat with Jenny.

A gruff laugh burst into the moment. Harry turned an eye to Paul.

'Something you want to say?' he asked.

'Yes, there is, actually,' Paul said. He leaned forward to eyeball Harry. Then he jabbed a finger at Keith. 'He's too soft, that's his problem. Always has been. Let it happen, he did. It'll just happen again, I said, you mark my words. And it has, hasn't it? But you still should've caught the one responsible, shouldn't you? Brought him to justice.'

Paul's words sat in the room unchallenged.

'We'll do the best we can,' Harry said.

'Aye, but that's not always enough, is it?' Paul replied.

'No, it's not.' Harry was an honest man and sometimes these things had to be acknowledged. 'But that doesn't stop us from trying.' He looked then at Keith. 'Clare mentioned something about Helen and Anthony? Your wife and son, yes?'

Harry knew the barest of details, those being that Keith lived alone, and had lost his wife in a car accident. About his son, though, he had no information at all.

'The accident happened in Hawes,' Keith said. 'It was a hit and run a few years ago.'

'That before I was here, then, too.'

Keith gave a nod.

'She was a very special woman. I miss her.'

'Of course,' said Harry. 'It must have been horrendous for you. I'm sure it still is. And your son?'

'That useless streak of piss was the one who broke into his place two years ago!' Paul said. 'His own father's house, would you believe! Him and that dickhead mate of his. And we've not seen hide nor hair of him since, have we, Keith, the little shite! I tell you, if I see him, if I get my hands on him, I'll give him something to think about, I promise you that for nowt.'

Harry was taken aback by this, remembering another detail from Gordy. He decided to ignore Paul's anger for the moment.

'Your son broke into your house two years ago, then?' he asked, looking at Keith.

'It's a long story,' Keith said.

'I've nowhere else to go,' replied Harry.

For a moment, a quiet stillness settled into the room, the only sound that of the fire crackling its way through some logs, filling the air with the sweet smell of burning wood.

'When we lost Helen, it was hard,' Keith said. 'For us both. Harder for Anthony, though. He was only thirteen. He never really got over it, I don't think. Not sure how he ever could be expected to either.'

'I lost my own mother,' Harry said. 'My brother, he'd have been around the same age as Anthony when it happened.'

'Then you understand.'

'I understand that grief affects us all differently,' said Harry. 'I left the Paras and entered the police force to catch the man who'd killed her. My brother, his life spiralled, and he ended up in prison.'

'I'm sorry to hear that.'

'Don't be,' said Harry. 'He's doing fine now. Better than fine, actually. Though it took a while. So, Anthony, then ...?'

'He became distant,' said Keith. 'Pushed me away. I was grieving in my own way, too, but he'd always been closer to her, you see? When we needed each other the most, we drifted apart.'

'That must have been very difficult for you.'

'He got into fights at school, ended up being expelled, left home at sixteen. Then he fell in with the kind of friends no one should have. One in particular, he was the worst. Drugs were involved, I think. I'd only ever see him if he wanted money.'

'And you'd always give it to him, wouldn't you?' Paul said. 'Every single time, like a great soft idiot. Honestly, Keith, you need a slap almost as much as—'

'He was my son!' Keith said, and Harry heard a lion's roar in the meek man's voice for the first time. 'Of course I bloody well gave it to him! Wouldn't you?'

Harry noticed something in what Keith had just said.

'You said "was" ...'

Keith sucked in a few deep breaths, calming himself just enough to speak again.

'After that break-in two years ago, that was the last I saw of him. And I miss him. Terribly.'

'And you've not seen him since?'

'He took money, his mum's jewellery, things he could sell, and that was that,' said Keith, lifting his phone. It was an old thing, battered and bruised, Harry noticed. 'He has my number. I won't change it. Or this phone. I read his messages still, listen to his voicemail, pretend it's really him, that he's coming home.'

'Did you try to stop him?'

'With every beat of my heart,' Keith said, his voice cracking with emotion. 'But all I saw were lights disappearing into the distance. He was gone.'

Harry said nothing for a moment, taking it all in. Then a thought struck him.

'This is a difficult question, but one I have to ask, particularly in light of what you've just told me: do you think this break-in tonight could've been your son?'

Keith turned to look at Harry and he saw tears in the man's eyes. A smile dared to bend his mouth, but the only happiness there was the kind lost to memories of better times remembered in pain.

'You know what? I wish with every part of me it was,' Keith said. 'At least then I would know, wouldn't I, that he had been here, that he'd come home? Yes, that would be something. It would be everything.'

'I could do with a description anyway if that's okay?' Harry asked. 'Or a photo, perhaps? Just in case.'

'There are plenty of photos back in the house,' Keith said. 'You'll probably see some scattered on the floor. Though most of those show him with long hair.'

'He cut it, then?'

'It was short when I saw him last,' said Keith. 'When he, well, you know.'

Harry understood.

'What about this friend of his that you mentioned.'

'What about him?'

'Could he have done this?'

Keith shrugged.

'Do you have any idea what they took this time?'

'Not a clue,' Keith said.

'He's still in shock,' said Clare.

'I'm fine, Clare, honestly.'

'No, you are not fine, not at all,' Clare corrected him. Then she turned her eyes on Harry, the brightness of them glaring at him like a lighthouse in a storm. 'And I think you'll be on your way now, won't you, Mr Grimm? You've plenty to be getting on with. A busy night of it, I'm sure.'

Harry took the hint, closed his notebook, and stood up.

'We'll do everything we can to find who did this,' he said. 'But in the meantime, if we have any questions, or if you remember something and need to give us a call, we'll be in touch regularly.'

'That's good,' Keith said. 'Thank you.'

Harry, with nothing else to say for now, made his way out of the room, Clare close behind him. In the hall, she reached past him and opened the front door. The night slipped in on a breath of cool air.

'We'll look after him,' Clare said.

'Of that, I have absolutely no doubt at all.' Harry smiled, then he stepped outside into the cool darkness and made his way back across the road.

CHAPTER SIX

HARRY WAS SITTING IN HIS KITCHEN NURSING THE LAST few drops of a very strong black coffee. The previous night had been interesting to say the least. He was weary as well as baffled, and the caffeine wasn't having the desired effect as yet. So, he finished what was left in his mug and poured another.

The Burning of the Bartle had been a strange affair, that was true, but the burglary over in Thoralby had affected him more than he'd expected it to. After all, no one had really been hurt, and if anything had been taken or broken, it could be replaced. Sentimental items were more problematic, but still, it was a burglary, not something a lot worse, which it could easily have been had Mr Sunter managed to tackle the thief to the ground.

The thing was, the man's sorrow had brought back a lot of Harry's own feelings about what had happened to his mum, how it had impacted him, but more so Ben. And how lucky they were that both he and his brother were living a new life, and well. Ben had a job, he had a girlfriend, he was happy. And that made him wonder about what had happened to Anthony, Mr Sunter's son. Had the break-in the night before been him again? There was no reason to suspect so, but also no reason to not think it might have been. And then there was the mention of this mysterious friend. Regardless, Keith was still a broken man, not just from the tragic loss of his wife, but also from what had gone on with his son. He was grieving for losing them both.

After chatting with Keith, Harry had headed back over to his house. Happy that DI Haig was fully in control, which she always was, he'd then taken her advice and headed home. He'd considered going back to bed, but his brain had been too busy, so he'd left Grace alone with her snoring and settled down in the lounge with Smudge to just think. And that hadn't lasted long because Grace had then woken him up at just gone eight.

'I don't remember kicking you out of bed.'

'You didn't.'

'Work, then?'

Harry gave a nod.

'You okay?'

'Just a burglary,' Harry said. 'Gordy called to let me know, so I headed over.'

Grace slumped down next to him, and Smudge crawled up next to her, resting her head on her lap.

'Anyone hurt?'

Harry shook his head.

'Not really, nothing serious, anyway. A few cuts and bruises, that's all. Whoever did it managed to get away.'

'They do that a lot, I'm guessing.'

'Far too often,' Harry said. 'And they're not exactly easy to catch. CCTV helps, but there's bugger all of that in the

Dale. We'll do our best, but sometimes, it's just damage limitation. Help the victim deal with what's happened, advise on security, provide support, that kind of thing.'

Grace twisted round to stare at Harry.

'This one's affected you though,' she said. 'I can tell.'

'How?'

'You're more sad puppy than angry bear. And if you don't mind me saying so, that's more than a little unsettling.'

Harry laughed, the sound bounding out of him so uncontrolled he was a little taken by surprise by it.

'Sad puppy? Me?'

'Usually, you're a bit more gruff,' she said. 'In a good way, though. Angry about what's happened, determined to do something about it. But now you just seem, well, not really that.'

'Maybe it's because I'm hungry.'

Harry pushed himself up out of the sofa and headed to the kitchen. He grabbed the little vintage egg poacher he'd purchased a few months back from an antiques shop over in Middleham.

'Poached eggs on toast sound good?'

'With coffee?'

'Of course.'

Harry got on with breakfast.

Grace came over.

'You sure nothing else is bothering you? Your decision to stay up north maybe, instead of heading back south?'

'Best decision I've made in years,' Harry said. 'You don't need to worry about that.'

'And you're still looking at buying somewhere?'

'I am,' Harry said.

He'd surprised himself with how quickly his decision to

turn down a job in Bristol had then morphed into an urge to find somewhere more permanent to live. The flat had done him and his brother, Ben, well. It was small, though, what with Smudge in his life now. And there was Grace, too. It was far too early days to be talking about moving in together, that was for sure, plus she had her own place, over in Carperby. And she hadn't batted an eyelid when he'd mentioned to her that he was looking to move. In fact, she'd positively encouraged it.

Eggs done, coffee brewed, Harry dished out breakfast then revealed the particulars of a handful of properties for sale in the Dale. He had booked viewings of them for later in the week.

'Any take your fancy?'

'Can't tell from a few photos and some bad copywriting,' Harry said.

'It'll be good for you to do it,' said Grace, shuffling through the papers. 'Buying your own place, it's a way of saying that somewhere is your home, isn't it?'

'About time, too, if you ask me,' Harry said. 'Not that I'm settling down. But some roots would be nice, or at least a place to plant them.'

Harry thought about Ben then, but his brother hadn't said much about it all. He suspected he was more focused on getting to the end of his probation in a month squeaky clean, not that it looked to be any sort of problem. He had a good life up here in Hawes, with the job down at Mike the mechanic's garage, and his blossoming romance with Liz Coates, the other Police Community Support Officer on Harry's team.

Harry felt something warm lean against his leg. He glanced down to see Smudge's deep brown eyes staring up at him. To emphasise whatever point she was trying to make, she raised a paw and rested it on his leg.

She'd grown, Harry thought, reaching down to stroke her soft head and then scratch behind her ear. Her behaviour was also seemingly being kept in check thanks to the training Grace had been putting in. Harry had been doing his best with it all, following Grace's instructions for what to do and what to absolutely not do at all. But there was a big difference between a professional gamekeeper who was used to dogs, and a DCI who'd never owned one in his life and who, it turned out, was also a bit of a soft touch.

Breakfast done, Harry tickled Smudge under the chin, then took the house details from Grace and showed them to the dog.

'What do you think?' he asked, shuffling through them slowly. 'Any preferences?'

Smudge's eyes didn't shift from Harry's.

'You don't really care, do you?' he said.

Smudge's tail wagged at the sound of her owner's voice.

Grace laughed and Harry gave Smudge another head scratch, then stood up, placing their breakfast crockery into the small dishwasher.

'I need a shower,' Harry said.

'Makes two of us,' said Grace, stretching. 'Mind if I join you?'

SKIN STILL TINGLING a little from the scalding temperature of the water he'd stood under for perhaps a few minutes longer than he should have, and from being in there with Grace, Harry was now dressed and standing in the hall ready for the day ahead. He pulled on his coat, slipped the

house details into a pocket, then opened the door. He immediately wished he hadn't.

Outside, the August day was as dark as a coal mine.
Something angry was crawling its way quietly across the
Dale, Harry thought, devouring what had been the balmiest
of weekends. He'd seen the weather warnings over the last
few days, found them hard to take seriously. They'd become
progressively worse, though the arrival of the apparent apocalyptic conflagration had been held back by the sweet kiss of
summer sun. Now, though, he could smell rain in the air, a
metallic tang which brought with it a distant scent of peat
and ice.

'Sure you have to go?' Grace asked.

'I'm on duty,' Harry said. 'On at midday, as a matter of
fact, and that's exactly ten minutes away.'

'And duty calls.'

'It always does.'

Harry zipped his coat, pulled the collar up, and stepped
out into the day. A gust of wind thumped into him, trying to
snatch the door from his hands. He took a last look at Grace
and Smudge, the dog staring at him with her nose in the
breeze thrusting itself into the flat, her soft velvet-like ears
flapping, her eyes narrowed, then he closed the door.

Stepping away from the flat, Harry pushed on, the wind
dancing around Hawes marketplace as it chased after pedestrians, trying to steal hats, making footsteps unsteady, and
snatching litter from the bins.

The road was quiet, the Dales somehow enforcing the
notion that Sunday was still a day of rest. He walked down
the road to where he'd parked his old Rav4 and was just
walking past it to head to the office at the Hawes Community
Centre, when his phone buzzed.

'Grimm,' Harry said, answering it before the buzzing got on his nerves.

'Boss, it's Jadyn.'

'Constable Okri,' said Harry. 'I was just on my way to see you. Assuming, of course, that you're in the office.'

'I am. Well, I still am, but I'm on my way out,' Jadyn said. 'That's why I've called, I knew you'd be in soon.'

Harry heard urgency in the constable's voice. His mind went immediately to the burglary in Thoralby.

'What's happened? Is it Mr Sunter? Is he okay?'

'Mr Sunter? Oh right, yes, he's fine, I think. That's all sorted now. Forensics has been and gone.'

'So, what is it?'

'We've had another call come in,' said Jadyn. 'Another break-in.'

Harry's heart sank and he took his phone away from his ear to stare at it in disbelief.

'Boss?'

'I'm hoping this isn't a sign that today is only going to go downhill from here,' Harry said. 'Where did it happen?'

'Down dale, over near The Forbidden Corner.'

Harry had seen signposts to the place, but never been.

'A theft of what, exactly?' he asked.

'A shotgun,' Jadyn said.

'Bloody hell,' Harry said.

'Thought you might say that.'

CHAPTER SEVEN

AGNES WASN'T ENTIRELY SURE WHAT HAD COME OVER her the evening before. The Burning of the Bartle was a strange custom, true, but it rarely affected her in such a way. This time, however, the sheer animalistic, primitive nature of the entire event had really swept her up. From somewhere inside her, a deep-seated anger about owners who simply refused to clean up after their dogs—particularly with one of them being her bloody neighbour—had broken free and run a little too wild. It wasn't as though it was the kind of crime that shocked a nation. It was, in many ways, a small thing, but it was something she dealt with daily, and she'd had enough of it.

Maybe it was a sign of something else though? Money was tight. It always had been, but it had only grown worse over the past few years. They got by, but only just. And it didn't help that a few things had gone missing. None of it had been big or hugely expensive—well, what on earth did they own that was?—or even sentimental, but it niggled that someone had sneaked in and helped themselves.

Agnes guessed that if she hadn't headed back to the pub, she would have still felt fine, but talking to that Steve Hill, well, he'd just made her blood boil, hadn't he? She'd noticed Andrew trying to keep things saner, but he'd been fighting a losing battle. What did they know about anything?

It had felt good to say what she had. That policeman with the ruined face, poor man, he'd listened well enough, even offered to come round for a chat about it all. So that was nice, wasn't it? They were lucky to have good police in the Dales, but still, a little help would make sense, she thought. And sometimes, a little direct action was exactly what was needed, wasn't it?

Following what had happened at the pub, she'd been unable to rest easy ever since, hadn't slept well. She'd only gone for a drink because everyone else had headed to the pub after the burning, and she'd sort of just got caught up in the cheery throng. At points, the crowd had been so thick, she'd felt sure she could have just lifted her feet off the ground and been carried along.

She'd seen Andrew talking in the corner, crept closer to listen in and throw in her support for what he was saying, when it had all gone just a little bit wrong. She'd not realised who he was talking to. If she'd known, she'd have stayed clear. It was that Steve Hill's fault, wasn't it? He was a mean old grouch at the best of times. He'd never liked Danny.

And then, of course, there was Christopher Black. Was it not enough that his farm had gobbled up most of her and Jonathan's own little corner of heaven? Probably not. A man like that lived for greed, growing fat on it by the day. Smug, too. The bastard. A smug, fat bastard, that's exactly what he was, and she half wished she'd called him that to his face. Not that she could reach that high. Why was he so bloody tall? An irrelevance, she knew, but it still annoyed her. He had everything, including height. She certainly didn't have that. It was no surprise the man had never been married, and the thought of it made her shudder.

So, the chapel was what she had decided she'd needed, and the chapel was where she had headed that afternoon after a light lunch of a cheese sandwich and a glass of home-made lemonade. To think, to have a little prayer about it all, and to help her decide what she was going to do about everything.

Worship, if it could be called that, had started at two pm on the dot. There was certainly no clapping or any of that kind of silliness, thank goodness. Instead, it was a little service put together by a local preacher she'd never heard of, someone from another circuit over beyond Sedbergh. He wasn't too bad either, she'd noticed, even chose some good hymns, and she'd belted those out with abandon. *How Great Thou Art* had always been a favourite.

The sermon had been a mix of good and bad. The good stuff had been the jokes, the bad were all the references to obscure Bible passages no one had ever read. And judging by how the preacher talked about them, he hadn't either. He'd had an air of Terry Wogan about him, she'd thought, albeit a Terry Wogan in a threadbare suit smelling of pipe tobacco and, for some strange reason, chocolate brownies. But once the service was over, there she was, back home again, wondering just what she was going to do.

From where she sat at the kitchen table on a chair with legs that wobbled alarmingly, Agnes heard movement upstairs. Danny was up there, buried in his room, reading probably. That was his escape. Always had been. A natural reader, he'd devoured books from an early age. He'd never really taken to movies or the television. Computer games didn't hold his attention. Too busy for his brain, they'd been told. Too much stimulation. But books? They were a safe, quiet world he could pop into and wander about in. She envied him. She loved him. Her only child. And he loved those goats, didn't he? Which is why she was so desperate to protect them. She'd do anything for him, absolutely anything.

The sound of a door opening. Boots dropping onto the floor. Footsteps. A man walked into the kitchen, weariness etched into every line on his face and held there by love.

'Hello, Love,' he said. 'Danny upstairs, then?'

'He is,' Agnes said. 'How's your day going?'

'Well, I've maybe helped stave off bankruptcy for another few days anyway. I could do with a shower, but there's a few more jobs to be getting on with first.'

As husbands went, Jonathan was a solid bet, or at least that's what her mother had said when she'd first met him. They'd been seeing each other for a few months before she had brought him home and he'd not been put off by the formality of the greeting, the table laid for afternoon tea, the questions.

He was a quiet man, and strong. He didn't seem to get riled about anything. He'd loved her all their years and been the kind of dad to Danny that made her heart sing just to think about it. Anything and everything that had needed to be done for their son, he'd done it. Never a complaint, never a moan. His son, his family, always came first.

'I went to chapel,' Agnes said.

'Hope you said a few good words about me,' Jonathan said, pouring himself a glass of water, sitting down for a moment's rest. 'Lord knows I need them.'

'You don't need me to do that. God knows you're a good man.'

It was true, Agnes thought, he was.

'God knows that I'm not, as well,' Jonathan said.

He drank his water.

'The rough and the smooth,' Agnes said. 'God knows we are all both of those.'

Agnes saw that look flicker in his eyes again, the one he did his best to hide. She'd never been quite sure what to make of it. Not that he had ever been one for secrets, but it did tell of something hidden, and that had niggled at her recently. It was a look both haunted and hunted, though she'd never known by what, never asked either. Never seen the need. Until now, though. But she still couldn't ask. In case she was wrong. Maybe there would be another way. Neither of them had ever said that maybe they should sell up, but they were both thinking it, and dreading it. Putting it off in the hope of tomorrow being a little brighter.

Jonathan sighed, placed his empty glass on the table, stretched, and stood up. 'I'd best be off again then. Once I've done the jobs I mentioned, I'll go check over the goats.'

'Danny will want to come.'

'He'd better too,' Jonathan said, his smile warm and knowing. 'He's the only one who can handle old Martha. She's getting worse, you know. Grumpy and just hateful, if you ask me. She's a mean one.'

'Danny loves her.'

'And she loves Danny, I know,' said Jonathan. 'But the look she gave me today? I swear she channels heat from the devil himself! Anyway, just let him know I'll be down with them in a couple of hours. Send him over.'

'I will.'

Jonathan made to leave, then paused at the door.

'Oh, and I might head out with the gun one night this week,' he said. 'Not sure when, yet. Not today, obviously, seeing as it's Sunday.'

'Rabbits?'

Jonathan gave a nod.

'They aren't half making a proper mess. A few hours lamping and I reckon I can clear them out well enough.'

'Good for the pot, too,' Agnes said. 'And the freezer.'

Cheap, too, she thought, which was always good.

'They are that. I'll be gone for a few hours. You'll just have to keep the bed warm.'

'I always do.'

'You do indeed,' Jonathan said.

Agnes saw a twinkle in his eye, one that had had her to bed often enough for a bit of slap and tickle.

Jonathan headed back out into the remains of the day.

Alone again, Agnes leaned back in her chair. She had a good husband, a son she adored, crippling debt, and a bunion on her foot that she was fairly sure was becoming self-aware. It wasn't much, no, and she was sure many, if not most, folk would think she'd settled for second best. But she hadn't. This was her world, and she needed to protect it. And that decided it for her. This meeting on Monday was important, and she'd get the keys to the Temperance Hall for it to make sure it went ahead, not so much because she cared about the Dale, which of course she did, that went without saying, but for her son, her husband, her family. First, though, she would head to see that detective. And if nothing came of that, well, she would have to see, wouldn't she? And with that, she grabbed her keys and headed off into the day.

CHAPTER EIGHT

THE JOURNEY OUT OF HAWES AND DOWN THROUGH Wensleydale grew increasingly gloomy, clouds tumbling their way across the sky thick as soup, to then roll down the fells in ominous shadow. It ended in a darkness so absolute and oppressive Harry wondered if maybe he'd fallen asleep in the passenger seat only to wake up with evening already frowning down on the world. And to think, how bright and summery yesterday had been. It hardly seemed possible that everything could change so quickly and with such drama. And yet it did, and often.

As Jadyn slowed down to turn off the road and down a gravel drive, large drops of rain began to thump down, bursting into small crowns on the windscreen.

'Doesn't bode well, does it?' Harry said, leaning forward as though getting a closer look at the rain would give him a deeper understanding of why it was falling.

The weather had the air of bad omens about it, not that he believed in such. But two break-ins so close together? That had him a little worried. Events like this sometimes came in waves. And the power of them could smash their way through a community with little anyone could do to stop them. The pieces left behind always took so long to pick up.

'Floods around here can be pretty spectacular,' Jadyn said, slowing down further for the rough lane rumbling grumpily beneath them like it was annoyed they were there at all. 'You should visit Aysgarth Falls when the rains have come in. Amazing stuff. Scary, too, all that water heaving itself down the valley. Imagine what it would be like to get caught in it.'

'No,' Harry said. 'I won't.'

'You'd be smashed to pieces,' Jadyn continued. 'Wouldn't stand a chance. There's always a few sheep that get washed off the fells when it's like this. Poor buggers.'

The farm ahead of them was an impressive sight, Harry thought as they approached it, the rain quickly moving on from a faint spattering to a downpour. The potholes in the lane filled up quickly, grubby water thick with dust and dirt from the hot weather of the previous days.

The house was all gable windows and front lawn, a place that, to Harry, was all about showing off to others. It looked cold in spirit and temperature, a building only, rather than a home, where fires would only ever be lit if a visitor was deemed important enough to warrant one. He knew he was jumping to a lot of conclusions, not just about the house, but about the owner, particularly as they'd not even seen inside the place. But his gut was rarely wrong.

Jadyn eased the vehicle to a stop and switched off the engine.

'And you're sure it's a shotgun that was stolen?' Harry said.

'I am,' said Jadyn. 'Why?'

Harry scratched his chin, frowned.

'Just look at the place, though,' he said. 'Surely, it's got security?'

'Only one way to find out,' Jadyn said, and he launched himself out of the vehicle to run to the shelter of the impressive stone porch at the front of the house.

Harry glared at the weather for a moment, then climbed out of the vehicle and walked with purpose through the stinging rain to Jadyn.

'You didn't run,' Jadyn said, staring at Harry.

'Of course I bloody well didn't,' Harry said. 'It's only rain, isn't it?'

'What if it's acid rain?' Jadyn asked.

Harry stared at the police constable.

After a pause that lasted just long enough to feel awkward, Jadyn said, 'Shall I ring the bell?'

Harry gave a firm nod.

'I think that's for the best.'

The bell was a ceramic button set into the stonework of the porch. Jadyn pressed it and from somewhere deep in the house Harry heard a metallic tinkling. A moment later the sound of footsteps approached.

The door opened. Standing in front of them was a man just a shade shorter than Harry. He had a look of meanness about him, Harry thought, as the man stared out at them from under eyebrows thick enough to use as yard brushes.

'Yes? What is it, then? If you're selling something, I'm not buying, whatever it is.'

'Mr Steven Hill?' Jadyn said. He then added, with what Harry thought sounded like boundless pride, 'We're the police.'

'I can see that well enough,' Mr Hill said. 'I'm not blind, you know. It's not Steven, either, it's Steve.'

'We're here about the theft,' Jadyn explained.

Mr Hill frowned, rubbed his chin. 'Are you, now? And why's that, then?'

'Because you called us about it,' Jadyn said, his voice giving away his confusion about where the conversation was going. 'And we're here to find out what happened.'

'But I've told you what happened, haven't I? Said everything that needed to be said on the phone talking to whoever it was who answered it. Even gave a description of who I think did it. And I know who did, don't I? Too bloody right I do. Don't have his name, but it's him, I know it.'

'I know, but—'

'So, shouldn't you be out trying to find my gun and that bloody thief?' Mr Hill asked. 'Instead of standing here on my doorstep wasting my time having me talk about it all again? I mean, what's the point of my calling you people in the first place and telling you about what happened, if I then have to go over it all again with you now? Or is wasting my time a hobby of yours? No wonder things are so bad around here.'

Harry decided to step in.

'Mr Hill? I'm Detective Chief Inspector Grimm. We need to check through the details of what happened, then we can go from there. This shouldn't take too long. May we come in?'

Mr Hill turned his attention from Jadyn to stare at Harry, his eyes narrowing to thin, black lines. They reminded Harry of arrow slits in castle walls, mean and dangerous and with no way of seeing what lay behind them. Mr Hill had given them a lot of information already. Harry, however, wanted to go through things step by step so as to not miss anything.

'You're that one from the weekend, aren't you?' Mr Hill said. 'At the Bartle? I saw you. Couldn't miss you if I'm honest, what with, well, you know, all of that going on.'

He gestured at his own face, clearly talking about Harry's own.

'Yes, I was there,' Harry said, ignoring him.

'You're wrong, you know, about this place not needing folk like me to do something about crime, leaving all of it to you instead. And what happened here? Well, it just goes to show we're right, doesn't it?'

'It's our job, Mr Hill, not yours,' Harry said, and he stepped forward.

Mr Hill didn't budge an inch and Harry paused his advance.

'So, you don't want our help then, is that it? Not good enough for you?'

'That wasn't the point I was making at all,' Harry said. 'Vigilante action is never a good idea.'

'That's a big word for nowt more than us local folk taking back some control.'

'Something always goes wrong,' Harry said, 'no matter how well-intentioned. And my aim in what I said was to protect all of you from something bad happening that you can't then undo.'

'We can look after ourselves,' Mr Hill said. 'This is Yorkshire, remember? We know what we're about.'

'You'd be surprised how quickly things can get out of hand.'

'Would I now?'

Mr Hill leaned his head forward, staring those narrow

eyes even harder at Harry, then he stepped back and said, 'Best you come on in, then. I'll get a brew on. The way the weather's coming in, you'll be needing something warm inside of you, that's for sure.'

A few minutes later, Harry, Jadyn, and Mr Hill were all sitting together in the kitchen.

'So, about this shotgun,' Harry began, having taken a slug of the tea to warm him up from the chill of the rain seeping through his clothes.

'What about it?'

'We'll need the details of the gun itself,' Harry said. 'And a look at the safe would be useful, too, so that we can get an idea as to what happened.'

'Take fingerprints, that kind of thing,' said Jadyn.

Mr Hill laughed.

'No, I'm serious,' Jadyn said.

'I wasn't laughing at that,' Mr Hill said. 'It was the mention of the safe that tickled me.'

'Not sure why that would be funny,' said Harry.

'You see, they took that as well,' Mr Hill said. 'There is no safe.'

CHAPTER NINE

HARRY WASN'T SURE HE'D HEARD CORRECTLY.

'It's gone?'

'Ripped it out of the wall and the floor,' Mr Hill said. 'Not easy to do, either. I mean, that's the point, isn't it, of a gun safe? To be difficult to remove, like. My old dad, he used to keep his gun under his bed, just in case.'

'Just in case of what?' Jadyn asked.

'Exactly,' Mr Hill replied.

Harry stood up.

'Where is it, then?' he asked.

'The safe? No idea,' Mr Hill said. 'It's gone, hasn't it? Good luck to them getting into it. Though I reckon a good angle grinder would have you through it in a minute or two.'

'What I mean is, can you show us where it was?' Harry said. 'And do you have any idea when this happened, exactly?'

Mr Hill led Harry and Jadyn from the kitchen and down the hall to a cupboard under the stairs that faced the front door they'd entered through a few minutes before. He opened the cupboard and there Harry saw among the clutter of an old vacuum cleaner, lots of boxes, some toilet rolls, and far too many carrier bags, some shattered brickwork and holes in the wall and floor where the safe must have been before it was ripped out.

'Happened early this morning, while I was out at church,' Mr Hill said. 'Always head over for communion. Start the week proper, you see. I must've left the front door open.'

'Why do you say that?'

'Only way they could've got in, isn't it?' Mr Hill said, holding up a set of keys, which were attached to a chain clipped to his belt. 'I mean, here's the key right enough. Took it with me to church. So, I must've forgotten, surely. Door was hanging open when I got back, like the house just wanted any Tom, Dick, or Harry to wander in and have a nosy around.'

'Does anyone else have a key?' Harry asked.

Mr Hill shook his head.

'I live alone. No other bugger to give one to, have I?'

'And you have the keys on you all the time?' Jadyn asked.

'Too damned right, I do,' Mr Hill said. 'I lost them once last year, but never again, that's for sure.'

'Lost them?' Harry said. 'When?'

'Buggered if I can remember that. But they turned up again. I'd left them in my old tractor, would you believe! They were right there, staring at me, if something can stare at you from the floor of a tractor. Felt like a right daft pillock. I didn't leave my house on account of the place not being secure. Was just about to have all the locks changed and then there they were, like they'd been there all along.'

Harry frowned.

'And you're sure you've no memory of when this was?'

'Who do you think I am, Mr Memory Man? I said I couldn't remember, didn't I? Can't see why it matters. Nowt to do with this, is it?'

'All details are important,' Harry said. 'No matter how small.'

'They are indeed,' said Mr Hill. 'This'll bugger up my insurance, that's for sure. Nowt I can do about that, though, is there? Forgetful in my old age, I think. But then we never used to lock doors round here. Was never the need, you see? Seems we have to lock everything down now, doesn't it? Sticky-fingered buggers strolling around just waiting to get their hands on things that aren't theirs.'

'What time were you at church?' asked Jadyn.

'Eight. Left here at seven-thirty.'

'And which church was that?'

'St Oswald's, over in Askrigg,' Mr Hill said. 'The vicar there, she does a grand job with the sermon. Could do with a bit more fire and brimstone now and again, but other than that, she's great. And there's always a nice mug of good coffee at the end of it. Sometimes doughnuts, too. Bit of a treat, that. You know what, I reckon if more churches were like hers, more folk would go, you mark my words. Doughnuts, that's the answer.'

'That'll be Anna's church,' Harry said.

'You know her, then?'

'This is Wensleydale, Mr Hill,' Harry said. 'I've not been here long, but I've been here long enough to know that everyone knows just about everyone else.'

Harry examined the cupboard which had, according to Mr Hill, contained his gun safe. From what he could see, the safe had been wrenched away from the wall, by a power tool of some kind. There was no way anyone was going to be doing that kind of damage with a hammer and chisel.

'Just one shotgun, yes?' Harry asked. 'In the cabinet, I mean.'

'Just the one,' said Mr Hill. 'Miroku 20-bore. Cartridges, too. The gun's nowt special, but it does the job, I promise you. Lighter than a 12-bore, great for game shooting, nice and quick you see, easy to whip through the air. Fine for rabbits, too. You can spend a fortune on a gun, but if you can't shoot, then that's your problem, isn't it? Not what you're using. No point blaming the tool if you can't use it. I used to be quite the shot back in the day. I've tried over-and-unders but never got on with them.'

'Would it be possible to see your licence?' Harry asked.

Mr Hill opened his jacket and pulled out a plastic wallet from a pocket.

'Here,' he said, handing it over.

Harry opened the wallet to find a shotgun licence staring back at him. A quick glance over and he handed it back, all of it in order.

'I don't need to tell you that this is a serious crime,' he said.

'Well, all crime's serious, isn't it?' Mr Hill said.

'It is,' said Harry, 'and I'm not suggesting otherwise. However, if it had been a few gold rings and a diamond necklace or two, I wouldn't be standing here worrying that they were going to be used out on the streets somewhere, possibly taking lives, would I?'

Mr Hill said nothing. Harry knew he was maybe being a little sharp with the man, but sometimes it was necessary.

'Was anything else stolen?' Jadyn asked.

'I'd have told you if it was, wouldn't I?'

Harry saw a thought crease Jadyn's brow.

'What are you thinking?' he asked.

Jadyn looked at the front door and then back at the mess in the cupboard under the stairs.

'I'm not sure.'

'Talk it through,' Harry said, encouraging the police constable to say what was on his mind.

Jadyn was quiet for a moment, caught up in his thoughts.

He then pointed at where the shotgun cabinet had been. 'Whoever did this,' he said, 'knew what they were looking for and where it was going to be.'

'Why do you say that?'

Jadyn looked up at Harry.

'Because it's like what you've told me, isn't it? To look for something that isn't there, but should be, or something that is there, but shouldn't.'

Harry saw Mr Hill shake his head as though trying to dislodge an uncomfortable thought.

'Come again?' the man said. 'Looking for something that's there but isn't and shouldn't? What kind of double-talk bollocks is that, now?'

'Go on,' Harry said. 'Explain what you mean.'

'If this was a crime of opportunity, which theft and break-ins often are, maybe they saw the door open or whatever, then first there's the fact that we're all the way down here at the end of the drive, isn't there? And the only way to see that the door was open would be to actually drive up to the house.'

Harry felt a smile begin to form but kept it hidden as Jadyn talked.

'You wouldn't see it from the road, would you? Second, if it was that, if they'd driven past and seen the door open, which I've just said is impossible, then they'd have been all over the house looking for anything of value, wouldn't they?'

'Maybe they have been, then,' Mr Hill said. 'You want to have a look about, like?'

Jadyn shook his head.

'No need.'

He pointed at the cupboard under the stairs.

'Looking in there is hardly the first port of call, is it? They'd have been after high-value stuff, things they can grab and sod off with and flog for cash sharpish. Televisions, laptops, jewellery, that kind of thing. They'd not be looking under the stairs. No one keeps anything of value in a cupboard like that. It doesn't make sense.'

'Well I did,' said Mr Hill. 'You saying I don't make sense, is that it?'

'I think what Constable Okri is pointing out, Mr Hill, is that as break-ins go, this one looks planned. And I'm inclined to agree with him.'

'Oh, so you're inclined now, are you?'

'I am,' Harry said. 'Now, you said earlier you'd given a description of someone you saw and that you know who it was but don't have a name. And yet you said you were at church when this all took place.'

'I've a camera, haven't I?' Mr Hill said.

At that moment, Harry wanted to grab Mr Hill and shake him hard enough to dislodge his head.

'A camera? Why didn't you mention this earlier?'

'You didn't ask earlier.'

'Well, I'm asking now.'

Harry sometimes wondered why people could be so deliberately obstructive. With Mr Hill, it was clearly just a part of his nature, but it wasn't making things any easier.

Mr Hill led Harry and Jadyn out of the house and into the yard.

'Over there,' he said, pointing a gnarly finger at an old barn currently in the process of some building work.

Harry looked and, sure enough, saw a camera.

'It's not pointing at the house,' he said.

'Of course it isn't,' said Mr Hill. 'It's pointing at the yard. That's where the expensive stuff is. I'm having that barn there converted into a little holiday rental. Nice little earner, I reckon.'

'You could have two cameras,' Jadyn suggested.

Mr Hill glared at the constable.

'I'm not made of money,' he said.

Harry wasn't so sure, having seen the house and now the work going on with the barn conversion.

'Anyway,' Mr Hill said, 'there it is, and I caught him, like. Look.'

He pulled out his phone and a few moments later had opened saved files downloaded from the camera on the barn.

Harry looked at the grainy image.

'There he is, the cheeky bugger,' Mr Hill said. 'Bold as brass, like.'

Harry watched as a figure walked across the phone screen. It was difficult to make out many details. But whoever it was, they walked around the yard, stood still for a while, keeping their face away from the camera itself, then wandered off screen again, back towards the house. Whoever it was, they were wearing what looked like a leather biker's jacket and jeans.

'We'll need a copy of this,' Harry said. 'Jadyn? Can you sort that?'

'Absolutely.'

'And you think you have an idea who that is, correct?' Harry asked.

'A weasel who needs his neck wringing, that's who,' answered Mr Hill, spitting the words. 'Honestly, if I get my hands on him, I'll ...'

The man's voice faded, burned up by the anger fuelling it.

Harry looked again at the grainy image on the phone screen.

'So, you don't know who it is, then,' he said, trying to encourage Mr Hill to clarify what he was saying.

'Oh, I know who it is,' Mr Hill said. 'Of course I bloody well do. I've run him off my land a few times, sneaking around. Found him in a barn once. He couldn't get out of there quick enough. I think the fact that I was carrying my now-missing shotgun helped persuade him it was a good idea to leg it.'

'And you reported him for that? Did he take anything?'

'He didn't have a chance,' Mr Hill said. 'Out of there like a ferret, he was.'

'So, what makes you think this is the same person?' Jadyn asked.

'My gut, for one,' said Mr Hill, his words falling over themselves. 'Never wrong, that. My eyes, for another. And they don't lie, do they, the eyes? Seen him before, like I said, usually sneaking around with Sunter's lad. Been a good long while, mind.'

'Keith Sunter?'

Mr Hill gave a nod.

'His lad, Anthony, right waste of space. That's not him on the camera, though, it's his mate, like I said.'

'Why do you say that?'

'That jacket of his. Wore nowt else. No idea what he's called, though. All I ever knew him as was *that little shite*, if you know what I mean.'

'Keith hasn't seen his son in over two years,' Harry said.

'And I've not seen his mate here for at least that long myself.' Mr Hill tapped a thick finger on the screen of his phone. 'But it's him, that's Anthony's mate, I promise you. And he's just the kind of someone that you, Mr Policeman, should be locking up and then throwing away the key, that's for sure.'

With nothing else forthcoming from Mr Hill, Harry led everyone back to the house. He quickly went over everything they'd discussed then made another call to the Scene of Crime team to turn around and come back out to Wensleydale again. With that done, he rang the office. Detective Constable Jenny Blades would be in, and he wanted her out here with Jadyn.

'Jen? It's Harry.'

'Were your ears burning?'

'Why?'

'I've just had someone come in asking to talk to you about something. Said it was very important that it was you she spoke to. I told her you were otherwise engaged and to call back later.'

'Who?' Harry asked.

'Mrs Hodgson,' Jen said. 'I think she's hanging around for a while on the off chance you'll be back sooner rather than later. Popped over to Spar I think.'

'I don't know a Mrs Hodgson,' Harry said, then realised that yes, he did, as the Burning of the Bartle floated to the top of his mind.

'Well, I may as well come over, then,' he said. 'If she comes back, tell her to wait. I shouldn't be long.'

'No problem.'

'And when I do, I want you over here with Jadyn,' Harry said.

'The break-in?'

'Yes,' Harry said.

'Something up?'

'I'm not sure,' Harry said. 'But I'd rather have two pairs of eyes on it that I trust, than just the one.'

With instructions left with Jadyn, Harry headed back up the Dale to Hawes. He found himself thinking that, as weekends went, this one was certainly measuring up to be unforgettable, and not for any of the right reasons. And he couldn't help but wonder if all of this was only the beginning. Of what, though, he had no idea.

CHAPTER TEN

When Harry arrived at the Community Centre in Hawes, he found Jen sitting in the office with Mrs Hodgson waiting for him. She was wearing a threadbare, ankle-length wax jacket and a wide-brimmed hat that looked as though it had spent a good deal of its time being enthusiastically chewed, though by what, he didn't know. On her feet were a pair of red Wellington boots.

There was an air about her, Harry thought, of someone with a purpose. Whatever she was here for, he knew by the way her jaw was set that she wasn't going to leave unless it was dealt with. At a glance, he put her age at somewhere in the mid-to-late fifties, though the laughter lines at the corners of her eyes seemed to him to be born as much of worry and tiredness as laughter and smiles.

'Boss, this is ...' Jen began, but the woman stepped forward and held out her hand.

'Agnes Hodgson,' she said, her voice firm and confident as she introduced herself. 'We met yesterday, at the Burning of the Bartle.'

Harry shook the offered hand.

'That we did,' Harry said. 'How can I help?'

A look of mild confusion inched its way across Agnes's face, one eyebrow raised just enough.

'You mean you don't remember?'

Harry shook his head.

Agnes held up a small, green bag in her right hand and then, to Harry and Jen's horror, she stretched up and thunked it softly against his face.

'Dog shit,' she said. 'That's what.'

Momentarily stunned by what Agnes had just done, Harry watched as she then did her best to wave it in front of his eyes like a tempting treat. A scent from it wafted under his nose, a truly stomach-churning mix of air freshener and the less than appetising contents.

'What the bloody hell do you think you're doing?' he said, stepping away to stare daggers down at the woman, wiping his forehead with his cuff.

'Dog shit, remember?' Agnes said, waving the bag around now. 'Like I told you on Saturday night. I want something done about it.'

Harry took a deep breath to calm himself down, but immediately regretted it, the rich stink from the bag in Agnes' hand catching the back of his throat and clinging on like it had teeth.

Harry immediately wished he hadn't shaken the woman's hand. Those bags were fragile, feeble things, something he knew from experience, clearing up after Smudge only to find out too late that the bag had a hole in it. Wiping soiled fingers on wet grass just didn't cut it.

'And what about it?' Harry asked, wondering if Agnes was the kind of person who spoke only in sentences that sounded like they all ended with an exclamation mark. 'There's a bin outside, if that's what you're looking for. By which I mean, use it. And now, please, before we go any further.'

'Well, there's more where this came from, I can tell you,' Agnes continued. 'It's everywhere. It's on my shoes, ends up in my house, on my carpet. I even found it on my reading glasses once. How is that even possible? Well, I won't put up with it anymore. It has to stop. No more dog shit, do you understand? And I want you to do something about it. Not just from walkers, either, but that next-door neighbour of mine.'

To emphasise the point she was making, Agnes again waved the bag at Harry.

Harry, his voice in check after his initial shock at being tapped on the head with a bag of dog excrement, stepped back, out of the way. That he'd made the journey over to only be assaulted by such a stench wasn't exactly putting him in the best of moods for the rest of their conversation, never mind the rest of the day.

Agnes lowered her hand. She made no attempt to do as Harry had instructed and remove her little parcel from the premises.

'What I want to know is,' she said, the bag dangling from her hand, 'why so many of them end up hanging from the trees and what you're going to do about it?'

'Ma'am, the police have plenty to be going on with as it is,' said Harry. 'I don't think we can spare the time to go picking up dog mess as well.'

'Well, something needs to be done,' Agnes said. 'And I'd rather you look into it than have to do something about it myself. I mean, I've tried, but nothing seems to work. There's always more of it, everywhere.'

'I made it fairly clear that any such action on the part of the general public is best avoided,' Harry said. 'So, whatever you're thinking of doing, I'd very much discourage you from doing it.'

'And that's why I'm here,' Agnes said, as Liz walked into the office.

She wasn't in uniform.

'Oh, hi,' Liz said, and Harry saw surprise in her eyes. She looked past him then and waved to Jen.

'You're not on duty today,' Harry said.

'No, I just popped in to show something to Jen.'

Harry glanced over at Jen and saw an awkward smile on her face.

'And would I be right to assume that whatever it is, is none of my business?'

Liz didn't answer. Instead, she looked at Agnes.

'Hi Agnes,' she said. 'What's brought you here, then? I don't think you'll be able to persuade Harry here to buy any of your goat cheese. We've only just managed to get him onto Wensleydale, but you never know.'

'Goat cheese?' Harry said. 'What?'

'I don't just have goats because of my son, Danny,' Agnes said. 'They're not a hobby, they're a business. I make my own cheese. Lovely stuff it is, too. Artisan.'

She said that last word as though it was a badge of honour.

'Of course you do,' Harry said. 'And I'm sure it is.'

'If I'd known, I'd have bought some with me.'

'Known what?'

'That you wanted to try some.'

'I don't think I said that I did.'

'I'll fetch some over in the week,' Agnes said, undeterred. 'You'll love it. Nice and ... tangy, yes that's the word, isn't it? Tangy.'

Harry did not want to talk about cheese. Especially not cheese described as tangy. Neither did he want to talk about dog shit. Today was getting weirder by the moment.

'So, why are you here, then, if it's not a social call?' Liz asked.

Harry knew what was coming next, was about to warn Liz, but it was already too late.

'Dog shit, Elizabeth, that's what's brought me here. Not goat cheese, dog shit. There's so much of it. Everywhere. I can't walk without stepping in it or having to avoid it hanging from a tree. Who does that? Who hangs dog shit from a tree? I want something done about it. Walkers, that neighbour of mine, it has to stop. Right now.'

Liz's eyes widened as she looked at Harry.

'You know each other, then, I assume?' Harry asked.

'Everyone knows everyone around here, you know that,' Liz replied. 'Certainly up this end of the Dale, anyway. Not so much the further down it you go, over towards Leyburn and whatnot.'

'I live down dale,' Agnes said, 'but I was born in Hawes, you see? And I'm over here a fair bit to the Mart. Today's a special trip, though. I thought it was best to strike while the iron's hot, as it were.'

'Then perhaps, Mrs Hodgson, you'd like to have a chat with PCSO Coates here?' Harry suggested. 'If so, then tomorrow would be good, when she's on duty.'

Agnes snapped her eyes up at Harry's.

'Oh no,' she said, 'it's you I want to talk to. You're the boss, yes?'

'Detective Chief Inspector,' Harry said. 'So, yes, that would make me the boss.'

'Then you can do something, can't you?'

'Well ...'

'Good,' Agnes said. 'I'm assuming you have an interview room or something? Somewhere we can go to have a nice little private chat?'

Harry tried very hard to hide the sigh that threatened to escape.

'Before we go any further,' Harry said, standing with Agnes outside the interview room door, 'I'm afraid I'm going to have to insist that what you're carrying be deposited appropriately outside the building. It's a health hazard.'

'But it's important,' Agnes said. 'It's evidence, isn't it? And I can't be throwing that away.'

'Evidence of what, exactly?' Harry asked.

'Littering, for one. And you're right, it is a health hazard, full of disgustingness.'

Harry was pretty sure that wasn't a word.

'Which was my point exactly,' he said. 'So, I'm afraid I'm still going to have to insist. That bag, and its contents, they're going outside in the bin before we go any further with this little chat. I hope you can understand why?'

Agnes paused, poop bag in hand.

'I could show you where I found it,' she said. 'And there's plenty more, that's for sure. You can test it or something, can't you? Trace it back to the dog that did it? Would that be enough? Evidence, I mean, if we catch the culprit? To put them away? And for a bloody long time, too, I hope. Makes my blood boil, I can tell you that for nowt!'

Harry gave a nod, just to get her to do as he had requested.

'Yes, I'm sure that would be very useful,' he said. 'For now, though, there's a bin outside. Just use that. There's a toilet here as well, you'll see it just down here at the end of the corridor, so you can wash your hands after. Then I'll see you in this room here when you're done.'

Harry opened a door to show where they were going to have their chat. Agnes stared into the room for a moment, gave an approving nod, then turned around and headed for the main doors.

CHAPTER ELEVEN

In the interview room, Harry stood waiting for Agnes to return from her errand. The afternoon was getting on and soon evening would be knocking at the door. He was imagining being back in his flat with Grace and Smudge when Agnes entered the room. He gestured to a chair opposite, and she sat down. Harry followed suit. A moment later, Jen popped in with a fresh pot of tea and a couple of mugs.

'I'm heading off now to catch up with Jadyn,' she said. 'Want me to bring in some biscuits before I go?'

'No, I think we'll be fine,' Harry said. 'Liz has gone now as well, yes?'

'She has,' said Jen.

'I like the sound of biscuits,' said Agnes, interrupting. 'What have you got?'

'Nowt much, to be honest,' said Jen, before Harry could do anything to stop her. 'Custard Creams, chocolate bourbons, and I think that's about it. Usually, we've a bit of Cockett's cake, but not today, I'm afraid. I'll need to have a word with Matt about that. It's his turn, I think, to buy it.'

'You do know that this isn't a café, don't you?' Harry said. 'People come here for police business, not to sit down for a natter and a bite to eat.'

'We can't be having a cup of tea and a chat without biscuits now, can we?' said Agnes. Then she looked at Jen and said, 'Sounds perfect. Oh, and can you bring some sugar in, please?'

Jen left the room. Harry couldn't say for certain, but he was sure he heard her stifle a laugh as she went.

'So,' Harry began, looking to hurry things along a little. The crime of owners not cleaning up after their dogs was not really something he wanted to dedicate too much time to. 'How exactly can we help you today, Mrs Hodgson?'

'First of all, call me Agnes,' came the reply. 'And I'm here because I think something needs to be done. About all the dog—'

Harry held up a hand.

'Yes, well, I think we both know why it is you're here,' he said. 'You've definitely made that more than clear. I'm just not sure what you are expecting us to do about it.'

'But you're the police, aren't you?'

'Not all of it, no,' Harry said.

'And it's disgusting, isn't it, how people don't pick up after their pets? Revolting, in fact. It has to be stopped.'

'Well, there are a number of waste bins around for people to use,' Harry offered. 'And if you see someone not clearing up after their dog, you can always report it.'

Agnes laughed. The sound bounced around the room as though desperately trying to find a way out.

'Yes, but that's not much really, is it?'

'That's the law as it stands,' Harry said. 'Though if you have any suggestions, I'd be more than happy to hear them.'

Jen popped round the door with a plate of biscuits and left without a word.

Agnes was into the biscuits immediately.

'Yummy!' she said, nibbling on a Custard Cream. 'I don't really buy biscuits for myself, so it's nice to have them as a treat, isn't it?'

Harry was beginning to wish he'd volunteered Jen to sit here with Mrs Hodgson. He removed his notebook, if only to hurry Agnes along with whatever it was she wanted to say.

'It's the thin edge of the wedge, though, isn't it?' Agnes said, tucking into another biscuit. 'Who knows where it might lead?'

'I think a lot of the time people just forget,' said Harry. 'I'm sure we've all done it.'

'You may well have done, but I certainly haven't.'

'You have a dog yourself, then?'

'Always,' Agnes replied, which struck Harry as an odd reply, but she gave him no time to enquire further. 'And I think something more needs to be done.'

Harry picked up his mug, went for a biscuit, then remembered what Agnes's hands had been holding earlier. He retracted his hand and gulped his tea.

'So, what would you suggest?'

'You need to arrest people. Just get out there and arrest them. Read them their rights, bring them in, lock them up for a few hours. That'll show them. It'd show him, that's for sure.'

'Him?'

'My neighbour, Mr Christopher Black,' Agnes said. 'His dogs are always loose, always doing their business on my fields. So, that's what I want; I want you to arrest him. Today, if that's at all possible.'

'That's not really how the police, or the law, works,' Harry said, not sure now whether to laugh or to shake his head in despair.

'Well, if you can't do that, how am I supposed to deal with it? And what about all those people wandering the lanes and footpaths and just letting their dogs do their business all over the place? Can you arrest them?'

Harry wasn't sure what to say. Which didn't matter right then, because he wasn't given the chance to speak.

'You could have a local register, couldn't you?' Agnes suggested, and it was clear to Harry that she had given this some serious thought. 'Every dog owner has to have their name on a register. Holiday-makers, too, because they shouldn't be given special dispensation just because they're not here all the time.'

Harry held up his hand to interrupt. Agnes ignored it and kept on talking.

'So, you have this register, yes? All the dog owners are on it, my neighbour for example, and then all you have to do is draw up a timetable of when and where they walk their dogs. Any mess found, you'll know who's responsible. It's quite simple, really.'

'Is it, now?' Harry said.

'Yes, it is.'

'And I assume we would be drawing up this register and timetable?'

Agnes's face lit up.

'You know, I knew you'd think it's a good idea!'

'No, that's not what I'm saying at all.'

Agnes was on her feet.

'I'll leave you to it, then,' she said, reaching for a few more biscuits and then shoving them into a pocket.

Harry stood up.

'Mrs Hodgson,' he said, 'I think you need to be clear on the fact that we will not be drawing up a register of dog owners or any kind of dog-walking timetable.'

'And you'll have a word with my neighbour?'

'We'll see if we can send someone round for a chat with Mr Black, yes,' Harry said. 'At least to establish the facts. And I'll ask my team to keep a particular eye out for a while for dog owners not cleaning up after their dogs. How does that sound?'

Agnes was already at the door.

'Thank you for all of your help, Detective,' she said. 'I very much look forward to hearing how you get on with it all and seeing our footpaths and my fields clean once again. Well, I'd best be off.'

As she was striding off towards the main doors, Harry caught up with her.

'Thank you for popping in,' he said—though he had no idea why—and opened the door for her to leave.

'Oh, it's been a pleasure,' Agnes said. 'With you sorting this little problem out, I don't need to worry about what those others are going to be getting up to. They'd only make things worse, like you said.'

Harry paused, the door half-open.

'What others? And what exactly are they getting up to?'

'What we were all talking about on Saturday,' Agnes said. 'There's quite a few keen to get going on it all. Part of me thinks it's a good idea, another part needs to be convinced.'

'All of you should know it's a bad idea,' Harry said. 'Was I not clear about that?'

Agnes looked up at Harry, then squeezed his arm with her hand.

'Don't you worry yourself about it,' she said, and with that, she was gone.

CHAPTER TWELVE

HARRY WOKE UP EARLIER THAN USUAL AND WASN'T entirely happy about it for two reasons. One, was that Grace wasn't at his side, as she'd headed home the evening before after he'd returned from work. Having a nice, warm cuddle before getting out of bed was something he rather enjoyed. Not that he was going to admit it to anyone. Two, was that Smudge had somehow managed to sneak into his bedroom in the middle of the night and was currently curled up at the foot of his bed. Also, it was Monday, and Harry had never been a huge fan of Mondays. Okay, so that was three reasons, but who was counting?

Sitting up, Harry shuffled his feet to shift Smudge, who was curled up next to them for warmth.

'Come on, you furry idiot,' he grumbled. 'Get off there and back into your own bed.'

Smudge didn't budge, the dog's stubbornness becoming something Harry was increasingly aware of.

'I know you can hear me.'

Still nothing, just a deep, contented sigh.

Harry swung his legs out of bed and slouched off for a shower. He turned the water up extra hot, enjoying the almost painful sensation of it burning into his skull. He closed his eyes and thought back over the weekend. The Burning of the Bartle had certainly been interesting, true, but with two break-ins and the chat with Agnes Hodgson, he'd pretty much forgotten about it. After that, the rest of Sunday had fizzled to nothing, and he'd headed home to fall asleep on the sofa.

As to the week ahead? Well, there would be plenty to be going on with, for sure, including reports from the SOC team about the break-ins, but he'd worry about all of that once he got to the office. Now, though, it was time for breakfast and a dog walk. So, he turned the blistering heat of the shower to freezing, caught his own breath from the shock of it, forced himself to endure it as long as he could, then stepped out and headed through to his bedroom.

'Bloody hell, Harry! Put some clothes on!'

Harry jumped at the sound of Ben's voice.

'I'm wearing a towel, aren't I?'

'You know Liz is here, right?'

'I wouldn't be walking around like this if I did, would I?' Harry said. 'I obviously went to bed before you two came home.'

'Well, she is, and I can't see her wanting to see her boss striding around like that, can you?'

'Well, next time, put a note under the door, then,' Harry said. 'I'm not psychic.'

'I did.' Ben pointed to the floor in Harry's bedroom. 'See? There it is.'

'Oh.'

'Exactly.'

Harry said nothing more and headed into his bedroom, shutting the door behind him. A few minutes later, and fully dressed, he headed out into the kitchen, Smudge at his heel.

'Just because I'm in here doesn't mean you get food,' Harry said, smiling.

The dog's wagging tail suggested she thought different. It was time for her to eat as well anyway, so he filled her bowl and Smudge just as quickly emptied it.

Harry quickly scoffed some toast then sorted himself out a coffee in a travel mug and headed through to the hall. He checked his watch; it had just flicked past seven. Smudge was already sitting by the front door.

'Fancy a walk, then?' Harry asked.

Smudge answered with the soft thump-thump-thump of her tail against the floor.

Outside, the warmth of Saturday was barely even a distant memory. The rain of the day before had eased through the night but was now threatening to return with a vengeance. Harry wasn't really in the mood for it. He felt like he needed a few more days of sunshine. Not just to laze around in, but to have it warming his back as he worked in the Dale. There was plenty enough wind and rain the rest of the year, so it seemed a shame to have waved goodbye to the sun. There was no way it would show its face today, that was for sure, the sky heavy and angry, a grey mass of operatic threat.

Heading through town, Smudge at his side, Harry was in the mood for a good, long walk, regardless of the weather. He had plenty of time before needing to be at the office and decided that he'd head up to the end of town, across the field behind the cemetery, then back along Old Gayle Lane, and finally across the footpath from Gayle and back into

Hawes. It was a nice little walk, and Smudge always enjoyed it.

At this time of the day, it was never really all that busy, though there would always be a few folk out offering their good mornings. Harry thought how little things like being seen around, just enjoying the countryside helped people see him, and the team, as more approachable. It was a community they served, and they were a part of it.

From the marketplace, Harry led Smudge down Penn Lane and paused for a look up Gayle Beck to the bridge on the other side of town. The water was a trickle, light bouncing between the small ripples on the surface. He could smell rain in the air and wondered how long it was before the promised downpour would be unleashed.

Further on, and opposite the playground, Harry spotted someone kneeling in the small pedestrian island in the middle of the road. The island provided a safe passage for anyone looking to make their way across from the old railway yard to the playground opposite and then on into town. It was also home to several perfect little flowerbeds, all well cared for and surrounded by cast iron railings painted green, a footpath cutting through the middle. There was also a plaque which he'd never really taken notice of before.

Harry decided to go over and say hello. As he did so, Smudge shoved her nose through the railings, then stretched out a paw to tap the arm of the person on the other side. Harry recognised them immediately as they looked at Smudge and then up at him.

'Mr Sunter,' Harry said, unable to disguise the surprise in his voice. 'It's you.'

'It is,' Keith replied, looking up from what he was doing.

He reached through the railings and patted Smudge on the head.

Harry wasn't quite sure what to say next. He'd seen the man early Sunday morning, and not in the best of states physically and mentally, and understandably so. Now here he was, kneeling in the dirt on a cold and soon to be wet day, sorting out some flowers.

'I thought you'd be at home.'

'The flowers needed seeing to,' Keith said. 'I've looked after this patch since we lost Helen.'

Harry remembered then about the car accident. His eyes fell on the plaque and he saw the words *Helen Sunter: You hold my heart still, and I will tend to your white rose.*

'This was where it happened, you see?' Keith said. 'They'd been in town for a few things, had lunch together, her and Anthony. They were crossing the road and a car just came out of nowhere. She pushed Anthony out of the way just in time. She wasn't so lucky.'

'Must've been awful,' Harry said, taking in these additional details of what had happened and understanding a little more about why Keith's son, Anthony, had gone so off the rails.

'Not the best, no,' said Keith. 'So, anyway, this used to be just grass, nothing special. But it's special now, isn't it? More than anyone will ever know, actually.'

He rested a hand on the freshly dug soil, then patted Smudge on her head once again and she nuzzled in.

'You're a friendly one, aren't you?'

Smudge took this as a sign that they were now best friends forever and offered her tummy up for a tickle. Keith obliged.

Harry shook his head in mock despair.

'She thinks everyone is her friend.'

'And I'm sure they are, too,' said Keith.

'Not exactly the best day for it, though,' Harry said, glancing up at the sky. 'And you're sure you're not too sore after what happened on Saturday night to be down there digging in the dirt?'

Keith glanced around at the small island of grass and flowers.

'I'm fine,' he said. 'It doesn't take much time, and I think it's nice to keep it looking good. It's taking my mind off things, too.'

Harry looked then at the flowers, dozens of them shining out with the most perfect white petals, daring the grey clouds to smudge them out with the promised storm.

'They're roses, aren't they?'

'They are,' said Keith. 'You're a gardener, then?'

Harry laughed. He knew nothing at all about gardening.

'I've never owned a garden, never even bought a house plant,' he said.

'That's a shame,' said Keith, and stood up and a wince of pain flashed behind his eyes. 'You'd be amazed at the difference they can make. Anyway, as you're here ...'

Harry watched as lines drew themselves into the features of Keith's face, turning his calm, almost monk-like visage into one considerably more serious.

'About what people were saying, and what you said yourself, on Saturday evening, at the Burning of the Bartle.'

'Oh, that,' Harry said, hoping he'd heard the last of all that. Clearly not, though, he thought. Then he remembered something from his visit to Steve Hill's. 'You mentioned Anthony's friends when we last spoke, one in particular?'

'He had so many friends when he was younger,' said

Keith. 'But after his mum was killed, he shut himself off. Then the ones he started hanging around with, I never really got to know, didn't want to either.'

'There was one who stood out, yes?'

Keith was thoughtful for a moment.

'Yes, there was. Ian, I think his name was. A fair few years older than Anthony.'

'What did he look like?'

'Goodness, I'm not sure I can remember. It's been a long time since I've seen him.'

'There's been another theft locally and someone was seen at the property. We've learned that this someone had previously been seen hanging around with your son.'

'And you think it was Ian? I can't really remember much about him. Short hair, like Anthony, but that's about it. Didn't really want to take much notice or get to know him.'

'That's it? Nothing else?'

'No, wait, there was that jacket of his, wasn't there? Yes, that was it. Anthony wore it a couple of times as well, from what I remember, like it was a badge of honour or something.'

'And what kind of jacket was it?'

'Like one that a biker would wear,' said Keith. 'You know, black and whatnot. Not that he had a bike, so far as I know. Reeked of weed. I could smell it on Anthony when he wore it.'

'You're sure about that?'

'Yes,' Keith nodded. 'It was a scruffy, stinking thing. Like its owner.'

Well, that was something, anyway, Harry thought, remembering the grainy images captured on the camera over at Hill Farm.

With nothing else to say, he said goodbye to Keith and

continued on his way. Hawes stretched out before him, leading him on. He walked up the hill towards the Auction Mart, then took a right across the field behind the cemetery, the path one of ancient flagstones worn by a hundred lives and more. Then Old Gayle Lane called him onwards and with Smudge to heel, he allowed himself to slip deeper into the day, awash in a cool breeze damp with the rumour of rain, the fells and fields peaceful, yet alive with the sounds of a world waking.

CHAPTER THIRTEEN

Back in Hawes marketplace, Harry headed over to the Community Centre, passing the pet shop on his right. As always, this brought a whine from Smudge, and she tugged at the lead.

'I'll grab you something later, you daft bugger,' Harry said, and together he and a momentarily disappointed Smudge walked on to the office the police team used as their base.

Inside, Dave Calvert, a man built like an ocean liner, was chatting with Detective Sergeant Matt Dinsdale. Harry had met him on his first day in Hawes. And on that same day, Dave had, without being asked by anyone at all, taken it upon himself to ensure that the new DCI had someone to socialise with who wasn't on the team.

'And here's the man himself,' Matt said, glancing over.

The first thing Harry noticed was that Dave was dressed from head to toe in camouflage. The second thing was that he was holding a brace of rabbits in one of his massive meat-hook hands.

'How do, Harry,' Dave said, striding over to then duck down to the floor and make a fuss of Smudge. 'You survived the Burning of the Bartle, then? Bit of a weird one, that, if you ask me. Haven't been in years. It's a night out though, isn't it?'

Harry looked Dave up and down. 'Last time I saw someone dressed like that, I was getting shot at,' he said. 'And best not to talk to me about the Bartle, not yet anyway.'

Harry saw Matt narrow his eyes at him, picking up on something hidden behind what he'd just said.

Dave rose to his feet with the faintest of groans.

'Been out for a spot of early morning shooting,' he said. 'Always try to get out with the gun when I'm back home if I can. A bit of fishing, too, if I'm in the mood. This was just a bit of pest control and a good walk in the early morning air. You can't beat it. You'll have to tag along sometime.'

'Might take you up on that,' said Harry.

'Matt here was just showing me a couple of pictures of the wee one as well.'

Harry peered over at Matt with a grin.

'By a couple do you mean hundreds?'

'I'm a new dad,' said Matt. 'What do you expect?'

'Well, yes, it was a few more than a couple,' Dave said, 'but I'm not complaining. No kids of my own and it's always good to see bright new eyes coming into the world, don't you think?'

Dave worked offshore, so wasn't around often. But when he was, he certainly seemed to make up for it, Harry thought. As for Matt, well, having become a dad a few weeks back, and regardless of the weariness in his eyes, it was clear that he and his wife, Joan, couldn't be happier. Though Harry would prefer to not see so many photos, mainly because to him, all babies looked much the same, all squishy and pink. And there were only so many times he could say, *Hasn't she grown?* and, *She's got her mother's eyes,* or whatever else people were supposed to say in those newborn baby photo situations.

'What about those wildlife cameras of yours?' Harry asked.

A while back now, Harry had received a call from Dave, who'd been out one night checking some cameras up in the red squirrel reserve in Snaizeholme. That phone call eventually led to Harry finding and adopting Smudge.

'Oh, they're fine,' Dave said. 'Got some great footage of the badgers the other day. You'll have to come and have a watch if you've a free evening.'

Harry ducked answering that by jabbing a finger at the rabbits.

'And you're just carrying those around with you, is that right?'

'These?' Dave said, lifting the rabbits to head height. 'Well, I was driving through, and I just thought I'd pop in and give you them.'

Harry wasn't sure he'd heard right.

'The rabbits? Give them to me? Why's that, then?'

'I've only been back a few days and the word's got around that you're staying here, permanent, like,' Dave said.

'Has it, now?'

'Which is fantastic news all round, I reckon,' Dave continued. 'So, I was just thinking to myself that what old Harry needs is something tasty to celebrate with. So, here I am, bearing gifts!'

'Well, that's very kind, Dave,' Harry said, having never been given dead rabbits as a present before. 'But—'

'And I'll take no buts,' Dave said, holding up a hand to forestall Harry's reservations. 'You just take them. I'll not take no for an answer, either. And what say we make an evening of it?'

'An evening of what?'

'I'll bring around some beers and we'll have a proper slap-up meal, like. What do you say to that? I've a crate in from the Wensleydale Brewery. Their Wensleydale Gold is an absolute gem of an ale, I promise you. Nectar, it is. Tastes like sunshine.'

'You've a whole crate?' Harry said, smiling inside at Dave's poetic description of a bottle of beer.

'Well, I'm not suggesting we drink them all, no, because that would be foolish. But we could certainly put a good dint in it.'

Harry wasn't sure how, but one minute he wasn't holding any rabbits at all, and the next he was. He was aware of the weight of them, of their smell. It wasn't unpleasant as such, sort of an earthy, grassy aroma with a hint of fur and, behind it, the metallic tang of blood. Smudge, however, was very interested in them, sniffing the carcasses with mounting enthusiasm, her tail almost a blur. Harry kept them well out of her reach.

'I've never cooked rabbit,' he said. 'Actually no, that's a lie. Survival training in the Paras. But that's a long time ago.'

'It's easy peasy,' Dave said, a phrase that didn't exactly fit with the man's huge frame.

'I remember our survival instructor telling us it tasted like chicken.'

'Well, it doesn't,' Dave said, shaking his head in mild despair. 'I mean, why on earth would it?'

'Well, it didn't,' Harry said, 'but I think that was down to us cooking it over a fire. I'm still amazed none of us got food poisoning.'

'It tastes like rabbit, is what it tastes like,' said Dave. 'And it's delicious. So, are you free one night this week, then?'

Harry liked Dave an awful lot. He was a difficult man to say no to. The enthusiasm in the man's eyes for what was clearly now a planned evening of feasting and merriment was impossible to ignore.

'I'll have to check,' Harry said. 'See what Grace and Ben are up to first. But I don't see why not.'

'Well, if we just grab some veg and do those as a stew,' Dave said with a nod at the rabbits in Harry's hand. 'Serve them up with loads of mash, there'll be plenty to go around. Have you got any bay? You need bay. I've a bay tree at home, so I'll bring some of that over as well. Love the smell of the stuff. We could do it in cider. You know what? That's exactly what we'll do. I'll bring that around with me as well, it's no bother. What do you say, Harry?'

'Like I said, I'll have to check with Grace and Ben.'

Dave was already at the door.

'Grand!' he said, as though everything was now arranged. 'Then I'll see you later in the week.'

He pushed his way out of the office and headed off into the day.

Matt laughed as Harry stood there holding the rabbits.

'And what am I supposed to do with these for the rest of the day, then?'

'Don't suppose you've a poacher's pocket in your jacket, have you?' Matt said.

Harry had no idea what Matt was talking about and just stared back.

'I'll take that as a no.'

'He's a force of nature, that man,' Harry said as Jim walked in. At his side came Fly, his young sheepdog, slinking in as quiet and gentle as a spring breeze, to sidle up next to Smudge. Harry watched as the two dogs touched noses. Fly flopped over onto his back. Smudge rested a paw on his chest, her tail thumping gently, conqueror of all.

'You didn't shoot those, surely?' Jim asked, pointing at the rabbits.

'Of course I bloody well didn't!' Harry said. 'For one, I don't have a shotgun or, in fact, a licence to own and shoot one.'

'Dave's just been in,' Matt explained.

'He's a hell of a shot, is our Dave,' Jim said. 'Probably bagged those out on our farm, then. Thought I saw him out there when I was checking on the sheep earlier this morning. He's got permission to shoot whenever he's home. He's not been around for a while. Looks like he's still got his eye in.'

'Interesting though this all is,' said Harry, 'none of it answers what I'm supposed to do with these in the meantime, until whichever evening it is that Dave is apparently coming round to help me eat them.'

'You don't need to do anything with them at all,' Matt said. 'It's not like they're going anywhere, is it? Just hang them somewhere for now. They'll be fine.'

Harry stared at the detective sergeant.

'What, like a slightly macabre wall decoration? It's not even Halloween.'

Jim walked over and took the rabbits from Harry.

'I'll put them in the back of my Landy,' he said. 'They'll be fine in there for the day, I'm sure. Not like it's going to be a warm one, is it?'

Jim headed out with the rabbits and Harry wandered over to the kettle.

'It's just boiled,' Matt said.

'You want another?' Harry asked, noticing the mug in Matt's hand.

'Is Wensleydale the jewel in the crown of Yorkshire?' Matt asked. 'Is fruit cake without cheese a travesty? Is—'

'I'll just take that as a yes, then,' Harry said, cutting in.

By the time Jim had returned, the rest of the team had started to show up. And it was a full house today, with everyone arriving in good fettle, as Harry had heard people say, though he'd not once used the word himself. Not yet anyway.

'We'll be needing the board, then,' Jadyn said, and Harry could see that the police constable was already standing ready, pens in hand.

'It's been a busy one, I hear,' said Gordy. 'Another break-in. On the bright side, Detective Superintendent Swift is on holiday this week, so he won't be over here—'

'Getting in the way?' Harry said, finishing the sentence for her.

'On the subject of getting in the way,' said Liz. 'A call came in yesterday to say that someone from the SOC team will be in first thing to go through what they've found at both crime scenes.'

Harry's heart sank.

'You're not one for expressions,' Gordy said, 'but that one, I think, suggests you're not happy with this news.'

'I'm not sure I'm ready for Mr Bennett,' Harry said.

Gordy leaned in.

'Speak of the devil ...'

Harry looked over his shoulder and standing just inside the door was the man himself.

'Good morning,' the pathologist said, announcing his arrival with the kind of smile Harry wanted to reach out and rip off like an old plaster.

'Best you take a seat,' Harry said.

'No, I think I'll be better over here, if you don't mind?'

Bennett moved then to stand beside the board.

Jadyn looked more than a little put out.

'Maybe later,' Harry said. 'For now, take a seat.'

The tone of his voice was enough to have the man do as he asked.

Harry gave everyone a few minutes to sort themselves out, grab a brew, then settle down. He walked over to stand in front of the board, nodding to Jadyn to grab a seat himself.

'Well, then,' he said, looking now at his team. They were all staring back at him expectantly. 'It's been a bit of a weekend if I'm honest. And I know there are other jobs to be on with, but we can leave the Action Book till later, I think. First though, we'll go through what happened over at—'

The office door burst open.

'Sorry,' said a voice everyone recognised. 'Did my best to get here in good time, but my mum wasn't entirely thrilled that I was coming at all. You know what she's like.'

Harry watched as Rebecca Sowerby, limping a little, but still walking with purpose, made her way into the room, and slumped down into a chair. A movement caught him out of the corner of his eye. When he looked, he saw that Bennett had his hand in the air, like a child in school asking to be excused to go to the toilet.

'Yes?' said Harry.

'I'm not sure she's supposed to be here,' Bennett said. 'If

I'm correct, she's still officially off. At least that's how I understand it.'

Harry looked then at Sowerby and saw a jaw set firm, but a pleading look in her eyes.

'She's here because I invited her,' Harry said. 'Can never have too many minds working on something, wouldn't you agree?'

'Well, yes, but—'

'Excellent,' Harry said. 'Then how about we crack on?'

CHAPTER FOURTEEN

HARRY GAVE A QUICK RECAP OF THE WEEKEND'S EVENTS, just to fill everyone in with the barebones of it all. He then handed it over to Gordy to go through the break-in over at Keith Sunter's place in Thoralby.

'We have very little on this for now,' Gordy began, 'but when is it ever anything else? What we know is that Mr Sunter, who lives alone, attended the Burning of the Bartle on Saturday evening. He then headed home. At some point in the night, he woke courtesy of Mother Nature. He heard something downstairs while he was in the bathroom.'

'You mean the intruder didn't wake him up?' Jim asked.

'Wears earplugs,' said Gordy. 'A light sleeper, apparently. He heard a sound downstairs, went to investigate, and came face-to-face with someone in his house.'

'What time was this?' Liz asked.

'He called it in at around one,' Gordy said. 'Paramedics arrived before me, and I was there by approximately one-thirty. So, we assume the intruder broke in just after midnight, maybe twelve-thirty.'

'Did they take anything?' Jadyn asked, pen already squeaking its way across the board.

'We won't know for certain for a couple of days, I don't think,' said Gordy. 'But we think the appearance of Mr Sunter was enough to send them on their way empty-handed, which is something, I suppose.'

'What about a description?' asked Matt.

'A dark, possibly black, hoody,' said Gordy. 'And jeans.'

Matt laughed.

'The go-to uniform of any burglar,' he said. 'We may as well just put a sign up outside asking them to hand themselves in, because we won't find them with that description, will we?'

Gordy continued.

'The damage was all downstairs. They broke in through a window, then turned the place upside down. It seemed to me that they were looking for something, but I can't say what or why.'

'I think I should point out as well, that Mr Sunter suffered a similar burglary two years ago,' said Harry. He looked then at Jen. 'You attended to that one, I think, yes?'

Jen looked thoughtful for a moment as she tried to remember that far back, then said, 'I did, yes. Can't believe the same thing's happened to the poor man, either. He's had enough to deal with these last few years as it is. How is he?'

'Well, he had a few bumps and scrapes from trying to keep the intruder from leaving, but he seems okay. He'd dealt with most of his injuries himself by the time the paramedics arrived.'

'He's bloody good at first aid, is our Keith,' Matt said. 'He's who I'd want sorting me out if I injured myself out on the fells, that's for sure. We've used that Land Rover of his a few times as well; nice go-anywhere, tow-anything vehicle, that.'

'And he's definitely okay; I saw him this morning while I was out with Smudge,' Harry added, then explained about the chat he'd had with Keith on the little traffic island on the other side of town.

'It was horrendous,' Matt said. 'Helen was killed outright. It's a few years ago now. Anthony was what, thirteen? He'd be twenty now, I think, not that I've seen him in a good while. I don't think anyone has. No one talks about it much. The driver was over the limit by a few, by which I mean bottles, not drinks. Keith's tended to that little patch of land ever since, a little memorial to her.'

A cough caught Harry's attention, and he found himself looking at Mr Bennett.

'Yes?'

'We have photographs of the scene of the crime,' he said, and stood up, walked over to Jadyn's board, and proceeded to cover it with stills showing what Harry and Gordy had both seen at Keith's house.

'They can go on the wall,' Jadyn said. 'Might be better to keep the board free, if that's okay?'

'Can they? Oh, yes, of course.'

Bennett then moved the photographs as suggested.

'As you can see, the place was turned over quite thoroughly. So far, we've found no DNA other than that of the owner, Mr Sunter, and his son, obviously, seeing as he lived there at some point in the past.'

'What about on the window the intruder broke in through?' asked Matt.

'Yes, that was an obvious place for a cut, for some blood

or tissue samples, but not a thing, I'm afraid. Very disappointing, really.'

'Fingerprints?' Jen asked.

'Again, nothing,' said Bennett. 'Same goes for hair and anything else that might help. Somehow, whoever did this, they managed to do so without leaving so much as a trace of themselves behind.'

'Impossible.'

Sowerby had, at last, spoken, Harry thought with relief and also some trepidation.

'How's that, then?' he asked.

'I mean, just look at the photographs,' she said. 'You can't do that amount of damage without leaving some part of you behind, can you? Like I said, it's impossible.'

'And yet, here we are,' said Bennett.

Harry watched as Sowerby turned fiery eyes on the man.

'No, and here *you* are,' she said, her intonation clear for all to hear. 'There has to be something somewhere, you know that as well as I do.'

'Yes, but—'

'Have you ever come away from a crime scene with no DNA? Nothing at all?'

'I didn't say there was no DNA,' Bennett replied. 'There's plenty relating to the owner, Mr Sunter and his son, just nothing else. No, that's not quite true, we did find some material that we matched to sheep, in the lounge I think.'

Harry laughed.

'He told me that a sheep broke into the house once,' he said.

'It happens,' said Jim, as though it was the most normal thing in the world. 'Best you don't ever come round ours, you'll find all sorts.'

Sowerby was on her feet and looking at the photographs.

'Something the matter?' Harry asked.

'I'm not sure, but maybe, yes.'

'How so?'

Sowerby leaned in then, her nose almost touching the photos.

'What do you see?' she asked, without actually looking at Harry.

'A mess.'

'What else?'

'There's something else?'

'I think so, yes.'

Harry looked again, shook his head.

'Well, I'm not seeing it,' he said.

Sowerby then proceeded to point at each photo in turn.

'In each one, the place looks a mess, doesn't it? Like everything's been thrown around, tipped on the floor, pushed off shelves, that kind of thing. So, all in all, a normal, every-day, run-of-the-mill burglary.'

'I'm not going to disagree with you,' said Harry. 'It was a break-in, and that's what I'm seeing in the photographs. Plus, I was there, and this is what I saw.'

'Then explain that,' Sowerby said, and dropped her finger onto a plant in the corner of one of the photos of Mr Sunter's lounge. It was a small white rose plant, like the ones Harry had seen earlier that morning.

'What about it?'

Sowerby turned her head just enough to look at Harry, an eyebrow raised a little.

'You don't think it looks strange?'

'The pot plant?' said Harry. 'It's a plant and it's in a pot. Not much else you can say about it, I don't think.'

'Look a little closer.'

Harry was beginning to think he maybe shouldn't have wished so hard to have the pathologist back.

'Well?'

'Well, what?'

'You mean you really can't see it? At all?'

Harry sucked in a breath through his nose and exhaled very, very slowly.

'No.'

'Anyone else?' Sowerby asked.

The rest of the team stood up and shuffled over to gather around what she was pointing at. There was a lot of *ums* and *ahs* but no one offered anything until Jadyn spoke.

'It's standing upright,' he said.

'Exactly,' said Sowerby.

'So what?' said Jim.

'Look, see there?' Sowerby began. 'Everything around it is just scattered about, isn't it? And all of it looks like it came off that shelf there. And yet this pot plant is standing there like it's always been there. Except it can't have been, can it, because it's standing on some of the things knocked down from that shelf there? There's not even any soil from the pot on the carpet.'

'Which means someone must have placed it there,' said Jadyn. 'Right?'

'Right,' Sowerby agreed.

Harry allowed Jadyn the somewhat smug grin on his face for spotting something no one else had. Then he frowned and stared at the photograph.

'But why would the intruder do that?' he asked. 'Doesn't make sense.'

Sowerby shook her head.

'Not a clue,' she said. 'But it's not right, is it?'

No, it isn't, Harry thought, and stared a little longer at the photograph, moved his eyes across the others. Sowerby had a point. That pot plant made no sense at all.

'Maybe the intruder just loved plants and didn't want to damage it,' Liz suggested. 'My gran's house is full of them. It's like a tropical rain forest inside her front room if it gets too warm.'

'Mr Sunter could've done it himself,' said Jim. 'Just picked it up after the intruder had gone, that kind of thing.'

Harry had known of more bizarre things in his time. Like the time he caught a burglar on a property only to have them do their best to convince those trying to arrest him that he was actually sleepwalking and in the middle of a very bizarre dream involving Elvis Presley and the Seven Dwarfs.

'What if it was Anthony?' Jadyn suggested.

'I wondered the same, but Mr Sunter says that he's certain it wasn't,' Harry said. He turned then to Bennet as Sowerby and the rest of the team took their seats again. 'Anything else?' he asked.

Bennett shook his head.

'Moving on, then,' said Harry, and looked at Jadyn.

'Yes, boss?'

'You can run through this one I think,' Harry instructed, and rather than give Jadyn a chance to try and convince him otherwise, he sat down, folded his arms, and waited.

'Oh, right, okay then,' Jadyn said. 'The shotgun, right, yes?'

'That's the one,' said Harry. 'The shotgun.'

Jadyn shuffled awkwardly on the spot for a moment.

'Between the hours of eight and we think around nine-thirty, at the residence of Mr Steve Hill, of Hill Farm, a gun safe containing a twenty-bore shotgun and an unknown number of cartridges was forcibly removed.'

'If I know Steve,' said Matt. 'He won't be happy about that at all.'

'Strikes me as the kind of person who's not really happy about anything,' Harry said.

'Fair point,' Matt agreed. 'Don't think I've ever seen the man smile. Has a face on him like a badly butchered joint of beef.'

Jadyn continued with his brief on what had happened, and having covered what they'd found, including the camera footage, looked at Harry.

'Yes, I think that about covers it,' he said. Then he turned to Bennett. 'The stage, as they say, is yours, I believe.'

Bennett rose to his feet and produced another folder with more photographs.

'There was no messing around with that, was there?' Jim said, as the photographs were stuck to the wall. 'Not an easy thing to do, rip one of those out.'

'I'm hoping you're not speaking from experience there,' said Harry.

'We've a couple of gun cabinets on the farm,' Jim said. 'Only way to have them out of the wall would be to take half the wall with you.'

'Looks like they did, too,' said Matt. 'I'll be checking mine tonight, that's for sure.'

'And me,' said Liz.

Harry did a double-take.

'You've a gun cabinet as well?'

Liz laughed. 'Hands up, who doesn't have a gun cabinet at home?'

Jadyn raised a hand, as did Gordy.

'The rest of you all have shotguns at home?' Harry asked.

'I'm assuming the question doesn't include me,' said Bennett.

Sowerby said, 'Mum's always had a gun. Dad liked to shoot as well. Not got my own, but I used to go out with my dad when I was younger.'

'Couple of rifles, too,' added Jim. 'Firearms certificates for those, obviously.'

'There's a lot of local shoots around,' said Jen. 'Not just game, either, but clays as well. Very popular around here. There's a brother and sister from over in Middleham, both on national squads.'

'So, why choose this one, then?' Harry asked. 'I mean, if there are so many of the things around, why do this?'

Sowerby was on her feet again, looking at the photographs. She's keen, Harry thought. Restless, too, no doubt.

'What about the rest of the house? Was there any other disturbance?'

'No,' Jadyn said. 'Just what you can see there in the photos. Mr Hill thinks he left the door open.'

'Personally, I'm of the opinion that's complete bollocks,' said Harry. 'Said he lost his keys last year, found them again a few days later.'

'You think someone swiped them?' asked Matt.

'If they did, then there's a chance this was done by someone local, someone who knows him, maybe,' said Jim.

'Possibly,' said Harry.

'I'd agree with you on all of that,' Sowerby said. 'This wasn't a crime of opportunity, was it? They didn't just drive past, have a quick peek, then rip out that cabinet and sod off.'

'Why do you say that?' Bennett asked.

Sowerby pointed at one of the photographs. 'Because doing something like this requires tools. Chisel marks here, here, all over the place.'

'I can see that very well myself,' said Bennett. 'And I was there, remember? There was damage to the opposite side of the cupboard, too. And scuff marks, from where they had dragged it out, I would think.'

'Did you find any evidence of nylon?'

'Yes, actually, we did,' Bennett said. 'In the stonework as well as various fragments here and there.'

'Nylon?' Harry said. 'What made you ask that?'

'Tow rope,' Sowerby said. 'Kinetic probably.'

'You know, that makes a lot of sense,' said Matt.

'Good, I'm glad,' said Harry. 'Perhaps, then, you could explain to the rest of us as to why.'

'You've not used one, then?'

Harry shook his head. 'A kinetic rope? Not that I can remember, no.'

'We've used them in vehicle rescues,' said Matt. 'You'd be amazed at where people can get a vehicle stuck. Even supposed off-roaders who say they know what they're doing. A good number of them don't, and those who do seem to go out specifically to get themselves stuck in the most impossible and precariously dangerous of places.'

'Go on,' Harry said.

'The kinetic rope transfers kinetic energy through the rope, which is nylon, to the stuck vehicle,' said Matt. 'They stretch, you see? Like, massively in some cases. Big elastic bands, really. It reduces the shock loads on vehicles.'

'Not sure I understand,' said Bennett.

Matt turned his attention to the pathologist.

'Let's say you attach a piece of string or cord to a stuck

drawer, right, to help you yank it out? Well, you have to really yank it, don't you, and there's a chance the string or cord will snap or the drawer handle will come off. And if or when the drawer moves, it shoots out, doesn't it? Flies at you.'

'Can't say I've ever done that,' said Harry, 'but keep going, anyway. I think I'm following you.'

'Now, take a good bit of elastic. Tie it to the drawer. You pull on it, and it stretches. And the energy you're putting into it is transferred to the drawer. But instead of it just being yanked out, it should pull it out more smoothly, because you don't have that sudden jarring action of the string or cord. See? Nice and simple!'

Harry frowned. He thought he knew what Matt was getting at but thinking about it made his brain hurt.

'So, what's that got to do with this?' Gordy asked.

Sowerby said, 'I think that whoever did this, chipped away around the cabinet first, then used a kinetic tow rope to do the final bit and get it out of the wall. Which means they'd have used a vehicle to do it.'

'We have a few tread marks, outside the house,' Bennett said and stuck up a couple more photographs. 'They're not the best, as you can see, but then the weather was against us. That's why I didn't put them up immediately.'

Harry stared at them. They were next to useless.

'If what you're saying is correct—'

'It is,' said Sowerby.

'Then you're right. Whoever did this, they knew exactly what they were coming for and how they were going to take it. They came with the right equipment, did the job, and left. And they not only knew when Mr Hill would be out, but also had somehow acquired a copy of the key to get into the house.'

'And I reckon Jim's right with what he said,' added Matt. 'About them either knowing Steve or the house or whatever. There's a good chance they're local.'

'What about the camera footage?' Jim asked.

'I'll print some stills from it when we're done,' said Jadyn.

'On that,' Harry said, 'Mr Hill said he recognised the person as someone who he'd seen hanging around with Keith Sunter's son, Anthony. Keith has confirmed that his son used to hang around with someone matching the description of this person here. We've a first name, Ian, plus confirmation that he always wore a biker jacket like the one this individual is wearing in the camera footage.'

'Well, at least Ian's not a very common name,' Matt said, shaking his head with a sigh.

'Right then,' Harry said, 'considering what we've got, which isn't much, it looks like the rest of the day is going to be spent knocking on doors, doesn't it? Matt?'

'Boss?'

'Check through the Action Book. If there's nothing urgent, then I want everyone on this, half of you over in Thoralby, the rest over to Hill Farm. You never know, someone may well have seen or heard something. Stay in touch, let me know if you find anything, and then we'll reconvene tomorrow and see where we are. Any questions?'

No one said a word.

'Good, let's get to it, then,' said Harry, then looked over at Sowerby. 'Coffee?'

'Absolutely,' she said.

CHAPTER FIFTEEN

WITH THE TEAM ON WITH INVESTIGATING THE BREAK-ins, Harry walked Sowerby out of the Community Centre, down through the marketplace, and into the Penny Garth Café at the top end of town. He ordered them both a coffee.

'Good to see you today,' he said. 'If a little unexpected.'

'I wish I could believe you,' Sowerby replied, and took a sip of her coffee. 'I should've called ahead, I know, but when I heard that Bennett was over, I just couldn't help myself.'

'You heard? How?'

Sowerby smiled.

'That would be telling now, wouldn't it?'

'Yes, it would,' said Harry. 'Which is why I asked the question. Detective, remember? It's what we do.'

'You know as well as I do no one gives up their sources.'

Harry drummed his fingers on the table.

'How's your mum?'

The smile on Sowerby's face was enough of an answer.

'So, she's fine then,' said Harry.

'She's like the human equivalent of a battleship or a tank. Both, maybe. She's still got a limp from the broken leg, but it's not slowed her down any.'

'And how about you?' Harry asked.

After the injuries she'd sustained in an explosion during an investigation over in Swaledale, Sowerby had been off work and living with her mum. What she was saying about her mum was hardly a surprise to Harry, who'd met the woman enough times to know just how formidable a person she was.

'I try not to think about it, and when I do, I've got a few strategies to cope with it.'

'That's sensible,' said Harry.

They both sipped at their coffees. Eventually, Sowerby broke the silence.

'I'm bored,' she said. 'Really, really bored. And Mum is driving me mad. I love her to bits, but sometimes I could strangle her.'

'Probably best that you don't,' said Harry. 'Though arguably, of all the people I know, you're probably one of the best placed to make it look like an accident or that someone else did it.'

Sowerby gasped.

'Wow, now that's dark,' she said with a thin smile.

'Sometimes, it's the best way to be,' Harry replied. 'So, you've not moved back to your own place, then?'

Sowerby shook her head.

'I could, it's just that, well, you know, Mum is ... well, she's ...'

'She's what?'

'She's on her own, isn't she?' Sowerby said. 'And

although I know she'd say the opposite, I'm pretty sure she gets lonely on her own in that big old place of hers. So, I've been kind of just putting off going back.'

'You could move in permanently.'

'I could also shoot myself in the face.'

'Messy.'

'There is that.'

'Bennett would have a field day.'

Harry was pretty sure that Sowerby growled at the mention of the other pathologist's name.

'You don't like him, do you?'

'Does anyone?'

'No,' Harry said. 'And I'm only going to say this once, so don't expect it to become a habit, or something I'll admit to in public, but the sooner you're back, the better.'

'You miss me, then?'

'I didn't say that,' said Harry. 'So, don't go putting words into my mouth.'

'How's Grace?'

'Good,' Harry said.

'And that dog of yours?'

'An idiot.'

'Says the detective who swore he'd never get a dog.'

Harry sipped his coffee. Outside, rain was dashing itself across the café windows, turning the world beyond into a watercolour painting smudged by the hands of a child.

'It was good to have your input today,' he said. 'When are you back at work officially?'

'A couple of weeks,' Sowerby said. 'Doesn't mean I'll be over here to join in on your Monday morning meetings, though. I've a feeling that when I get back, I'll be spending a lot of time undoing whatever Bennett has been up to.'

'I think he wants your job,' Harry said.

'He can't have it.'

'I think I speak for the entire team when I say I'm relieved to hear it. So, what are you on with for the rest of the day?'

Sowerby went to reply when the café door opened and in walked Jim, somewhat out of breath.

'Thought you'd be here,' he said, walking over to stand awkwardly at the side of the table.

'Something up?' Harry asked.

Jim gave a nod.

'Yes, I think so. I'm not sure. It's just that, well ...'

Harry pulled a chair out and pointed at it.

'Park yourself down on that and get to the point.'

Jim sat down.

'I overheard someone in Spar,' Jim said. 'I was grabbing a few things for my mum and dad, and these two blokes were just talking about it. I didn't see who it was, though. Didn't want to appear too obvious if that makes sense.'

'Overheard someone saying what?' asked Sowerby. 'What were they talking about? Is this about the burglaries at the weekend?'

'Yes,' Jim said. 'I mean, not specifically, but I think so.'

Harry wasn't sure what the PCSO was getting at.

'Who was it?' he asked. 'What were they talking about? Was it the shotgun? If it was, then—'

'There's a meeting,' Jim said, cutting Harry off.

'Not sure I understand.'

'It's over in Askrigg, at the Temperance Hall,' Jim explained. 'Next door to the old Methodist chapel. Everyone's talking about it apparently.'

'What do you mean by everyone?' Sowerby asked. 'The whole of Wensleydale?'

'And you've not actually said what it's about, either,' said Harry.

Jim shuffled awkwardly in his seat.

'I'm just saying what they said. Something about sorting things out once and for all.'

'Well, that doesn't sound good,' grumbled Harry.

'One of them seemed convinced that we, as in us, the police, can't do anything,' Jim continued. 'The other one said something like it was about time, and that if the government wasn't going to help with more police, then what choice did they have?'

'About what?' Sowerby asked.

But Harry knew.

'That bloody Bartle,' he said.

'Who's Bartle?'

'More of a what, than a who,' said Harry. 'Though it's based on a who, apparently.'

He quickly explained where he'd been on Saturday night and what he'd heard people talking about.

'Struck me as a bit weird,' said Jim. 'Which is why I was running around Hawes trying to find you. It's probably nothing, but I thought it best to flag it up.'

'Oh, something like this, it's never nothing.' Harry sighed. 'And it's usually a lot more than just something.'

'So, I was right to come over and tell you, then?'

'That you were. And it looks like I'm going to have to get myself over to Askrigg, doesn't it?'

'You sound worried,' said Sowerby.

'That's because I am. I thought I'd made myself very

clear on Saturday at that Burning Bartle thing, but obviously not.'

'I've not had a chance to ask you about that,' said Jim. 'How was the Bartle?'

'Weird, if I'm honest,' said Harry. 'Bit of an odd thing to have as an annual celebration, isn't it? But then it adds a bit of local flavour, doesn't it? And it's not like where I'm from doesn't have its fair share of odd.'

'It does,' said Jim. 'Like Mischief Night. Little things like that make a place what it is, don't they?'

Mischief Night was the night before Bonfire Night, when kids would sneak around carrying out practical jokes. Though Harry didn't see the funny side of throwing eggs and flour at people's doors.

'Grace said the same,' he said. 'You should have a trip out to Glastonbury one day. Can't move for wizards and people walking around dressed in capes.'

Jim stood up to leave.

'I can go tonight if you want?' he said. 'Save you the bother. It's not a problem.'

Harry shook his head.

'No, I think it's best if I deal with it,' he said. 'There's a bit more chance they'll listen to a grumpy DCI than a keen PCSO.'

'Fair point,' Jim said and headed out into the day.

Harry sat quietly for a moment, swirling the dregs of his coffee around in his mug.

'It won't come to anything, surely,' said Sowerby.

'I'm not going to take that risk,' Harry said. 'All it takes is for one person to go too far, do something stupid, and we both know what we've got then, don't we?'

'A lynch mob,' Sowerby said.

'Exactly.'

It wasn't that long ago that Jadyn had ended up in the hands of something exactly like that, and the very thought chilled the marrow of Harry's bones.

CHAPTER SIXTEEN

SOMEWHAT PREOCCUPIED WITH THE UPCOMING meeting Jim had told him about, Harry's afternoon was spent somewhere between deep concern about what he was dealing with and frustration that the team had gained nothing from knocking on doors. But that was just the way of things sometimes. Investigations didn't happen like they did on television. You couldn't just head out and wham-bam find a clue or a witness or a suspect. Real life played by very different rules, and it wasn't about to share them with anyone any time soon. The only movement they'd had on anything so far was thanks to Jen who had headed over for another chat with Keith Sunter. She had made a point of asking him again if he was certain that it hadn't been his son who had carried out the break in, just to make sure, but once again he had been adamant that it wasn't. Harry wasn't exactly convinced and to him, Anthony was still a suspect, whether his dad said he saw him or not. But at the end of the day, it wasn't much of a crime to be investigated, with nothing having been stolen.

Back in his flat, Harry looked down at Smudge as he checked his watch. It was just gone six and he'd not yet had dinner. Grace was busy and over at her place after a day out doing whatever it was that gamekeepers did. Ben was nowhere to be seen. And now here he was having to head out to deal with a bunch of locals waving their pitchforks around and baying for blood. He'd had better Monday evenings. Hell, he'd had better weekends. So far, the week was playing out perfectly as one he was already looking forward to forgetting.

As for those properties he wanted to view, he'd managed to book a couple of viewings, but not till Wednesday. He had a feeling that by that time it would already be too late. But the job came first, as always. The one good thing was that Jim had taken the brace of rabbits home to clean and would be dropping them over to him tomorrow for the fridge. Harry knew how to gut and skin one, but he wasn't going to complain about not having to do it.

Half an hour later, showered, and with a disappointingly unappetising cheese and Bovril toasty inside him, Harry headed over to Askrigg in his old Rav4. He left Smudge at home to make sure that the sofa didn't do anything shifty while he was away. And he was confident that when he returned later, Smudge would have kept a solid eye on all of his furniture. She was good like that. The best, in fact. To date, she'd let not a single piece of it do anything untoward or wander off.

The evening was surprisingly light considering the gloomy weather. The heat of the summery weekend was well and truly gone, though, a memory of sun-blessed days replaced by a dreary grey dampness that grew through his bones like a fungus. Thick cloud had blanketed the Dale in a soft pillow of grey, the rivers were rising, and any animals unfortunate enough to still be out in it were seeking the shelter of wall and tree and tumbledown barn.

Taking the back road from Hawes, Harry rolled along, going neither too fast nor too slow, just doing his best to enjoy the undulating lane as it cut its way down along the valley's edge, a stone skipping along an ocean of green, all the more vivid now because of the rain. Fields glistened, trees wept, and puddles lay in front of him like mirrored portals to a darker plane full of ominous threats.

Above him and to his left, rose Little Moss, then Little Stags Fell, their sides scarred by rock escarpments and patches of woodland looking as though they could, at any moment, slip down towards the valley bottom, dragging with them great swathes of rock and soil and scree to drown anything in their path.

When he eventually rolled up the hill and into Askrigg, Harry parked his vehicle on the cobbles outside the church. He remembered a case they'd dealt with a good while ago now, a body found in the tower. And yet the darkness of such an event just didn't have the power to stain the beauty of the Dale itself, or a village like this.

Harry clambered out of his vehicle, heaving the door shut behind him before locking it. At the bottom of the hill, he spied the Askrigg Temperance Village Hall. The door was open, and people were making their way inside.

He had a choice. He could stride in there right now and attempt to put an end to whatever idiocy it was they were trying to start, or he could let the meeting go ahead, do a bit of a sneaky recce of it, and perhaps get a better idea of what everyone was planning. That way, at least, he'd have a full understanding of the issues that had led them all to think whatever they were doing, or thinking of doing, was a good idea.

Once the meeting was coming to an end, perhaps then he would make an appearance. That way everyone would have had their say, he would have a good idea as to who the ring-leaders were and putting a stop to it all might be a little easier. And a surprise visit was always more fun, wasn't it? Nothing like making an entrance, and if there was something that Harry knew he did well, it was that.

Checking his watch, Harry saw that he had just a few minutes till the meeting kicked off, so he hung back and waited. Then, when he saw the door to the hall close, he made his way down through the village. Opening the door just a little, he saw on the other side a small reception area, which meant that it didn't open straight into the main area beyond. And that gave him a space in which to hide out of everyone's way and just listen. He heard muffled voices, the scraping of chairs, and then the sound of a gavel, which struck him as a little more official and organised than he would have expected. Not a good sign.

'Right then,' a voice called out across the hubbub. 'Best we get on, if you'd all be so kind as to take your seats.'

Harry recognised the voice from Saturday evening, though he couldn't put a face to it.

For the next few minutes, there was a lot of muttering and general chatter while whoever was running the show tried to pull things to order. Then the gavel sounded once again, and a hush descended.

Harry opened the door to the hall just enough to have a peek and to hear a little better what everyone was saying.

The room was packed.

'As you all know,' said someone from the front, though

Harry couldn't see who it was as they were hidden by a sea of heads, 'we're here to discuss doing our bit to bring some local law and order to the Dale. It's been mentioned enough times over the years by some of us, so maybe we can do something about it now.'

Harry saw a hand shoot up.

'Yes?'

The owner of the hand rose to their feet.

'Bob Thwaite,' the man said. 'Here because, well, I don't know, if I'm honest. But I think I just need to say that I'm not sure any of this is really necessary, is it? It's all very well talking like we're out to get some Bartle character ourselves, but I don't reckon it's all that sensible.'

'And why's that?'

'Well, we've got the police, haven't we? And shouldn't we just let them get on with their job instead of getting in the way, like?'

'If you think that, then why are you here?' said another voice from the front. 'You know where the door is. You can use it to leave just as well as you can to come in.'

'I'm just saying what I think,' Bob said. 'These kind of things can get out of hand, can't they? And we don't want that happening.'

Harry liked Bob and was happy to hear a ripple of approval follow his words.

Someone at the front stood up. Harry definitely recognised the man from Saturday night and again from Sunday morning. It was Steve Hill, the farmer whose house had been broken into and had his shotgun forcibly removed from the premises.

'If you ask me, it sounds like you're scared, Bob.'

'Say that to my face, Steve, and we'll see who's scared.'

'I just did,' came the reply.

Harry had his notebook out now and was starting to jot down names and notes.

The discussion quickly descended into a chorus of shouting and accusations as others joined in. It was impossible to work out who was saying what or what it was they were actually trying to say.

Someone stood up at the front. Harry saw they were holding a gavel. This man was tall, Harry noticed, big, too.

'Bob, if you could take a seat and just listen, I think that would be for the best.'

Bob hesitated, then sat down.

'Okay, then, Chris,' he said. 'Let's hear what you've got to say.'

'Well then, this doesn't need to be a long meeting, and we've all got homes to be looking after, haven't we? Which is why we're here in the first place, to see what we all think about protecting them a little bit better than they have been of late.'

'Isn't this just Neighbourhood Watch?' a voice called out.

'No, it bloody well isn't!' said Steve. Harry was beginning to realise he was a man who very much liked the sound of his own voice. 'If Neighbourhood Watch was any good, do you think my place would've been broken into yesterday? Well, do you? No, of course you don't.'

'That's not what I'm saying.'

'Then, what are you saying? We can't just sit around and do nowt, can we? What use is that?'

Two more voices joined in.

'What are you suggesting, then?'

'That's what I want to know. That's why I'm here. We're not the police.'

These comments were followed by others from various parts of the room, though Harry was unable to see by whom.

Chris held up a hand to calm things down again.

'Has anyone heard of the Guardian Angels?'

The question was met with silence. Harry, though, had heard of them well enough to know it was not what he wanted to see starting up in the Dales. The notion of Wensleydale soon having patrols of people in bomber jackets and military-style red berets amused him almost as much as it horrified him.

Chris explained briefly about the Guardian Angels.

'They see themselves as a safety patrol,' he said. 'They've had training in first aid, law, and a bit of self-defence, you know, martial arts, that kind of thing.'

A small voice said, 'Are you suggesting we all learn Karate? I mean, I'm eighty-one and I don't think I'd be in for all those roundabout kicks stuff.'

'It's roundhouse kicks,' corrected someone close by.

'I don't care what it is, I'm not doing it. Do I look like Bruce Lee?'

'Bruce Tea more like, seeing as you drink gallons of the stuff.'

Laughter erupted then, and Harry was beginning to wonder if his initial worry about this meeting was more than a little misguided.

Steve, though, was on his feet.

'This is no laughing matter!' he said, his voice rough, gruff, and laced with just enough hot anger to have the room's attention. 'If you don't want to help, then politely bugger off. But we all know that the Dales isn't as safe as it used to be. All these holidaymakers driving through, newcomers moving in, and goodness knows what else. We need to do something. Yes, we have the police, but there's nowt but a handful of them and they can't be everywhere, can they? But if we were a part of something, if we were all out and about, keeping an eye, then we could make a difference, couldn't we?'

More muttering and it went on for a while until order was again brought from the front.

'I've been broken into,' Steve said. 'I know what it's like, coming home and finding that someone's been there, a stranger, going through your stuff, breaking things, taking whatever they like. It's not right. It's not!'

'Here's what I suggest,' Chris said, his voice loud and calm enough to demand attention, like a headteacher in front of a hall of teenagers. 'For now, those of us who are interested in doing something to help keep the Dales safe, will set up a messaging group so we can all contact each other with our phones. Then we'll decide who can be out and about, where and when. And if anyone sees anything or hears anything, they can contact the rest of the group who can swing by and help.'

'And call the police.'

Harry's voice hit the room with the impact of a wrecking ball. Every single person in the place turned to face him, eyes wide with shock and more than a little fear.

Harry waved.

'Hope you don't mind me joining you,' he said. 'But when I heard about this little gathering, I just couldn't resist.'

'There's nowt you can do to stop us,' Steve said, and Harry saw how the man was barely able to contain his anger at seeing him standing there in front of him. 'This is our Dale. We just want to look after it, that's all. It's not like you're doing that good a job, now, is it?'

Harry walked to the front of the hall, ignoring Steve, which only served to make the man's face turn an even darker red, and turned to face the crowd.

'For those of you who don't know me, I'm Detective Chief Inspector Harry Grimm.'

As he spoke, Harry cast his eyes over the faces and recognised a few. Agnes Hodgson was there. She waved, though it was a nervous wave rather than a warm one.

'I'm going to say here and now that whatever it is you're planning to do, don't,' Harry said. 'Although I admire you for wanting to do something, this really isn't it. Wensleydale doesn't need its own version of The Justice League.'

He let that sit for a second or two before speaking again.

'I've been listening to everything that's been said. I heard mention of Neighbourhood Watch. Though you may not believe it, it actually works.'

'No it doesn't,' someone shouted out. 'I heard Keith's place was broken into as well, Saturday night.'

Harry said nothing.

'Doesn't exactly bode well, does it?' the voice continued. 'If the bloke who's supposed to be running the Neighbourhood Watch can't even manage to have his own neighbours watch his house.'

Harry could see their point, but he wasn't about to agree with it.

'Heading out on some hare-brained scheme to patrol the Dales will only end in trouble,' he said.

'Will it, now?' Steve said.

'Yes,' said Harry.

He turned to face Steve down. The man was on his feet and bouncing a little with nervous energy.

'How's that then?' Steve asked. 'It's because you don't think we're up to it, that's it, isn't it? You think we're soft.'

'I don't think that at all, no,' Harry said.

'Yes, you bloody well do! Well, let me tell you, we know what this place needs and that's folk like me, that's what! And you can't stop us. You can't! I won't be letting anyone take anything from me again, I can tell you that for nowt!'

'What I think,' Harry said, as Steve's temper simmered just below boiling point, 'and I'm speaking here from experience, I might add, is that challenging someone you think is up to no good rarely ends well. People get hurt, people get killed.'

'I can handle myself.'

'And what would've happened if you'd arrived home and found whoever it was that broke into your house?'

'I'd have had them!' Steve said.

'What if they'd have been armed?' Harry asked. 'They took your shotgun, after all. They could've had it loaded and ready. Then what?'

'I'd still have had them! I would!'

Harry saw Steve puff out his chest.

'Would you, now?' Harry asked.

'Too bloody right I would!'

With no warning given, Steve lunged at Harry. Harry sidestepped the punch, catching the man as he fell past, and keeping him from smashing into the floor by guiding him down. Then Steve's hands were behind his back and Harry had him in cuffs. The whole thing had taken seconds.

Harry looked back out at the crowd, a firm hand on Steve's shoulder making it absolutely clear he wasn't going anywhere and shouldn't even try.

'Now, all of you, ask yourself what could have happened if our friend Steve, here, had seen me trying to break into a house, challenged me, and I'd whipped round with a knife? Not even a shotgun, just a knife, that's all. Something I'd grabbed from the kitchen, maybe. Because—and you may not realise this—but the majority of knife crime isn't from Zombie knives or anything fancy like that. No. It's from what you've got in your cutlery drawer at home. Which makes you think, doesn't it?'

'You can't cuff me!' Steve hissed. 'Take these off me, right now!'

Harry ignored him.

'It doesn't have to be a knife, either. It could be anything; a rolling pin, a bike chain.'

Harry glared down at the sea of faces staring up at him. He had them, he knew it, some with eyes so wide they were threatening to pop out of their skulls.

'I've seen violence you've only ever witnessed in the movies,' he continued. 'And worse. This is not a game. Start taking the law into your own hands and I guarantee that someone will get hurt. Someone will end up in hospital. Someone will die. And I really don't want to have to go around and break the news to any of you that your nearest and dearest died doing something admirable and understandable, yes, but ultimately absolutely bloody idiotic and dangerous.'

Harry let the silence sit in the room for a moment. Then he reached over behind Steve and released him from the cuffs.

'Off you go now.'

'I reckon I could still have you,' Steve mumbled.

'No, you couldn't,' Harry whispered, just loud enough to

stop Steve in his tracks. The stare he gave the man made it very clear he'd best keep walking.

Once Steve was back in his seat, Harry strolled back down to the doors. As he made to leave, he stopped and turned around.

'And one last thing,' he said, 'if I see or hear of anyone out there playing Superhero, they'll have me to answer to. And I promise you, you really don't want that. Understood?'

A few minutes later, and back in his vehicle, Harry thought about what had just happened. It was the oddest meeting he had ever been to, spiced with a little bit of unexpected excitement from Steve. He had a few names in his notebook and everyone in that room knew that he wasn't just onto them, he would be watching. Hopefully, that would be deterrent enough. Driving back home, a niggling voice in the back of his mind wasn't so sure.

CHAPTER SEVENTEEN

The following morning Harry was sitting in his kitchen deep in thought. The previous evening had been an interesting one, and he wondered what echoes from it he'd be running into over the next few days and weeks.

Hopefully none, he thought, but his gut once again told him hope was pointless. Something had been started, and he doubted that what he'd said to those gathered in Askrigg had finished it. It would have got to some of them, for sure, but others would ignore him. As experience had shown him more than once, sometimes when you tell someone not to do something, all it does is serve to make them more determined to do it. Human nature is an arse.

With Tuesday upon him, Harry started the day with a strong coffee and a couple of slices of toast. It was hardly a breakfast of champions, but it would have to do for now. That done and forcing himself to think about something else other than the night before, he was now staring at the details of a handful of properties for sale. These were the ones he had booked for a viewing the following day.

For sale...

Was he really considering buying a house of his own in the Dales? He'd been here, what, just over a year? This was as close as Harry ever got to an impulsive decision, and it was a little unnerving. He'd never bought a house before, never even considered it. Renting had just been easier, simpler, and tying himself to one place had just never been something he'd wanted to do, until now.

His years in the Paras had left him with a legacy of a life lived out of a bag. He wasn't one for possessions. He would always prefer to be able to just pack and go at a moment's notice rather than have to consider boxing things up, packing his life away.

Harry looked at each house in turn. None of them jumped out at him as a dream house, a place he could see himself living out his days. They were simple, had three beds, the gardens were different sizes, one had parking, the other two didn't. Actually, Harry thought, that was something to consider, wasn't it? Did he really want to be frustrated every time he came home as to where he could put his car? But then again, did it really matter? And did he want a garden big enough for a barbeque or not? One of them had a very nice bathroom, he noticed, another a decent kitchen. Would he have to decorate? Probably. Because that's what people did, didn't they? And that meant trips out to DIY stores to buy paint and brushes and a ladder and ...

Harry placed the house details back on the table and rubbed his eyes, leaning back in his chair, his head flopping back. The temptation right there and then was to just call the estate agent and cancel. There was enough going on as it was, without having to think about putting money into bricks and mortar.

That was another thing, wasn't it? All the savings he had would be going into this purchase. So, what if the housing market crashed? What if he needed more money to do work on the house but didn't actually have any? What if he moved in and then found himself hating the place? And what if work took a turn for the worse and he had to move? What then?

Harry laughed. He was running around in circles in his mind, trying to convince himself that buying a house was a good idea at the same time as telling himself it wasn't. Grace would laugh if she knew, shake her head.

Grace ...

The thought of her smile made him only laugh louder, thinking how she'd tell him to stop being an idiot, to stop putting things in his own way and to just get on with it all.

Standing up, Harry shoved the details into a pocket. He washed up his mug and his plate, considered having another slice of toast, then headed through to the hall. Work was calling so better to focus on that. Smudge was with him, sitting by the door, ready to head out with him. He clipped her lead to her collar, fastened his coat, then headed out into the day.

Stepping outside, Harry had the distinct impression that the day wasn't actually very pleased to see him. The wind thumped into him, knocking him back against his door and rain was in the air once again. It wasn't raining as such, not yet anyway, but he could taste it and knew that a downpour was very much on its way.

The road was busy, not just with traffic heading to market up at the auction mart, but with roadworks now being set up alongside the primary school. The height of the tourist season didn't strike Harry as the best of times to be carrying out repairs.

A few minutes later, Harry made his way over to the Community Centre to see a large man bursting out of the door, his face a rictus of rage.

'It's you I want, not that lot, not for this!'

Jadyn rushed out after the man, but he was already in front of Harry.

'You were at the meeting last night,' Harry said. 'Running things, if I remember correctly.'

'I was,' the man said. 'Chris Black. And you're coming with me. Right now.'

Jadyn was now at Harry's side.

'Sorry, boss,' he said. 'He saw you coming up the lane and just stormed out.'

'I didn't storm anywhere,' said Chris. 'I walked. With purpose.'

Harry glanced over the man's shoulder to see Matt standing in the doorway of the Community Centre. He didn't look best pleased.

'Well, I'm heading to the office,' Harry said, 'so perhaps it would be better if we headed inside together and then you can tell me what this is all about. At least then we'll be out of the way when the rain starts.'

Then, almost as if the weather gods had heard him, the first drops landed.

'Bugger the rain,' said Chris. 'You need to come out to my place right now. And then, when you've seen it, you can arrest her. That's what you can do. The woman's mad, I tell you. And she's going to have to clear it all up, that's for sure.'

Right then, Harry had no idea what Mr Black was on about. Also, he wasn't a massive fan of being ranted at. If there was ranting to be done, then he would do it, not the other way around. And he was starting to get wet.

'Inside, now,' he said, and he side-stepped the man and walked on into the Community Centre, Matt standing back to let him through.

'It's a mad morning, boss,' Matt said. 'You wouldn't believe half of what we've got coming in, and the rest of it doesn't make much sense either.'

Harry heard the door swing shut behind him, but didn't look to see if Mr Black had followed, and headed into the office. The rest of the team were all there, and busy by the looks of things. Jim was pulling a jacket on, clearly getting ready to head out, Jen was on the phone, Liz was writing something on another of the boards, one which Harry was sure had been blank the last time he'd seen it. Gordy was the only one not in the room, though she was sometimes away down Dale, dealing with other things.

Jadyn came over to Harry and apologised again about Mr Black.

'He's a bit uptight, isn't he?' Harry said. 'Now, what's the problem?'

Jadyn hesitated.

'Out with it,' said Harry.

'He says someone—Mrs Hodgson, he seems to think—has dumped a pile of dog sh—I mean, faeces, on the bonnet of his car.'

Harry wasn't sure he'd heard right.

'Come again?'

'Seriously, that's what he's here about,' said Jadyn. 'He's demanding that we go over and arrest her right now. And that's not the half of it, either. You wouldn't believe some of what we've got coming in. Liz was properly busy last night.'

Harry glanced over at Liz, who looked at him, shook her head, and rolled her eyes.

'He's got proof then, has he?' Harry said, back on Jadyn, remembering clearly almost every moment of his meeting with Agnes Hodgson on Sunday.

'No idea,' Jadyn said. 'But what he does have is a lot of anger. And he's big.'

Harry laughed.

'Right, let's get everyone together so that I'm up to speed with all of this.'

'What about Mr Black?'

'He can stew for a moment or two,' Harry said, then called everyone together. He waited for them all to take a seat.

'Right then, the primary focus of today should be a continuation of what we were on with yesterday, the break-ins. However, I can see that something's up, so I need someone to give me a run through as to what's going on.'

'I'll do that,' Liz said, 'but you won't believe it.'

'Try me,' Harry said.

Liz stood up and walked over to the board Harry had seen her standing by when he'd entered the room.

'I'll be as quick as I can,' she said, 'but you have to promise not to laugh.'

'And why would I laugh?' Harry asked.

'Because last night I arrested Batman, and that was merely the beginning of it ...'

CHAPTER EIGHTEEN

A FEW MINUTES LATER HARRY WAS TRYING HIS BEST TO take it all in.

'So, let me get this straight,' he said, 'and just so as we're all clear, last night you, Liz, arrested someone dressed as Batman. Only it wasn't actually Batman at all, but someone wrapped in a blanket to keep warm while hiding in a tree in their garden to—' He looked at Liz to finish what he was saying. 'What was it they were up to again?'

Liz opened her notebook and read from it.

'He said he was there *to keep an eye out for dodgy folk*,' Liz said. 'He'd scared the hell out of someone walking past after shouting at them from the darkness and demanding their name.'

'And he was armed with—?'

'Some newspapers he'd rolled up into a baton and wrapped in Sellotape,' Liz said. 'It would certainly give you a hell of a headache if he whacked you with it. I confiscated it, which he wasn't happy about, mainly on account of how long it had taken him to make it.'

'And after that,' Harry continued, 'you had to then confiscate a couple of cricket bats from two men spotted patrolling the green over in Bainbridge, and have a word with a farmer who was in the process of putting up a temporary barrier across the road over to ... where was it, now?'

'Deepdale,' Liz said. 'Out beyond Beckermonds. He wanted a checkpoint put up so that he knew who was coming and going.'

Harry shrugged. He didn't have the faintest idea where either of those two places were.

'And on top of that, we've now got Mr Black outside the office saying someone's covered his car in dog shit.'

'Oh, and we've also just had a call in about an abandoned pick-up truck and trailer out by Agglethorpe,' Liz said. 'Over between West Witton and Middleham. I was just heading out there to check it out myself when you came in.'

'An abandoned pick-up? Who called that in, then?' Harry asked.

'The farmer who found it,' Liz said. 'Fred Calvert. I thought Mr Black was here about it as well, but apparently not.'

'Why?'

'He's from out that way, too. Thought he might have seen it or something.'

'So is that Steve bloke whose shotgun was nicked,' Jadyn said. 'That's where we were on Sunday.'

'What Fred was saying all sounded a bit strange,' added Liz. 'But then, after the last few hours, I'm kind of used to it.'

'Strange how?'

'Apparently, the pick-up is empty and some stuff he had stolen from his farm a couple of years ago has all appeared back in one of his barns. Well, everything except for a chain-saw, that is.'

'You're right, that does sound strange,' Harry said, then he took a moment to think on what he'd been told.

'Well, whatever's been going on, it's pretty clear to me that all of this stems, not just from what people were talking about at that Bartle thing over in West Witton, but also the meeting in Askrigg last night, the one Jim overheard someone talking about yesterday.'

'You went, then?' Jim said. 'How was it?'

'It was a hall full of people talking a right load of complete and utter bollocks, that's how it was,' said Harry. 'I've a few names for us to keep an eye on, but thankfully, I don't think too many of them were really up for heading out into the night like a posse from a Western. Some were though, so I had words. But it doesn't seem to have done much good.'

'And how did that go down?' Matt asked.

'Well, Steve Hill threw a punch and ended up in cuffs, so that was a highlight for sure.'

'You cuffed Steve? He'll be fuming about that for weeks!'

'Good,' Harry said. 'If his punch had landed, being in cuffs would've been the least of his worries. Anyway, my concern now is that after everything I've just heard, it looks like we've got a situation that could quickly get out of hand. Maybe it already has. But I'll not allow Wensleydale to be turned into some idiotic version of that movie Kick-Ass. Fun and exciting though it may be for people to talk about what they'd all like to do if they could get their hands on criminals, if we've got some of them actually acting on what they're talking about, then eventually someone is going to get hurt.'

'What do you want us to do?' Matt asked.

'First, what I don't want is to make a big deal about any of this. Carry on working through what we are on with regarding those break-ins. Jen, I want you to pull out details of the burglary over at Mr Sunter's two years ago, please; worth comparing, see if there's anything similar about the two events. It still strikes me as a little odd. And I want someone to contact the SOC team, see if they've found anything else. I doubt they have, but it's worth a shot. I'm sure there's a few doors that could still be knocked, as well, so go out there and knock on them.'

'What about last night's events?' Liz asked.

'Sounds to me like you dealt with it all accordingly,' Harry said. 'And well done on all of that. Though, maybe keeping a straight face through all of it was the hardest thing.'

Liz laughed, nodded.

'What I suggest,' Harry continued, 'is that we leave Batman and the others alone for a day or two, let them stew on the fact that we know who they are and what they were up to. Word will get around about what happened, and it might stop others from being complete idiots.'

'We've Mr Black to deal with,' Jadyn said.

'And I'm sure that you can do that very well with Matt here,' Harry said.

'It would be my pleasure,' said Matt, and Harry rather liked the grin which appeared on the detective sergeant's face.

'But he was pretty adamant that he wanted you on this,' Jadyn said.

Harry heard the worry in the constable's voice.

'Want and need are two very different things,' said Harry. 'And anyway, I'm needed elsewhere.'

'You are?'

'Yes,' Harry said, and again looked over at Liz. 'I'll come along to keep you company, if that's okay.'

'Only if Smudge can come with us as well,' said Liz, which was when Harry noticed that his dog was lying under the PCSO's seat.

There was a hard knock at the office door.

'That'll be Mr Black,' Matt said. 'He's one of those people who doesn't like it if he doesn't get his own way or is kept waiting.'

'Then I'll leave him to you,' Harry said. 'Liz?'

Liz stood up and Smudge followed her as she walked over to stand with her commanding officer.

'The rest of you all know what you're on with. Stay in touch and if anyone sees Batman again, please, do me a favour and take a photo.'

CHAPTER NINETEEN

Outside, the day was growing darker, giving Harry the impression that they were stepping into a gloomy evening rather than an early morning.

'Wind's getting up,' said Liz, her hair dancing as they made their way over to Harry's Rav4. Really, they should've been taking one of the official police vehicles, but he was on autopilot and behind the driver's seat before he realised what he was doing.

'I leave this here more often than I do down by the flat,' he said. 'Just seems easier.'

'You should think about getting something a bit better though,' Liz suggested as she clipped Smudge into the backseat, then came to sit beside Harry.

Harry raised an eyebrow at Liz and tapped a meaty hand on the dashboard.

'There's nowt, I mean, there's nothing wrong with this,' he said, catching the Yorkshire in his speech. Some days he heard not only phrases but the accent creeping in, too, as though the place wasn't just getting under his skin but becoming a part of who and what he now was, changing his DNA. 'It'll do me for now, anyway.'

'Ben and Mike would be able to sort you something, I'm sure,' Liz said. 'Why don't you ask them?'

'Because I don't want to,' Harry said, immediately realising his reply was a little sharp. So he softened his voice and added, 'Watching my pennies right now, as you know.'

Not that a few quid would make much difference to the thousands he was going to say goodbye to as a deposit if he found somewhere he not only liked but could actually afford.

'The house-hunting?' Liz said. 'How's that going?'

'I've a couple booked in for a viewing tomorrow,' Harry said.

'That's good. Exciting times for you.'

'I suppose so, yes,' agreed Harry, and started the engine. 'So, where are we going, then?'

'Just head out of town,' Liz said. 'Towards Leyburn.'

Harry started the engine and rolled the vehicle out of the marketplace. Then, barely thirty seconds later he was forced to come to a dead stop. In front of them was an articulated truck, one of its rear tyres blown out.

'Can you get past?' Liz asked.

'Not even by breathing in,' said Harry.

'Best turn around, then,' Liz said. 'We'll head up to Gayle, over the bridge, then down Old Gayle Lane.'

Harry did a three-point turn and headed back up into the marketplace.

'Best you get someone from the office down here sharpish,' said Harry. 'Traffic will be backing up soon. Though there's not much they can do about it right now.'

Liz called it in and soon Jen was on her way down to at

least try to keep people calm while the truck driver fixed his tyre.

Harry headed up through town. The roadworks outside the primary school were still being set out, so the temporary traffic lights weren't there to delay him quite yet. But someone in a caravan was, and Harry waited as patiently as he could for them to burn out their clutch as they turned left and headed up into Gayle in front of them.

'Now there's something that's never attracted me,' he said.

'They probably missed the turning into Old Gayle Lane, just before you get to Hawes,' Liz said. 'There's a caravan site just up there.'

Harry knew it, though had never had reason to visit.

'Why choose to spend a week or more in a tin shed on wheels, though?' he asked, not looking for an answer. Liz didn't provide one.

Passing the Wensleydale Creamery, the caravan seemingly going ever slower, Harry was half tempted to overtake it, but decided to just stay where he was. Impatience this early in the day wasn't a good sign, so he needed to rein that in as best he could. Which was when he saw movement in the back of the caravan.

Harry did a double-take.

'Did you see that?'

'Yes,' Liz said. 'And I can't quite believe it.'

'Someone's in there, aren't they?' Harry said and shook his head in disbelief.

'Looks that way.'

'If it's kids, you're going to have to hold me back from the parents,' Harry growled. 'Who the hell tows a caravan with passengers inside? Bloody idiots!'

Liz reached into the footwell and pulled out a light to attach to the roof of the Rav4. Harry swung out past the caravan as she dropped the light onto the roof and switched it on. The car pulled to a stop by the kerb and Harry and Liz were out in a beat.

'Right then,' Harry said, 'let's see how large a pile of horseshit nonsense they try to pile in front of us as an excuse, shall we?'

The driver of the car wound down his window.

'Is something the matter, officer? Is there a light out? I checked them before we set off. I always do. And everything was fine.'

The man, Harry saw, had clearly left retirement age a good while ago. Judging by the length of his beard, he'd stopped shaving quite a few years before that point. He was also smoking a pipe, the smell of it wafting out to greet Harry with a rich scent of cherry and vanilla. It was surprisingly pleasant.

'Probably got Hobbits in the back,' Harry muttered, glancing over at Liz.

She stared at him, frowning. Then she saw the beard and a smile broke through her confusion.

'Can I ask you to step out of the car, please, sir?' Harry said.

'Well, you can't have pulled me over for speeding, that's for sure.'

'I'll be needing you out of the car all the same,' Harry repeated, as Liz walked around to the passenger side and then on towards the caravan's door.

The driver opened his door at which point there was a yell from Liz and the next thing Harry saw was a figure hoofing it out of the caravan and along the pavement.

'I've got this,' Liz shouted, and scooted off after the runaway.

'I don't suppose you can explain to me why there was someone in your caravan, can you?' Harry asked.

The driver rubbed his beard, scratched his head, smoked his pipe. To all the world, it looked to Harry as though he was about to impart on him some great wisdom. Instead he said, 'No.'

Harry needed more.

'So, you had no idea at all that someone was in there?'

'I've been on the road for a couple of hours at least,' the man said.

'I'm not sure what that's got to do with it,' Harry said as he watched Liz tackle the escaping figure and bring them to a stop. She could certainly sprint, Harry thought.

'I'm travelling on my own,' the man continued. 'Bit of a road trip, you know? Just me and some good books, tasty wine, that kind of thing. And whoever that is, they must've been in there since the A1 at least. Not that I checked. I mean, why would I? Maybe I'd left the door open after setting off this morning. Just needed a loo break, you see, and a bit of a nosy around the shop. Always try to stop every couple of hours. Got myself a nice new audiobook to listen to and some chocolate. Oh, and a coffee. Got to have a coffee in the morning. Bit of a habit of mine since my wife died. She would always make the coffee in the morning. Reminds me of her, you know? The smell of it, that familiar routine.'

Harry was only half-listening to the driver ramble on as he watched Liz walk back with the figure beside her, arm held firmly in her hand. As yet, Harry couldn't tell if it was a man or a woman. They were carrying a small backpack.

'So, you had no idea someone was in your caravan?' Harry asked. 'At all?'

'Of course not. Why would I?'

Harry would reserve judgement for now.

Liz arrived at the car. Harry could see now that the figure was a young man, probably in his late teens or early twenties, he guessed.

'Well, then,' Harry said, 'it looks like we've got ourselves a little bit of a pickle here, doesn't it?'

'Let me go!'

The young man squirmed in Liz's grip, but she held on tight.

'Either you stop struggling,' Harry said, 'or I'll come over there and cuff you. Your choice.'

The young man stared back at Harry from beneath hair black as pitch. The shadows beneath his eyes were almost as dark.

'You wouldn't dare. I've done nothing wrong.'

'I would and you have,' Harry said.

Liz looked over at Harry.

'I'll give Jadyn a call. We'll sort this out. Shouldn't take too long. That way you can head on to where we were supposed to be going until we saw our new friend here trying to get comfy.'

Harry walked over to the young man.

'Just out of interest, how long have you actually been in there?' he asked, gesturing to the caravan with a jab of his thumb.

'I wasn't doing anything, and I didn't nick anything neither!'

'That's not the answer to the question,' said Harry. 'And it's either, not neither.'

'What?'

'Just answer the question.'

The young man struggled again against Liz's grip, though there was less effort in it this time.

'Couple of hours, maybe,' the young man said. 'I just needed somewhere dry to sleep, that's all. That's not a crime, is it? It was a wet night.'

Harry could see that his clothes were still damp.

'And your choice of the day was a moving caravan, was it?'

'It's better than kipping under a bush. I've done that often enough as it is. Sick of it.'

'Homeless, then?'

'No, of course not,' the young man sneered. 'I own a three-bed semi in Manchester and this is my idea of a luxury holiday. You should try it sometime.'

'Getting lippy with me isn't going to help,' Harry said.

'But I've done nothing wrong, have I?'

'Stowing away in a caravan is bloody dangerous, you know that, right?'

'I'm still here, aren't I?'

'Your weight shifting around in the back could've made the whole thing unstable,' Harry explained. 'You ever seen a vehicle and trailer jack-knife? You'd have been tossed around in there like a rabbit in a spin dryer! We'd have been lucky to find enough pieces to put you back together to identify you.'

'Why would you need to?'

'So that we could tell your nearest and dearest you died being an absolute bloody idiot, that's why!' Harry said, his voice the echo of thunder. 'Liz?'

'Jadyn's on his way,' she said. 'And I've just sent you directions to Mr Calvert's farm.'

'Excuse me?'

Harry turned to see the driver staring at him, pipe stuffed into his mouth, the clouds of smoke twisting around his head like a dragon's breath.

'Yes?'

'Well, can I be on my way? You don't need me now, do you?'

Harry saw Jadyn's car driving up the hill towards them. He walked over to his Rav4.

'Keep me posted on all this,' he said. 'And I'll be wanting a statement from Gandalf here as well.'

Then he climbed into his vehicle and headed off up into Gayle.

CHAPTER TWENTY

Following Liz's directions, Harry headed to the bridge over Gayle Beck. Gayle itself was a higgledy-piggledy mix of houses in a surprisingly small space. They clearly built the estate leading up into the village from Hawes in the sixties or seventies, though Harry wasn't entirely sure when exactly. It ended abruptly at Harker Hill, giving way to considerably older dwellings, both small cottages cosied up together against the elements, and larger, grander places Harry knew he could only ever dream of owning. Though, if he was honest, the smaller cottages were probably out of his price range, too. The river was up, and to his right he saw that the ford was completely impassable. Thick brown water tumbled down it like molten toffee, cresting in white tufts of foam and spray as it gabbled and tossed itself between pebble and bank.

The weather was going through some kind of identity crisis, Harry thought, as the rain had stopped for a moment, though the dark clouds seemed lower now, more ominous. To Harry, it was as though the sky was pressing down on the world below, sinking ever closer until soon everywhere would be swamped by the thick gloom. It wasn't helping him look forward to the day ahead.

After the bridge, Harry headed left along Old Gayle Lane. It was a road he knew well, courtesy of his on-off relationship with trying to keep fit. Right now, that relationship was very much off, though he'd be trying to rekindle it soon, or at least that's what he told himself every weekend.

He swept along past the back entrance to the auction mart, narrowly avoiding being hit by a tractor driven by a maniac. With it being market day, the place was a bustling throng of trucks and tractors and four-wheel drives, sheep and cattle and noise. If there was ever a place that could be called the beating heart of the Dales, he thought, then that was it, right there. The smell of the place was ripe, but it wasn't unpleasant either, Harry thought, as his nose caught the scent of animals and diesel, hay and straw.

Soon back on the main road, Harry took a right and sent himself on towards Bainbridge. A huff and a scratch from the backseat were the only signs that Smudge was with him.

Driving along, Harry wound down the window to enjoy the cool, damp air. Spots of rain were in it again, but for now, he didn't really care. The breath of the Dales was refreshing and various scents rippled through it, from the heather of the moors to grass and leaf and thick, damp earth.

Through Bainbridge and Aysgarth, then Harry turned off at West Witton, which only reminded him of the Burning of the Bartle. He couldn't believe that such an event could have caused so much trouble these past few days, and he hoped things would quieten down soon.

With Pen Hill rising to his right, Harry recognised the roads from his and Jadyn's visit to Mr Hill's farm the day before. The theft of a shotgun worried him, not so much the act itself, or the impact on the owner, but the final destination of the gun. He'd dealt with the aftermath of what shotguns could do, capable of untold damage to the human body, ruining the lives of the family and friends of those whose lives had been so cruelly taken.

As per Liz's instructions, Harry rolled along towards Agglethorpe, until he saw the reason for his journey down through the Dale, a rusty red pick-up truck, a trailer attached, abandoned at the side of the road. He felt fortunate to not be coming out to a traffic incident, with some poor sod having raced along the lane and straight into it. Beyond the pick-up and trailer, surrounded by fields populated with sheep, he saw a clutch of buildings gathered around a house; a small farmyard, and as Harry drew closer, he heard dogs barking.

Pulling up a little way from the pick-up, Harry parked, then climbed out of his vehicle. On the backseat, Smudge didn't stir, curled up as she was in a ball of thick, black fur.

'Won't be long,' Harry said, barely noticing how he talked to the dog almost as much as he talked to anyone else in his life.

In response, Smudge thumped her tail a couple of times, but otherwise didn't move.

With his shoulders hunched against the wind, Harry blinked as a drop of rain splashed into his eyes. Others were following close behind, and Harry wanted to get back into the Rav4 and wait it out in the warmth with Smudge, who was clearly a better judge of these things. Though looking at the sky, and remembering the forecast, that wait could very well be for the rest of the day. Best to get on, he decided. After all, this wouldn't take him long, he was sure. An abandoned vehicle was hardly a crime of the century.

Harry was about to just walk over and give the scene a once over when something caught his eye. He'd been expecting nothing more suspicious than a pick-up and trailer abandoned by someone who they would then have to track down, if only to establish just what the hell they thought they were doing leaving it there in the first place. Now though, he saw that not all was as it should be.

For a start, both front tyres were blown out. Not flat, like the driver had been unfortunate enough to have a double puncture and then simply sodded off home in a grump. The tyres were shredded and torn. Even from where he was standing, some twenty metres away, Harry could see holes in the rubber. Not something caused by a rough road and a pothole or two, that was for sure, and anyway, the road the pick-up was on was metalled and smooth. Harry had an inkling of an idea as to the true cause, but right now, it just seemed too far-fetched. After all, this was Wensleydale, and he was fairly sure folk didn't generally drive around shooting tyres out for a laugh or because they'd had a disagreement with someone over their driving.

Edging closer, and considerably more cautious now having spotted the tyres, Harry took in the rest of the vehicle. The driver's door was hanging open. The trailer was empty. It did look abandoned. But those tyres, they just didn't sit right in his head. Something about them was definitely off.

'How do,' came a voice from Harry's right, down a lane between himself and the farmyard.

Harry looked up to see a man approaching, at his heel a border collie with its head down and eyes focused on him. The man was dressed in a grease-stained boiler suit of inde-terminate colour and wearing black Wellington boots covered in bicycle repair patches.

'Morning,' Harry said, with a wave. 'I'm—'

'Oh, I know who you are,' the man said. 'Detective Grimm, if I'm not mistaken, which I'm not.'

Harry wasn't quite sure how to take that.

'Detective Chief Inspector Harry Grimm. Was it you who called in about this?'

'It was,' the man said.

'Mr Calvert?'

'That's me,' the man said. 'You here to tow it away, are you? No way you'll be driving it with the tyres like that. Look at the state of them. Can't have happened on the road here, though, can it? No potholes on it for miles. And it won't have happened down my lane neither, if that's what you're thinking.'

'I'm not,' Harry said, but Fred clearly wasn't listening.

'I look after it, you see,' Fred said. 'My responsibility. And a tidy road says a lot about the farm it leads to, I think, don't you?'

Harry closed the distance between them and took out his notebook.

'Would you mind if I took down a few details?'

'Yes, I would,' the man said, then jutted his chin towards the pick-up. 'This is nowt to do with me, if that's what you're thinking. And my privacy is exactly that. Private.'

'Just a telephone number, that's all,' Harry said. 'I've already got your name.'

'Already given it, haven't I?' Mr Calvert said. 'Not that I wanted to, but somehow your police people got the information out of me.'

'Well, the information hasn't been passed on to me quite yet. I was in a rush to get out here as soon as possible.'

'That'll be for you to sort out then, won't it?'

Harry said no more, just stared. The rain had now upped its game, moving from a mild threat to aggressive, and threatening worse to come. Though the man in the boiler suit didn't seem to notice. He just stood in front of Harry, still and calm, oblivious to the sky opening up on them, as impervious to the weather as an ancient standing stone.

At last, the man gave his telephone number, then added, 'And less of the formal Mr Calvert, if you don't mind. My name's Fred, so use it. Fred Calvert. No relative of Kit Calvert, in case you're wondering. There's plenty of us about, like.'

Harry wasn't wondering at all. He hadn't the faintest idea who Kit Calvert was. He knew another Calvert though, that being big Dave, but he wasn't getting any sense of a family resemblance.

'So, when did you find this, then?' Harry asked, keen to get back to the reason he was there.

'This morning,' Fred said. 'I'd been out in the fields, checking up on things, as you do. And when I came back, there it was.'

'What time was that?'

'Haven't a bloody clue,' said Fred. 'Not a fan of watches.'

'Any particular reason?' Harry asked, immediately regretting doing so.

'Don't rightly need one, if I'm honest,' Fred said. 'Don't want my life timetabled or being clocked off hour by hour. Not for me, that.'

'So, you've no idea at all, then?'

'Well, I left the house when it was still dark,' Fred said, 'and when I came back, it was just getting light. So, I'm guessing that would put it at between five and six in the morning, wouldn't it?'

Harry pondered on this for a second.

'But you only called it in about an hour ago,' he said.

'I had things to do,' Fred said. 'Can't be phoning the police every hour of the day, now, can I? I'm a busy man. There's just me on the farm, you see. Don't get a moment to myself.'

'Not sure that's what I was suggesting,' said Harry.

'Well, it skipped my mind, to be honest,' Fred continued. 'People always seem to park in the stupidest of places, don't they? So that's what I thought when I first saw it, just some idiot parking up to head off on that path just over there, probably with their dog or something. I reckon some folk, townies usually, think they can just park anywhere, no regard for other road users, people who actually live around here. But then, when I saw that it was still here, I headed over for a closer look. I saw those tyres, you see, the open door, too, and the blood. I thought then that I'd best give your lot a call to come and sort it out. I've certainly not got the time, that's for sure.'

Harry snapped to attention.

'Blood?'

'What about it?'

'No one mentioned blood.'

'I'm pretty sure that I did,' Fred said. 'But, then again, maybe I didn't.'

Harry clenched his jaws. The rain was coming in hard now. He was very aware that any blood, or any other such evidence, was now at risk of being washed away for good.

'Where is it?'

'Driver's side,' said Fred, pointing at the vehicle, as though suggesting he didn't think Harry knew where that was.

Harry dashed over to the pick-up. He spotted a patch of blood on the ground. So far, the door had sheltered it from the rain, but that wouldn't be the case for much longer.

Grabbing an evidence bag from a pocket, Harry ducked down to the ground to take a sample. He couldn't just scrape up some bloody mud, though. So, he pulled out something else he always carried with him, a small plastic Ziploc bag of cotton swabs. He dabbed the end of four of them in the blood and stowed them safely away in the evidence bag.

Aware then that he needed to protect the scene as best he could, and with no other choice he could think of, he pulled off his jacket and lay it over the blood, propping it up with some larger rocks, which had tumbled from a wall nearby, so that it didn't contaminate the area. Also, he didn't really want blood on his jacket, mainly because that meant having to buy another jacket if the stains didn't come out. And Harry hated buying clothes.

He stood up.

'You'll catch yourself a chill standing out in the rain like that,' Fred said. 'Weather's only going to get worse.'

'I need to call this in,' Harry said, already making his way back to his vehicle.

'Well, why don't you do that up at the house?' Fred offered. 'And, while you're there, maybe you can help me with what's happened in my barn before we get a brew on.'

'And what exactly has happened in your barn, Mr Calvert?' Harry said, the rain already soaking through to his skin.

Fred's voice then took on a mysterious air, as though he was sharing the creepiest, most unnerving of tales.

'Things,' he said, his eyes widening as he spoke, 'have appeared ...'

CHAPTER TWENTY-ONE

Having quickly set some cordon tape around the pick-up truck and trailer, and with Matt and Jen on their way over following his call, Harry then followed Fred up the lane to the farmyard. It was an orderly place, with everything just so; vehicles parked neatly either on the yard or in an open-fronted shed. Harry couldn't see anything that had just been left lying around or piled up to gather mould or rust. This was a well-cared-for farm sat deep in the bosom of green fells. So much so that it looked as though the slopes had grown up around it.

'The barn's over there, other side of the road,' Fred said, as Harry came to the front door of the house. 'Just come in a moment while I fetch you a coat.'

When Fred returned, looming up out of the grey light inside the house, he handed Harry a garment which had very obviously once been a jacket, but should've been committed to the waste bin a good long time ago. It had two arms, yes, and would keep out some of the rain, but it was held together with so many scraps of black tape Harry wondered if the wind would just rip it apart. There was a smell to it as well, an animalistic hum of fur and urine, the pockets stuffed with straw.

'It's my ferreting jacket,' Fred said. 'Usually carry one in each pocket, you see. The straw keeps them warm.'

Harry took the jacket with as much gratitude as he could muster and pulled it on. The stink of it clung to him immediately, rising gleefully up to his nose and then further, his eyes close to watering with its acrid tang.

'Right, we'll head to the barn first, then I'll sort you out with a tea and some cake,' Fred said, then pushed past Harry and strode across the yard to unlock the door to the barn in question.

Once inside, Harry was pleased to be out of what was now clearly turning into a storm. Though the wind was seemingly unhappy at their escape and hammered at the tin roof above their heads.

Harry glanced around. The space was dry and surprisingly warm, the floor cast over with dry straw and grey dust. A quad bike was parked over at one side. He saw other bits of equipment too; a small generator, a trailer to attach to the back of the quad bike, and various other things he had no doubt were very useful, but to him were a complete mystery. It all looked much like the rest of the farm; ordered, cared for, in its place. At the far end was what looked to be a small office room, built from a few lengths of wood, the windows mismatched and cracked, panes more suited to a greenhouse.

The thing was, as Harry stood there taking it all in, he couldn't see what the problem was. Everything, to his eye, looked absolutely fine and normal. This was just a barn on a Wensleydale farm, nothing odd about it at all.

'See what I mean?' Fred said.

Not really, no, Harry wanted to say, but instead said, 'I've been informed that you've had some things returned, items that were stolen from your farm a couple of years ago, I believe.'

'That's exactly what's happened,' Fred said. 'Really has me puzzled, that's for sure.'

'I can understand why it would,' said Harry, more than a little puzzled by it himself. 'And you think the pick-up and trailer have something to do with it?'

'I reckon so, yes,' said Fred. 'Plus, there's tracks from its tyres leading up to the barn. Well, there was, but the rain's getting rid of all that now. Means I've got two quad bikes now, seeing as I claimed for that one when it went missing. I've no idea what the insurance will say about this one appearing again. Though if they try and blame me, suggest I'm pulling a fast one, we'll be having words.'

'Can you remember the date when the original burglary took place?' Harry asked.

Fred frowned.

'Actually, I can,' he said. 'Same weekend as that Bartle thing that people go to. Not my idea of fun, I must say, so I've never bothered with it.'

Harry paused, his pen hovering over his notepad.

'You're sure about that?' he asked.

'I don't say anything unless I am,' said Fred.

Harry moved on.

'As well as the quad bike, then, what else has been returned?' he asked.

Fred reeled off a few other items in front of Harry. 'I was surprised to see any of it back, as you can imagine, but the quad bike and that generator? They're worth a few bob, aren't they? So, what I want to know is, where's this stuff been for the past two years? Doesn't make any sense.'

'No, you're right, it doesn't,' Harry agreed.

'Well, whoever it was, they even brought back my old air rifle,' said Fred and Harry saw it propped up against the wall. 'Great for keeping the rats down, it is, so those little buggers have had the run of the place for a good while. That's about to change now though, isn't it?'

Harry said nothing in reply.

'The only thing I've not found is the chainsaw,' said Fred. 'Which is a shame, really, because I could be doing with that right now. There's a tree that came down yesterday in all this weather we're having, and I'll be needing to head out to get the thing chopped up and stacked up to season good and proper for the fire. Damp wood doesn't burn.'

'Right, I see,' Harry said, jotting everything down in his notebook. 'Chainsaw still missing. Anything else?'

'Is that not enough?'

'It's just a question, that's all,' Harry said. 'Any other details you can give me that you think might be useful, even if you don't think they're important.'

'No, I've said my piece and now I need to get on,' said Fred.

'Well, if you do think of anything, then please give the office a call.'

'Don't want to be using the phone too much now, do I?' Said Fred. 'No idea what could happen.'

Fred, Harry was beginning to realise, was a man of very deep, and very specific, suspicions.

'Such as?' Harry asked.

'Haven't a clue, and that's the problem, isn't it?' Fred

said, tapping the side of his nose and then pointing at Harry as though he was the wisest person in the room.

'And you're absolutely sure that the chainsaw hasn't been put somewhere else perhaps?' Harry asked, holding his hands up to quell the storm of Fred's indignation before it had a chance to crash down onto him. 'The reason I ask is that it's my job to ask, that's all. Detective, remember? And I can see that you're a very organised man, Mr Calvert. But things do end up in places they shouldn't, as I'm sure you know. And maybe, whoever brought all of this back has put it somewhere else.'

'Well, they haven't,' Fred said, then he pointed at the wall. 'See that?'

Harry stared. He saw a hook. Then he saw that on the wall an outline had been sketched out in faded black paint. The outline was roughly the shape of a chainsaw.

'And it's always hung there, has it?'

'It has,' Fred said. 'And you'll see that it's not, so that means it's not here. And as I'm the only one who lives and works here, then you can understand my wondering as to its whereabouts. Because I've checked everywhere in this barn, in the other barns as well, even in the pick-up and trailer themselves, and it's nowhere to be found.'

Harry took a wander around the barn.

'You live alone?'

'I'm the only one here, like I said. Man and boy. Took over from my father when he died. Mum passed away a few years ago now.'

'I'm sorry.'

'I'm not.'

'Oh, right,' Harry said, a little taken aback.

'You know, I reckon she was looking forward to it,' Fred

said. 'All she ever seemed to talk about was buggering off to have a natter with old Saint Peter. Proper Methodist, she was. Chapel every Sunday at two, and never touched a drop.'

Harry checked the barn door, saw no sign of forced entry, not that one was actually needed, the door was held fast by only a large, cast-iron latch.

Whatever had gone on here, it was one of the most bizarre things he'd ever been called out to investigate. A part of him wondered if Fred Calvert was simply having him on, except that the man was clearly telling the truth.

So, why had all of this been returned? And by whom? Why would someone steal it all in the first place, not flog any of it, wait for a couple of years, then come back and return it? A guilty conscience was one thing, but this, it just didn't make any sense, did it? Harry suspected that there was a lot more going on here than was visible on the surface. What, though, he hadn't the faintest idea. Add to it all the abandoned pick-up truck and trailer and what he had was a bit of a puzzle.

A distant rumble shook itself free from the clouds, then spent a few moments rolling around far above.

'Thunder as well,' Fred said, looking up, shaking his head. 'Looks like we're in for a proper day of it, doesn't it?'

Just beneath the sound of the rain, wind, and now thunder, Harry heard the thrum of an engine. He headed outside to see Matt pulling up, with Jen sitting beside him.

'Why don't you head back to the house,' Harry suggested. 'Give me time to chat with my team.'

'I'll put the kettle on,' Fred said. 'You'll all be wanting a brew, I'm sure. I know I certainly do.'

Fred headed off to the house as Matt came over, leaving Jen behind in the car and, luckily for her, in the dry.

'So, what've we got?' Matt asked. 'Nice jacket, by the way. Not sure how much protection it'll give you against all of this.' He looked up at the sky, his shoulders hunched up against the tumult. 'Coming down like stair rods, now, isn't it?'

'Stinks to high heaven,' Harry said, turning up his nose as another waft of animal stench drifted under his nose from what he was having to wear. 'Amazing what you'll do to preserve a crime scene, isn't it?' He nodded over to the pick-up and trailer. 'As to this? Well, right now, I've not the faintest. But there's blood by the driver's side and no driver, and that's enough to have me worried in and of itself, but the rest is just bizarre, with stolen items returned, a missing chainsaw. And get this; the burglary during which the items were originally stolen happened the very same night Keith's place was broken into two years ago by his son, Anthony.'

'That's not a coincidence, is it?' said Matt.

Harry shook his head.

'No such thing.'

'You'll be wanting me to see if I can find the owner of the van as well, then?' Matt asked. 'And by that, I mean calling the office to have Jadyn get on with it, obviously.'

'I will,' Harry said. 'That blood is a real worry. Either we've someone with a head injury walking around, dazed and confused ...'

'Or something else,' Matt said.

'It's the something else that's bothering me,' said Harry. 'Particularly after that meeting over in Askrigg last night. Here, have a look at this.'

Harry took Matt over to the pick-up and pointed at the tyres.

'Bloody hell,' Matt said. He crouched down and had a

closer look, using his pen to poke at the shredded rubber. 'No pothole did that.'

'Then what do you think did?' Harry asked.

Matt looked up at Harry, eyes serious.

'We both know the answer to that, don't we?'

'That we do,' said Harry. 'And you can see marks on the wheels themselves, too.'

Matt leaned in for a closer look.

'Yeah, it's been peppered,' he said. 'A shotgun did this. Point blank range, too, to cause that kind of damage. Though it looks worse than that, don't you think?'

Harry wiped rain from his eyes, scratched the scars on his face, a tingle beneath the skin coming on stronger than usual, a sign that the wounds would never truly heal.

'How do you mean?'

'They've been driven on,' Matt said. 'The tyres aren't just shot out, they're shredded.'

Harry had another look.

'Nothing about this makes any sense,' he said.

'And we both know what that means, don't we?'

'That's what's bothering me.'

'Do you want to call him, or shall I?' Matt asked.

'I don't need to answer that, do I?'

Matt took out his phone.

CHAPTER TWENTY-TWO

With Jen in the car as the Scene Guard, Harry led Matt up to Fred Calvert's farmhouse. On the way, Matt gave a quick call to the office and spoke to Jadyn. As for Jen, she would call him as soon as the pathologist, Mr Bennett, arrived. Harry had been half tempted to just call Rebecca instead, but that was pushing it, he thought. Not just with the powers that be, but also with her mum. With the way the week was going, he was becoming increasingly pleased that he wasn't having to explain it all to Detective Superintendent Swift. He'd be able to put that off till next week, at least.

'Through here,' came Fred's voice, as Harry and Matt stepped in through the open front door.

Harry, with Matt in tow, walked deeper into the house and through to a kitchen.

'What do you think?' Fred asked.

Harry stared. The kitchen was blue. Not just the cupboards either, but the walls, too. He had the odd sensation that he had somehow walked into a swimming pool.

'You wouldn't believe it, but I was down at the refuse

site a few weeks back, like, and someone was throwing out a couple of large tubs of paint,' Fred said, his voice lit with glee. 'So I thought to myself, you know what, I'll have those! So, I had a word, brought them home, opened them up. The kitchen needed a bit of a freshening up so that's what I was on with a couple of weekends ago. And I've plenty left over, so if I've time I might splash a bit elsewhere, too.'

'Well, you've definitely done a thorough job,' Matt said, and Harry was impressed with the man's diplomatic approach to praise.

Fred nodded to a dining table in the centre of the room.

'Sit down and serve yourselves,' he said. 'I'll just nip out with a mug for that poor lass you've left in the car.'

Harry sat down as instructed and poured out two steaming mugs of tea.

'I see he's provided cake, too,' said Matt. 'I'm impressed. A good host.'

'This isn't a café,' Harry said.

'No, but it could be,' said Matt. 'There's plenty of walkers in the area and there will be footpaths through his fields. You could make a killing, easily.'

'You should tell him,' Harry suggested. 'Anyway, how's little Mary-Anne doing?'

Matt pulled out his phone to reveal a photo of a very pink and very squashed baby's face.

'She's lovely, isn't she?'

'Yes, she is, I'm sure,' Harry said, cleverly disguising his thoughts about this particular photo.

'Joan's doing so well with it all. We're both tired, obviously, but she's knackered. Not that she shows it much or complains. She has everything organised and right now all

I'm doing is just trying to keep up. She's the most amazing woman.'

'Which makes one wonder why she married you, really, doesn't it?'

Matt laughed as Fred walked back into the kitchen.

'You've not started on the cake,' he said. 'Something up with it?'

'We were just being polite,' Harry said.

'Don't be daft,' Fred said, and cut himself a large slice which he then stuffed into his mouth before sitting down opposite Harry and Matt.

'Makes a change to have visitors,' he said.

'My colleague here was saying how you could open a café,' Harry said, 'what with all the footpaths around and about.'

'Are you mad?'

'But I thought—'

'I said it made a change. I didn't say it was nice.'

All at once, Harry felt more than a little unwelcome, retracting his hand halfway to the cake.

Fred laughed, the sound akin to that of a hyena choking on a packet of crisps, high pitched and filled with the crackle of phlegm.

'Your faces!' he said. 'Absolutely bloody priceless! No, it is good to have visitors. Don't get many if I'm honest. Obviously, I've a few friends around and about, but this farming life, it's a bit lonely, isn't it?'

Harry was already wondering why they'd agreed to come to the house. The promise of a warm mug of tea was perhaps not worth whatever it was Fred was going to ramble on about for the next few minutes.

'We'll need details of the chainsaw,' Harry said, hoping

to steer the conversation before Fred took it off course. 'And you'll need to contact whoever you have insurance with.'

'I tried speed dating once,' Fred said, clearly not listening. 'Have you ever done it? My advice: don't. Bloody awful. Five minutes chatting with someone then this buzzer sounds and you all have to move on to the next poor sod unfortunate enough to find themselves staring at you as you stare back. Everyone's all awkward in their Sunday best, a little bit pissed, too, just to steady the nerves. Some are taking notes. And there's always one who's super confident, isn't there? Well, that someone wasn't me. Been three times now, though.'

Harry finished his tea a little too quickly, the liquid scalding his throat.

'You know, I think we should go out and keep an eye on things,' he said, 'just in case.'

'There was this one lass, though,' Fred said, very much on a roll now, Harry realised, 'and she seemed keen on me. Not had that in years, I have to say. I mean, I'm old for one thing, aren't I? Well, I'm not old-old, but I'm definitely getting on a bit, with sixty just around the corner. We've even been on a few dates since, you know? She's visited the farm, too. I cooked for her. She didn't stay over, mind. I'm a gentleman, you see. Taking things nice and slow, which is for the best. Can't be rushing into anything, now, can I?'

Harry stood up, Matt followed suit, but Fred was still talking.

'And then there's the smell. That's the trouble with being a farmer, isn't it? There's always this stink around you. Not just of animal shit, either, but just general farm stuff, the chemicals we use, foot-rot spray, cordite from cartridges if you've been clearing out a few rabbits. I'm used to it, don't notice it at all, but others do, I'm sure.'

'Well, we'll be off, then,' Harry said.

Fred stood up and held out the plate of cake.

'You'd best take some of this with you,' he said. 'She made it for me, you see, the lass who I met speed dating. I can't really eat it all, not on my own, and I don't want her to think that I didn't like it, because I did, I mean I do, but there's only so much cake you can eat when you live on your own, isn't there?'

'Not sure I agree with you there,' Matt said, reaching for the cake, 'but I'll happily help you out.'

At the farmhouse door, Harry stared into a day quickly on its way to apocalyptic levels of rain. It was coming down so hard that looking across the farmyard was like staring at a painting ruined by water damage. The colours were running into each other, the greys of the buildings smearing across the yard to flow down the road and into the fields. The fells were hidden completely from view, the sky black and angry.

'Think I'll be spending my day inside, in front of the fire, checking through all my invoices and receipts,' Fred said, looking past Harry to stare into the storm. 'Can't say that I fancy your job today, though.'

'Makes two of us,' Harry said. 'I'll bring your jacket back as soon as I can.'

'Oh, don't worry about it. This rain will do it good. Give it a bit of a clean, like. Lord knows it needs one. I've not worn it for weeks because of the reek it's developed. Reckon it could walk if I gave it a chance.'

Harry briefly considered handing the jacket back to Fred, but a deafening peel of thunder changed his mind. He strode across the farmyard, which was already filling itself with a healthy collection of puddles to soak his feet in. With Matt at his side, they walked into the lane and as they approached Jen, who sent them a little wave, they saw another vehicle pull up behind her. The driver's door opened and out stepped a figure already dressed from head to toe in waxed storm-proof clothing, the hat spilling with rain like strands of silver hanging from its wide brim, the jacket ankle-length and worn with years of use. From a distance, and against the backdrop of a sky raw with anger, the figure cut well the silhouette of a Wild West marshal rolling into town seeking vengeance.

'Well, she didn't take long,' Matt said.

'Considering she wasn't even invited, it's even more of a miracle that she's here at all,' answered Harry.

And with that, Harry headed over to meet Rebecca Sowerby's mother, the District Surgeon, Margaret Shaw.

CHAPTER TWENTY-THREE

'Margaret,' Harry said with a nod.

Margaret closed the distance between them, sploshing her boots through deep, dark puddles, which hadn't been there when Harry had arrived earlier. She stared up at him through the rods of rain dripping from her hat, wide eyes set in a stern yet warm face. Short she may have been, but she carried the presence of someone twice her size.

'Before you say anything,' she said, 'I know you weren't expecting me. And I'm not here in my capacity as district surgeon either.'

'Good job really,' said Harry. 'Seeing as we don't actually have a body for you to confirm as deceased.'

'That makes a change.'

'It does.'

While Matt climbed into the car with Jen to get out of the rain, Harry waited for Margaret to tell him why she was there. When no answer seemed forthcoming, his patience ran out.

'I'm assuming you've an explanation for turning up not only unannounced, but uninvited,' he said. 'And I'm not being rude, I just want to know. Particularly for when Bennett shows up.'

'Rebecca is in daily contact with her office,' Margaret said. 'That's how she knew about what was going on at the weekend and headed over to see you all. Anything that comes in, she hears about it. So, this came up and here I am. She would've been here herself if I hadn't nipped out when she was having a nap. I've tried to hold her off, but as you saw, she's not exactly the kind of person who takes well to being told what to do.'

'Can't imagine where she gets that from.'

'I am not in any way, shape, or form as stubborn as my daughter.'

'No, of course you're not,' said Harry. 'How's that broken leg of yours, anyway? Didn't get much use out of those crutches you were sent home with, did you?'

'Crutches? Didn't bloody need them, did I? I'm a surgeon, medicine is in my blood! It was just a break, that's all. No point being all weak about it and making a fuss. Better to just crack on and—'

'—not listen to the doctors, who probably know what's for the best,' Harry said, cutting in.

Margaret stepped a little closer, fixing Harry with a steely stare.

'You can go off someone, you know that, don't you?'

Harry smiled.

'You're a spy, then, is that it?'

'Not exactly James Bond, I admit,' Margaret said, lifting her arms then like bird wings, before letting them splat back down against her jacket. 'And I really do look awful in a tuxedo. I do mix a mean Martini, though.'

'Now, why doesn't that surprise me?' Harry said. 'How's Rebecca? It was good to see her, you know, but don't tell her I said so.'

'I won't, I promise.' Margaret laughed, sucking in a deep breath through her nose. 'She's doing okay, though. Insists everything is fine, that she's good to go back to work, doesn't need to talk about what happened. It was easy when she had to stay in bed. But now? Well, now it's a bloody nightmare. Like having a tantrummy toddler in the house, only she's larger, older, and considerably better at yelling.'

'Not throwing things at you as well, is she?'

'I did once hear a croissant thunk into her bedroom door after I'd left her some breakfast,' Margaret said. 'Bit ungrateful if you ask me. Who in their right mind would throw away a delicious pastry? It was warm, too. Lovely stuff.'

'You're making me hungry.'

'You're always hungry.'

'It's the job.'

'It's also Wensleydale,' Margaret said. 'When I moved over here, I was a waif. Hard to believe, isn't it? But soon enough, what with cheese and cake offered every time you pop round to see someone, pie and pea suppers, the pubs serving good beer and good food, I then wasn't, if you know what I mean.' She tapped a hand on her stomach. 'Still, it's all worth it. And it gives me a good excuse to get out on the hills as often as I can for a good tramp around and about.'

This was all very interesting, Harry thought, but right now all he was doing was discovering an entirely new level of being soaked to the skin. Margaret's presence, pleasant though it was in the very small world of distractions he was happy to accommodate, was one he could undoubtedly do without once the Scene of Crime team turned up. Not that she'd get in the way, quite the opposite, but it could certainly put their backs up.

The pathologist, Mr Bennett, wasn't the most pleasant of individuals. In many ways, he was revolting, kind of like how Harry imagined an eel would be to deal with if it grew arms and legs, donned an ill-fitting suit, and decided that the best thing to do with its life was to rummage around in the remains of people, a good number of whom hadn't exactly died well. Knowing that the person he was covering for had sent her mother to spy on him might not put him in the best of moods. Still, it would certainly be amusing, Harry thought.

'So, what have you got?' Margaret said.

'This is a crime scene,' Harry said. 'You know as well as I that we're not supposed to do anything until after the Scene of Crime team has done their thing.'

'Oh, don't talk such nonsense!' Margaret said. 'Like there's much more damage we can do that hasn't already been done by this weather!'

'Even so,' Harry said, but Margaret didn't let him finish.

'We both know I'm not going anywhere until I've got something to take back to my daughter. Because if I don't, she'll be hell to live with, and that's saying something.'

'You've not kicked her out, then?'

'She's said she's going home in a couple of weeks,' Margaret said. 'We're both counting down the days.'

Harry remembered what Rebecca had said, her worries about her mum being alone. He wondered if those two weeks would extend indefinitely. He shivered then, the cold of the day now with its claws firmly in his bones.

'You sure about that?'

Margaret narrowed her eyes and Harry could hear her unspoken accusations.

'What did she say?'

'Nothing.'

'Out with it.'

'Nothing to get out.'

'Even with that face of yours, I can tell when you're lying,' Margaret said.

Harry sighed.

'Look, maybe you should just talk with her, that's all. I'm sure it's not been a bed of roses, having her back, but I'm also sure that you've enjoyed having her around.'

'Of course I have, she's my daughter.'

'And maybe she's enjoyed being around you, too. Just talk to her, that's all I'm saying.'

Margaret was quiet for a moment, folded her arms, unfolded them, then reached out to pinch the sleeve of Fred's jacket.

'Why on earth are you wearing this stinking thing?' she asked, clearly changing the subject.

'Had to put something over the blood to protect it. My jacket was all I had to hand. This is on loan.'

'Even so.'

'It's worse for me, I can assure you.'

'You don't need to.'

Harry led Margaret over to the pick-up, ducking under the cordon tape he had put up around the area.

'It was called in this morning by the farmer,' Harry explained. 'A Mr Fred Calvert. He found it here this morning after he'd come home off the fells. There's a patch of blood on the ground round the driver's side. And that's all we know.'

'How large a patch?'

Harry thought for a moment.

'About the size of a large frying pan,' he said. 'I took some samples as well, what with the weather turning as it has.'

'Could be an accident,' Margaret suggested. 'Those tyres certainly make it look like that.'

'Well, they would if that damage had been done by the road,' said Harry. 'Have a closer look. Tell me what you think.'

'I'm not a pathologist.'

'No, but you've been around enough crime scenes in your time to have a good idea about a few things, I'm sure,' Harry said. 'And I also know you'll give me an honest opinion.'

'No bullshit, you mean.'

'No bullshit.'

Margaret slopped her way over to the pick-up for a closer look, ducking down by the passenger door. She stared at the tyre, leaned in for a closer look at things, then stood up and came back over to Harry.

'Yeah, someone shot that out with a shotgun,' she said. 'There are holes in the wing which look about the right size for pellets from a cartridge. No need to look at the other one as I'm going to assume the damage is the same. But the tyres look ...'

She paused, thinking.

'They look like they've been driven on, don't they?' Harry said.

'They do.'

'The blood was just about enough to have me call this in,' Harry said, 'but the rest of it, the possibility of a gun being used, we need that confirmed. Like you said, it could just be an accident and we find ourselves with someone wandering around the fields dazed and confused.'

'Or dead in a ditch.'

'Or that, yes,' said Harry. 'We're on with tracing the owner now, but those tyres and that blood really have me worried.'

'And rightly so, too,' said Margaret. 'Bit of a quandary, really, isn't it? A proper puzzler.'

'I've an abandoned vehicle, a missing driver, a pool of blood, two tyres not only blown out with what looks like blasts from a shotgun, but also driven on, and a rainstorm to wash away just about any useful evidence that might help.'

Harry didn't mention Fred's returned items.

'It's going to be a fun one, that's for sure.'

'Not sure fun's the word I'm reaching for right now,' Harry said, as he saw Matt climb out of the car and approach them.

'Now then, Margaret,' he said. 'Solved the case for us then, have you?'

'The butler did it.'

'It's always the butler, isn't it?' Matt said, then looked at Grimm. 'Anyway, two things. One, everyone's favourite pathologist has just called in at the office to ask if anyone would be able to grab him a pie from Cockett's for his dinner this evening.'

Harry opened his mouth to fill the air with enough swearing to turn it blue for a year, but Matt kept on talking, giving him no chance to.

'However, you'll be pleased to hear that he had Gordy

there to deal with, so she politely suggested he continue on his way here and sort his own supper out once he'd finished.'

'You began with one,' said Harry. 'I'm assuming there's a two.'

'There is indeed,' said Matt. 'We've got a hit on the owner of the pick-up.'

CHAPTER TWENTY-FOUR

No sooner had Matt finished speaking than the Scene of Crime team arrived. They turned up in two large white transit vans, both of which looked much like crime scenes themselves, with rust patches, bumps and knocks covering most of their surface. Harry watched as two figures approached. He knew them both, disliked one of them immensely, and the other he found simply baffling.

'Ah, Mr Grimm,' the first man said, busily trying to zip up his jacket against the wind and rain. It was a bright yellow thing, and clearly very new. It was also a few sizes too small by the looks of it. 'Good to see you again.'

Is it, though? Harry thought.

'Mr Bennett,' he said, at least acknowledging the man.

'Lovely day you've picked for it.'

'I've seen worse.'

Bennett continued to struggle with his jacket and it put Harry in mind of a fish caught in a net. He soon gave up on the zip and just wrapped his arms around himself. The other man, for once, didn't exactly look filled with his usual macabre enthusiasm.

Bennett's eyes turned to rest on Margaret.

'Mrs Shaw,' he said, bristling just a little. 'I don't believe we have a body.'

'You don't,' Margaret replied.

'Then may I ask in what capacity you are attending the scene?'

'No, you may not,' Margaret said. Then she turned to Harry. 'I'll be off then.'

'Remember what I said,' said Harry.

Margaret looked at him for a moment, smiled, then turned and walked off back to her own vehicle.

'Not sure why you've called us, really,' Bennett said, as Harry watched Margaret drive away. 'Doesn't sound very important. Or look it, either. And remind me later to talk to you about your team back at the office. Not very helpful when I popped in, I must say.'

'Well, they're not much into running errands,' Harry said. 'They have this crazy, misplaced notion that their time is better spent doing the job they're paid for. I've tried to dissuade them from it, but you know how it is. People, eh?'

Bennett's lips went thin as thread and his pudgy face grew just a little red.

'Can I get on?'

The question was from the other man now standing with them. He was wrestling with a large camera and hadn't exactly come dressed for the weather.

'Nice shorts,' Matt said. 'Going to the beach, are we?'

'I was trying them on for my holidays,' the photographer said. 'I forgot I had them on.'

'Oh dear,' Matt said. 'Oh deary, deary me, that is a

mistake now, isn't it? You'll be catching your death if you don't watch it. I'd hurry along if I was you.'

'That's what I'm trying to do.'

'Well, don't just stand there talking then,' Harry said. 'Get a shift on so you can put away those pale-looking things as soon as possible.'

The photographer stared at Harry then down at his legs.

'They're not that pale.'

'I've seen healthier-looking sticks of celery,' Harry said.

With that, the photographer pushed past and dipped under the cordon tape. A moment later, bright flashes cast themselves through the downpour, freeze-framing random moments of time, the rain turning to diamonds as he took photos of the crime scene.

Harry stood in silence with Matt and Bennett. It was difficult to resist the urge to step just a little further away. He turned to Matt.

'I think we can leave all of this in the capable hands of Detective Constable Blades, don't you?' he said.

'Very much so,' Matt agreed.

Bennett stared at them both.

'With this weather, I can't see that we'll get anything of use,' he said.

'Giving up then, are you?' asked Harry.

'That's not what I said.'

'No, but you implied that your heart isn't really in it, and that's much the same in my book.'

'Are you questioning my professionalism?'

'Seem to be doing a grand job of that yourself,' said Harry, then pointed a finger at the pick-up. 'For starters, those tyres look like they were shot out. Shotgun, possibly. So, we'll be looking for confirmation as to what did it. Not least because we had a shotgun go missing earlier in the week. If you can give us an idea of what gauge it was, that would be useful, I'm sure. We also think they've been driven on. Stop me if I'm telling you how to do your job ...'

Mr Bennett went to speak but Harry didn't give him a chance.

'Also, there's the blood,' he said, and pulled a plastic bag from his pocket and handed it to Bennett. 'I took a sample before the rain really came on. As to the rest, I'm sure you'll find plenty to keep you busy. Fingerprints, hair samples, anything really. And make sure that my jacket is looked after, will you? I want that back in one piece.'

Bennett's pudgy face seemed to melt with confusion, like a cheap novelty candle left too long in the sun.

'What, you thought I was wearing this out of choice?' Harry said, pinching a piece of the material. 'Oh, and finally, once you're done here, I could do with your team having a look at that barn over there as well, if you'd be so kind.'

'The barn? Why?'

'A chainsaw's missing,' Harry said. 'And apparently, some previously stolen items have been returned. The farmer, Mr Fred Calvert, can give you further details on all that. I'm thinking that both events are connected.'

'Anything else?' Bennett asked.

Matt leaned in.

'Well, if you've a moment to spare, I could do with some sausages from Cockett's for dinner tonight, if you wouldn't mind? No, wait, my mistake. I can do that all by myself, can't I?'

Harry turned then, fully expecting to hear the sound of the pathologist's head exploding in both frustration and anger. With Matt by his side, he walked over to Jen, who lowered her window.

'We're heading off to check up on the details of the owner,' Harry said. 'I'm assuming you're good to stay put and keep an eye on things?'

'I'm warm and dry in here,' Jen replied. 'Sounds like the perfect job to me on a day like this. Though I'll be out for a run later so I'm hoping it'll have cleared up by then.'

Harry and Matt climbed into his Rav4. The vehicle was cold now and as soon as the engine was on, he turned the heating to full.

'It'll take a few minutes to warm up,' he said. 'Now, where are we heading?'

Matt checked his phone.

'Leyburn,' he said. 'None of this makes much sense, does it?'

'Not much, no.'

'It will do soon enough, though, I'm sure.' Matt read Harry the rest of the address. 'The owner's name is a Mr Ian Wray.'

'Ian?' Harry said.

'Yes, rings a bell or two, doesn't it?'

'Is that a good sign or not?' Harry asked.

'Could be both. I'll check.'

As Harry turned his vehicle around and Matt called the office, Smudge shuffled around and got comfortable again.

'We'll give the dog a leg stretch when we arrive,' Harry said. 'She could do with it.'

'She seems quite happy where she is.'

'That she may be,' said Harry. 'But she's been in here a while and the call of nature is better answered outside my vehicle than in.'

'Jim's going to see if he can find anything out for us,' Matt said. 'Might be nothing, but you never know.'

Harry made to pull away, but then caught a whiff of the jacket he was wearing.

'Just a minute,' he said, climbing out of the vehicle and pulling the jacket off. The sleeve he was yanking came away from the rest of the jacket. He threw it and the rest of the jacket into the boot.

'It was very kind of him to loan it to me,' he said, climbing back in beside Matt, 'but I'm not sure I wasn't better off without it.'

'It was starting to make my eyes water,' Matt said.

'You and me both.'

Once on the main road, the journey to Leyburn was slow, with Harry driving as cautiously as he could from puddle to flood and back to puddle again. At one point, they passed a couple on a tandem bicycle. They were wearing enough reflective gear to almost blind Harry when his headlights caught them.

'Never seen the attraction myself,' Matt observed as they sped past, giving a wide enough gap so as not to drench them even more. 'A bike ride is one thing, but imagine being stuck on one with someone else? Not that it's an issue for Joan and me, like, but still, can you imagine?'

'I'd prefer not to.'

'I mean, can you imagine us doing that?'

'You and Joan?'

'No, you and me.'

'Why on earth would we do that?' Harry asked.

'You'd probably pull rank and bagsy the front seat, and I'd be stuck on the back, getting covered in your sweat, doing all the work, staring at your arse.'

'Does your brain always do this?' Harry asked.

'What?'

'Talk bollocks?'

'Yes,' Matt said. 'Endlessly. It's why I have to share it sometimes, just to ease the pressure a little.'

They splashed on, taking the road over the River Ure and on through Wensley, after which they had named the whole of the dale. A little further on, Harry had to do an emergency stop as someone on the opposite side came round a bend on the wrong side of the road to avoid a large puddle.

'Why is it,' he asked, 'no matter what the weather, there's always some idiot in a rush, willing to risk life and limb to get somewhere a couple of minutes faster than they actually need to?'

'Well, that's never been me,' Matt said. 'Driving fast has never really been my thing.'

From Wensley, the road seemed to transform itself gradually into an ever-angrier river, as drains overflowed, and water swilled off the fields. The rain was so heavy that a haze was growing above the road, a thick mist of raindrops bursting on impact.

Leyburn swept up to greet them, hurrying them on to their destination. The marketplace was a spectacle of people either seeking shelter under shop fronts, or hurrying from shop to shop, braced under umbrellas, holding hats. Harry saw a small child swept up into the arms of an adult and hurriedly shoved into a waiting child seat in the back of a car, and a dog sitting to heel and looking none too happy about it either.

Following the rest of Matt's directions, Harry headed past the marketplace until a couple of minutes later they were heading down a narrow lane lined with a mix of houses and bungalows.

'It looks like a dead-end, but it isn't,' Matt said. 'The road's one of those that the council can't be arsed to maintain, so they keep it good up to a point and then it's a bit rough.'

Almost as Matt finished speaking, the road surface changed.

'Just keep going. The address is just a bit farther ahead on the left.'

And rightly enough, there it was, a small bungalow tucked beneath some trees like it was hiding from the world or ashamed of something it had done.

Harry pulled up and turned off the engine.

'Best we go have a nosy, then,' he said, and opened his door to push his way back out into the rain.

CHAPTER TWENTY-FIVE

Back at the office, after having persuaded Jim to head back to Mr Black's farm to check out his story about dog faeces on his car, Jadyn was now with Gordy in the interview room. In front of them was a young man who had refused to give his name so far. Since being found in the back of a caravan, he hadn't exactly been cooperative. They'd offered fresh biscuits. They'd even gone so far as to open a new jar of coffee, but still nothing.

'Look,' Jadyn said, leaning forward and clasping his fingers together, 'no one's going anywhere until you at least give us an idea of what you were doing in the caravan.'

'Then we'll be sitting here for ages, won't we?' the young man said. 'Not like I'm in a rush.'

'It can't harm anyone to give us your name, can it?'

The only response Jadyn received was a shrug.

He glanced at Gordy, eyes wide with desperation.

Gordy leaned in just far enough to get the young man's attention.

'The simple fact is, what you did was illegal. And the key

reason for that, as we've already explained to you, is because it's hugely dangerous. You understand that, don't you? Not just to you, either, but to the person driving the car. And he didn't even know you were there.'

'I was fine. I don't know what you're worried about.'

'You were not fine at all,' Gordy said. 'What do you think would've happened if there had been a crash? Have you thought about that?'

No response.

Jadyn was both annoyed and impressed by the young man's dedication to not giving anything away.

'Caravans aren't designed to survive collisions or impacts like a car,' Gordy continued, really rubbing the point in. 'You understand that, don't you?'

'Yes.'

'And you understand that if someone is rolling around in a towed caravan, it'll interfere with its stability. Which could easily result in the crash that you probably wouldn't survive.'

'Yes.'

'Not only that, because being in a towed caravan is illegal, any car insurance is null and void.'

'So, why don't you arrest me, then?'

'Because there's more to this than just hitching a lift, isn't there?' Gordy said. 'Yes, the police arrest people, of course we do, but we also try and help where we can. And we want to help, don't we, Constable Okri?'

Jadyn was surprised to hear his name, thinking Gordy was in control of things.

'Of course we do,' he said, then he added a little extra to show that he'd been taking notice. 'But we can't do that unless you help us first.'

'You know, I dealt with something similar once,' Gordy

said, leaning back. 'A few years ago now, I was behind a caravan on the motorway when the door popped open. It happens, usually because people forget to lock the door properly. And they're pretty flimsy things anyway, aren't they? Doors can just pop open. Except on this occasion, the reason was a little different.'

'If you're trying to scare me, it won't work.'

'It was a kid. 'No older than eight. A little boy, blond hair. He reached out to shut the door,' Gordy said. 'And slipped.'

There was enough of a pause between the word *door* and *slipped* to cause both Jadyn and the young man to turn expectantly.

'He caught himself just as he fell,' Gordy continued. 'Swung out on the door. Good job it was one of those two-piece ones, because the top half swung away and he managed to grab the bottom half, but only just.'

'So, what happened?' Jadyn asked, a little too keenly, he thought. 'Did he fall?'

'He still had his toes inside and pulled himself back in. Never been so terrified in my life. Pulled the car over sharpish, I can tell you. Turns out the parents had put him in there because he'd been making too much noise in the car. It was a punishment, and one that nearly killed him.'

The young man was unmoved. He slid down further in his chair, rolled up his sleeves, crossed his arms behind his head, and yawned.

Jadyn went to say something, but Gordy hushed him with a stare and a quick shake of her head. Then she tapped her forearm before pointing at the now-revealed forearms of the young man. On them, Jadyn saw ink.

'That's some nice artwork,' Gordy said.

The young man closed his eyes.

'I should've guessed from the haircut,' Gordy continued, 'but those tattoos have given it away, haven't they?'

The young man sat up, leaned forward, rolled down his sleeves, head down now. Something had changed, Jadyn noticed. Gordy was onto something.

'Which regiment?'

'What?'

'Listen to me,' Gordy said, her voice soft and calm, 'I know you're absent without leave. You've gone AWOL. Yes?'

Silence for a moment, then the faintest of nods.

'No one does that unless they're desperate,' Gordy said. 'It's no small thing to just pack up and leave your regiment, your mates, your life. And to hitch a ride in a caravan? That tells me you were desperate.'

The young man's chin was shaking now.

'Whatever's happened, we can help,' she said.

'You can't. No one will believe me, anyway. And I can't go back now, can I? I'll get beasted to death, I know I will.'

'Was it bullying, then? Is that what this is? The Army takes a very serious line on that. But you need to let us help.'

'They'll say I'm making it up just to get out, but I'm not!'

'Start from the beginning,' Gordy said.

'I ... I had to go. I couldn't stay any longer. I just couldn't!'

The young man jumped up from the table, knocking his coffee over. Tears were streaming down his face.

'I'll go get a cloth,' Jadyn said.

'You do that,' said Gordy, then stood up and quietly made her way around to the young man. As he left the room, Jadyn saw her rest an arm over his shoulders.

Back in the main office, and as he was just grabbing a

cloth, the phone buzzed. He answered it, listened, jotted everything down, then raced through to Gordy.

'A call's just come in,' he said. 'I need to get shifting.'

Gordy made sure the young man was okay and followed Jadyn out of the interview room.

'I'll get him returned to his unit,' she said. 'But what's going on? You look spooked.'

Jadyn steeled himself for what he was about to say.

'Someone was out running on the fells. Over Pen Hill.'

'In weather like this?' Gordy said. 'Has there been an accident, then? Wouldn't that be more for the Mountain Rescue team to sort out instead of you?'

'No,' Jadyn said. 'Not an accident.'

'What then?'

'A foot,' Jadyn said.

'You're making no sense,' said Gordy. 'You said it was a runner on Pen Hill.'

'It was,' said Jadyn.

'And they've broken their foot?'

Jadyn shook his head.

'No, they found one,' he said.

CHAPTER TWENTY-SIX

Having taken Smudge for a less-than-enthusiastic trudge in the rain, during which she had relieved herself within seconds of leaving the vehicle and then refused to go any further, Harry was now staring at the bungalow. It looked lifeless, he thought, a place forgotten by the world and unloved by whoever owned it. The weather only added to the depressing scene, a backdrop of soaked darkness more suited to a horror movie than real life.

'Doesn't look very inviting, does it?' Matt said.

Harry didn't answer and ambled up to the front door, observing the place as they drew closer. He noticed that the curtains were pulled shut, the windows filmy inside with dust and dirt. What passed as a garden at the front was hugely overgrown, weeds pushing through the path.

'And this is where Ian, Anthony's pal and the owner of the pick-up truck we've found, supposedly lives?' Harry asked.

'It's the address attached to the vehicle, yes,' Matt said

and pointed to a garage on their left. 'Want me to go and check it out?'

Harry shook his head.

'In a minute. Let's just check the house first, see if Mr Wray is in. If he is, then we'll be having a few questions for him, I think.'

At the door, Harry pushed the button of a small plastic bell set into the door frame. From inside the house, he heard a chime sound. But that was all. There was no sound of someone coming to answer the door.

Harry tried again. Still nothing. He banged his fist on the door like a hammer.

'Mr Wray?' he called. 'This is the police. Can you come to the door, please?'

'Don't think he's in,' Matt said.

Harry tried the door handle: nothing. But he wasn't about to take silence as an answer.

'Right, you stay here,' he said. 'Just in case someone pops out through the front. I'm going to have a look around the back, see if it's open.'

Harry made his way through an iron gate at the side of the bungalow. A narrow path, as overgrown as the front garden, led him round to the rear of the property. There, he found a patch of grass grown thick with weeds. The place was surrounded by trees, hidden from view. A garden shed sat just back from the house, the glass windows broken, the roof sagging. With nothing really grabbing his attention, he swung round to look at the bungalow. Here, the curtains were drawn back, though the windows were so grubby he doubted that any light had made its way through in months. He leaned in close, tried to see through the grime, but it was an impossible task.

A backdoor was just to his right. He slid along to it, found the window set in it to be in an even worse state, and was about to give up when he thought he may as well give the door handle a go, just in case. And, to his amazement, it opened.

Harry pulled out his phone to call Matt to come round.

'I was just about to call you myself,' Matt said.

'Why?'

'I noticed that the garage door was open, so I had a quick peek. I've found something. And you're going to want to see this.'

'What is it?'

'My guess is lots of things that don't actually belong to our sticky-fingered Mr Wray,' Matt said. 'The place is full. We're going to need a team out here to go through it all, cata-logue it, and cross-reference it to reports of break-ins, thefts. It's a hell of a lot of work we're looking at, that's for sure.'

''Well, it's not going anywhere for now,' Harry said. 'The bungalow's open. Round the back. Need you with me, just in case.'

Matt arrived a few seconds later, having jogged around.

'I'll go in first,' Harry said. 'Just be ready, okay?'

'I'm never anything else.'

Harry pushed the door fully open.

'Mr Wray? This is the police.'

No answer.

'Your door was open,' Harry continued. 'We need to ask you some questions. If you are home, please show yourself.'

The house, Harry thought, had a quietness about it only obtained after being empty for a very, very long time. There was a weight to the silence, as though the place was trying to keep hold of a terrible secret.

'Mr Wray, I need to tell you that we are entering your house. Do not do anything foolish. We just need to speak with you, please.'

Harry stepped into the bungalow, Matt on his heels.

They found themselves in a kitchen. It was a small space, the cabinets a couple of decades old, Harry guessed. There was a smell to the room, and it wasn't just coming from the pile of filthy crockery in the sink, or the pans of mould on the electric cooker.

'I'm thinking we don't open the fridge,' said Matt. 'Because whatever's in there is probably so out of date it could be classed as a biological weapon. Or alive. Or both. Either way, I've no urge to find out.'

Harry reached for a light switch, flicked it. Nothing happened.

'Electricity is off,' he said. 'So I'm with you on staying well away from the fridge.'

'Where is he, then?' Matt asked. 'If that's his pick-up we've found over at Agglethorpe, and this is his address, then why isn't he here?'

'He's clearly not been here in months, either,' Harry said. 'You can feel it in the air. It's damp, the whole place smells rotten and fusty.'

'Which means I'm even more confused about the pick-up.'

Harry pushed on from the kitchen through to a small hallway. Doors led off to a couple of bedrooms and a bathroom. The walls of the first bedroom were black with damp mould, the bed covered in a scrunched-up duvet. Clothes were scattered on the floor; a single trainer was lying on its side. He spotted something on the bedside cabinet.

'We'll need that tested,' he said, jabbing a finger at a

mirror on top of which was a razorblade and a rolled-up banknote held in place by a thin elastic band.

'Amphetamine?'

'Could be,' Harry said and left the bedroom. 'Cocaine seems a bit too rock and roll for a place like this.'

The next bedroom was much the same. A mattress on the floor, scattered clothes. So, at least two people had been staying here, Harry thought.

The bathroom was yet another room dedicated to mould and Harry could see that there was nothing worth looking at in there, not unless he wanted to go rummaging around in the overflowing clothes basket by the sink. And he was absolutely certain he didn't want to do that.

'Wherever Mr Wray is, he's clearly not here, that's for sure,' Harry said, making his way to the end of the hall. 'Best we check out the lounge though before we call it in.'

With Matt behind him, Harry pushed open the lounge door and stepped through.

CHAPTER TWENTY-SEVEN

JIM WAS STARING AT WHAT COULD ONLY BE DESCRIBED AS the largest pile of dog shit he had ever seen. Someone had gone to an awful lot of trouble to collect it all, then dump it on the bonnet of Chris Black's car. He was grateful for the rain; in the sun, the stink of the stuff would have been stomach-churning. The way it looked, though, wasn't much of an improvement, the rain serving to turn the stuff into more of a slurry, gradually spreading out across the car's metallic paintwork.

'I was going to clean it off,' Mr Black said, 'but then I thought no, because I needed you to see it. And there it is. There's something in it, too, poking out, but I didn't want to touch any of it. So, are you going to arrest her?'

'Who?'

'Agnes Hodgson, that's who!' Mr Black seemed oblivious to the rain, his voice loud and harsh and hot with anger. 'She did this, I know she did.'

'Do you have any proof of that?' Jim asked.

'Proof? I don't need any bloody proof!'

'Actually, you do,' Jim said. 'I can't just arrest someone because someone else thinks that I should. And anyway, I'm a PCSO, so I can't.'

'Can't what?'

'Arrest someone,' Jim said. 'That's not what my role is. I support the police and the community, sort of work like a liaison between them.'

'And you can't arrest someone? Like, not at all? Not even a little bit?'

'No,' said Jim. 'And you can't really arrest someone a little bit. Either you arrest them or you don't. And I can't.'

'Then what bloody use are you?' Mr Black roared. 'No wonder things are going to hell in a handcart if we've now got police who can't even make a sodding arrest!'

The section of the pile of dog muck with something poking out of it broke away from the rest, slumped slowly down, then started to make its way across the bonnet.

'Nice car by the way,' Jim said. 'Jaguar, isn't it?'

Mr Black wasn't listening. He was pacing, swearing at the sky. When he'd finished, he came over to stand in front of Jim. He was a big man, Jim noticed, imposing.

'Are you going to arrest Agnes Hodgson or not? And I don't care whether you can or not, because you're going to, simple as that.'

'I think you need to calm down a little, Mr Black,' Jim said. 'If we can go inside and talk through your reasons, then perhaps I can then go and have a chat with Mrs Hodgson, see if I can find out where she was at the time this happened.'

'Any alibi she has will be a lie,' Mr Black said. 'She hates my dogs, just because they go for a wander now and again. She reckons they bother her goats, but they wouldn't hurt a fly, I promise you. And there are plenty of dog walkers around, aren't there? So, any mess she finds in her fields, it's probably from them, not my dogs.'

'Has she threatened to do something like this before?' Jim asked. 'I know that she spoke with DCI Grimm on Sunday about it.'

'Oh, did she, now?' Mr Black said. 'See what I mean? She wants you to think I'm at fault.'

'No, I think she wants your dogs to stop using her fields as a toilet,' Jim said.

'What did you say?'

'That wasn't an accusation,' Jim said, stepping back, though he had clearly meant it as one. Mr Black and his demanding attitude were getting under his skin. 'I was simply stating the reason behind her visit.'

'So, she gets to see a detective and I get a plastic police-man, is that it?'

Jim took a slow, deep breath in through his nose and let it out again just as slowly. He'd been called that before. He was good at his job, dedicated. That someone would have the audacity to say what Mr Black had just said was enough to make his blood boil.

'Mr Black,' Jim said, working hard to keep his voice calm, 'if you want me to do what I can to help, then I need to ask you to calm down.'

'I am calm,' Mr Black said.

Jim was about to suggest once again that they head inside to talk, when a flash of yellow plastic and brass in the section of dog waste that had broken away from the rest caught his attention.

Jim turned from Mr Black and walked over to the car for a closer look.

'What are you doing?' Mr Black asked. 'I was talking to you.'

Jim wasn't listening. Instead, and to his amazement, he was now staring intently at the dog shit and the objects stuck inside it that had been revealed by the rain.

Mr Black came over to stand at Jim's side.

'What is it? What are you looking at?'

'That,' Jim said and pointed.

'I told you something was there, didn't I?' Mr Black said. 'And you've still not said what you're going to do about any of this.'

'Those are shotgun cartridges,' Jim said.

Mr Black leaned in for a closer look.

'They're what?'

'Shotgun cartridges,' Jim repeated.

'They can't be.'

'Well, they are. So, why would they be there?'

'Don't ask me. You're the police officer. No, sorry, you're not, are you?'

Jim ignored the jibe.

'Do you have a watering can or a hose or something?'

Mr Black pointed over to a wall.

'There,' he said. 'Why?'

Jim walked over and picked up the watering can, a green plastic thing with the rose long gone. He saw a tap sticking out of the wall and quickly filled the can, then headed back to Mr Black and the car.

'What are you doing?'

Jim lifted the can and proceeded to wash away the dog mess.

Mr Black nearly exploded.

'What the hell are you doing? That's evidence! You're destroying evidence! Stop! Right now!'

Jim didn't stop. He kept on pouring until he had managed to wash the three shotgun cartridges free of the excrement. And now that they were, he saw that they were protected from what they had been buried in by what looked like a Ziploc bag, the kind Jen was always using to fill the fridge up with her horribly healthy sandwiches.

From a jacket pocket, he pulled out an evidence bag then scooped up the cartridges and tied the bag off. He held the bag up for a closer look.

'Twenty-bore,' he said.

'I don't own a twenty-bore,' Mr Black said. 'Never have.'

Jim wasn't listening; he was remembering Jadyn's report on the theft over at Hill Farm on Sunday.

Mr Black was staring at the dog mess, then at the bag containing the cartridges.

'Look,' he said, 'I ... I'm sorry about all the shouting. Got a bit carried away, I think.'

'That's okay.'

'I heard about the break-in over at Steve Hill's place, and with everything that's been going on ...'

'News gets around fast anyway,' Jim said.

'It does,' Mr Black said. 'This doesn't really matter, does it? Not in the grand scheme of things. And the car's clean now. Maybe Agnes has a point. About my dogs, I mean.'

Jim was a little confused.

'I'll still go and speak with her,' he said. 'Just to clarify things. And to see about these, too.'

He shook the bag containing the cartridges.

'They're just some rubbish, that's all,' Mr Black said.

'Then why were they in a plastic bag?'

Jim knew then that he needed to speak to Harry. Whatever this was, the pile of excrement, the cartridges, it definitely wasn't normal. Mr Black had calmed down, so that was good. However, a chat with the boss might help. As he pulled out his phone, it buzzed in his hand.

'Jim, I mean, PCSO Met—'

'Jim, it's Jadyn.'

Jim could hear from Jadyn's tone that something was up.

'What's happened?'

'You still dealing with that dog shit thing?'

'I'm just about finished, I think,' Jim said.

'Something's come up.'

'What?'

By the time Jadyn had finished telling him, Jim was already in his Land Rover and heading up to Pen Hill.

CHAPTER TWENTY-EIGHT

HARRY STEPPED INTO A ROOM THICK WITH GLOOM. What little light was able to creep its way inside from around the curtains did little to help, skulking in the corners as though it was ashamed of what it might reveal.

'Here,' Matt said, handing Harry a small metal torch.

Harry switched it on, the beam cutting through darkness built from shadows and dust.

'You hear that?' Matt asked.

'As soon as we entered,' said Harry.

The air was still, but somewhere at the back of it, there was a soft hum. And Harry would bet the house he hadn't yet bought that it wasn't air conditioning.

'Flies,' said Matt. 'Probably more rotting food somewhere, judging by the rest of the house. Lives in a proper sty, doesn't he?'

Harry didn't answer, the beam from Matt's torch now resting on something on the wall.

'I don't think it's rotting food. Look.'

The wall on the opposite side of the room, which

contained a small, long-dead fireplace, was splattered in a violent explosion of black grime. The shattered fingers of it reached around the chimney breast and stretched up onto the ceiling, breaking then into scattered dots, a gore-born system of black stars on a cosmos of faded flowery wallpaper. The grime seemed to pulse as the flies feeding and breeding on it moved around haphazardly, looking for just one more little tasty morsel.

Matt walked over to stand at Harry's side.

'Bloody hell,' he said, his voice quiet, sombre. 'I wasn't expecting this.'

'I've seen the aftermath of plenty of gunshot wounds in my time,' Harry said, 'both in the Paras and in the police, and I'd put money on that being caused by a shotgun.'

'Close range, too,' Matt said, still staring. 'But then shooting anyone in here would be at close range, wouldn't it? Ian, you think?'

'This is his house,' Harry said. 'So, one would assume that, yes. But if so, then where the hell is his body? And why is his vehicle and trailer where we just left it?'

Harry cast the torch beam around the room, just in case he had missed the fact that they were being stared at from the shadows by the rotting fly-struck remains of who they'd come here to see. But he saw no body, just more of the room; a small coffee table, a television, and a sorry-looking sofa, stained and mould-covered, sat dejectedly against the wall.

'Well, whoever all that blood and whatever else it is belongs to, they're not here, that's for sure,' said Matt. 'And you don't walk away from something like that.'

'Which means we've got two options, doesn't it?' said Harry. 'One, is that Ian Wray was killed in this room and his body removed by the killer.'

'Or that he did this to someone else, took the body, and then did a runner.'

'Neither of which line up with his pick-up and trailer being found over in Agglethorpe this morning by Mr Calvert,' said Harry.

'Nothing lines up with that,' said Matt. 'Certainly not this.'

Harry walked out of the room, then led Matt back outside. The air of the garden was welcomingly sweet in the rain and helped to clear away the rotting flesh stink from inside the bungalow. Harry, though, couldn't shake the feeling that he urgently needed to take a shower, the grime of the place burrowing into his skin.

'Right, the garage, then.'

Matt took point and Harry followed. The detective sergeant opened the garage door. On seeing what was on the other side, the only thing Harry felt was more confusion.

'Whatever this week is turning out to be, I want it to stop,' he said. 'I want it to stop and I want to get off.'

The garage was crammed from floor to ceiling with piles of goods so precariously balanced, Harry worried that even a sneeze would send it all into an avalanche. At a glance, he spotted a record deck and various other bits and pieces of home entertainment equipment, clothing, suitcases, fitness equipment, vinyl records, and plenty of boxes full of other bits and bobs which Harry assumed had been liberated from people's homes, cars, and pockets over goodness knew how long.

'There's no way this is all from around here,' he said. 'This is from wider afield. It has to be. You can't be nicking all of this from an area as small and tightly knit as Wensley-dale, and not have us notice.'

'I agree,' Matt said. 'If all of this was being nicked in Wensleydale, it's all anyone would be talking about.'

Harry scratched his head, hoping it would loosen up an idea or two in his mind. It didn't.

'So, that's the burglary Saturday night at Keith Sunter's, the shotgun taken from Hill Farm, the pick-up at Fred Calvert's place, and now this, all in the matter of a few days.'

'And let's not forget the fact that both Keith and Fred's places were broken into on the same night two years ago either,' added Matt.

Harry shook his head and rubbed his eyes.

'The only name I'm coming up with right now is Anthony,' he said. 'But he's not been seen in two years by anyone it seems.'

Matt agreed. 'Maybe he and Ian had an argument that night two years ago, after the break-ins, Anthony shot Ian, and then he disappeared.'

'In the process taking Ian's body with him as a souvenir,' said Harry. 'Can this week get any weirder?'

Matt's phone buzzed, interrupting the conversation. He took the call, saying little, his eyes on Harry the whole time.

'About things not getting any weirder,' he said, when the call was done.

'Who was that? What's happened?'

'That was Jadyn,' Matt said. 'And I'll tell you on the way.'

'Why? Where are we going?'

'Pen Hill,' Matt said. 'Something is afoot ...'

WITH CORDON TAPE stretched out around the bungalow, Harry put a call in to have one of the team come over and secure the site. Liz was available so they waited for her to arrive before heading off. He asked her to bring a spare jacket over for him if she could. There was usually one or two hanging in the office, left by members of the team over the years, old things used as spares.

'And you don't want me to do anything?' Liz asked, standing with Matt and Harry, looking at the bungalow. 'Just act as Scene Guard, right?'

'Actually, yes, I do,' Harry said, thankful to be in a jacket that was some way to being waterproof. 'See if you can find out anything more about Ian Wray, the owner. Knock on a few local doors but keep an eye on the place.'

'Why? You think someone's coming back?'

'I doubt it,' Harry said. 'But no one is to go in there until the SOC team have arrived. They'll be over as soon as they're done at the other crime scene in Agglethorpe.'

'Bennett's going to love you.'

'It's what he's paid for.'

'To love you? I'm not so sure about that, boss.'

Harry smiled at that.

'And it's that bad in there is it?' Liz said.

'I just don't want anything disturbed, that's all,' Harry said. 'There's a story to tell in there and I want to know the start, the middle, and the end.'

'No problem.'

'See if we can pull up any other details on him, financial status, that kind of thing. And I want to know more about the house. The power's off. I'm assuming the water is, too, but there are no signs of the place being repossessed. It's just been empty for a long, long time and I could do with knowing for how long exactly.'

Harry turned to climb into his vehicle then a thought

crossed his mind thanks to movement on the back seat. He called Liz over.

'You mind looking after Smudge? If we're to be walking up Pen Hill to a crime scene, I don't think it's best I take her. She's better here with—'

'Of course I don't mind!' Liz said, and before Harry could say any more the PCSO had Smudge out and was holding her to her chest like a toddler.

Harry shook his head in dismay as Smudge licked Liz's face.

'See you later then,' he said.

Once they were back on the road, Harry listened as Matt told him what Jadyn had shared on the phone.

'A severed foot?'

'That's what the lad said.'

'And someone found it up on Pen Hill.'

'Apparently so.'

'Well, how the hell did that get there, then?'

'I can't imagine someone leaving it up there by accident,' Matt said. 'You'd notice, wouldn't you, if a foot came off? It's not something you'd only realise once you got home wondering why you'd found walking so difficult and fallen over a few times.'

'There is that.'

'Whatever this is, it's deliberate.'

'Not necessarily,' said Harry.

'A foot on Pen Hill got there by accident, you mean? How?'

'There was this car accident when I was down south,' Harry said. 'Middle of the night. Driver was going too fast down a lane, window was open, lost control and flipped the vehicle. His arm was taken off in the process. No one could find the damned thing until a few days later, when what was left of it was found half a mile away outside a fox den.'

'So, this could be something like that?'

'All I'm saying is that we just need to keep an open mind,' said Harry.

'And an eye out for ravenous foxes. Good advice.'

'The best.'

It didn't take long to get to where Jadyn and Jim were parked. Harry recognised it from where they had all gathered some time ago to have a little remembrance service for the previous DCI. Jim's Land Rover was pulled off the road and through a gate in a high drystone wall. Just up from the open gate was a small, white hatchback. Harry pulled through the gate and parked up next to Jim. He switched off the engine, steam coming off the bonnet.

Climbing out, Harry raised his eyes to look at the slopes of Pen Hill. They rose steeply above Wensleydale, an ancient mound of rock and peat and moorland, and Harry was struck by the loneliness of the place. It was beautiful, but stark, as though the hill held secrets, many of them dark. The summit was hidden in cloud. Harry wasn't keen on having to trudge up to the top but knew that's exactly what they would all be doing, and soon.

He glanced up at the sky, rain splattering his face.

'I'm not sure what I'm more baffled by,' he said. 'That we've got a severed foot somewhere out on the hill, or that someone was out running on Pen Hill in weather like this.'

Jim and Jadyn walked over.

'Jen does it all the time,' Jim said. 'Says it's good for hill training.'

'Well, it is a hill, after all,' Harry said. He looked to

Jadyn. 'So, where is this runner, then? And I'm assuming we have a name?'

'Angie Taylor,' Jadyn said. 'She's in her car over there. I'll go and fetch her.'

Jadyn jogged through the gate to the white car and a moment or two later returned with a woman dressed in running leggings, trail shoes, and a waterproof jacket. Her dark hair was cut short, sticking out in damp strands from the rim of her huge bobble hat. Harry guessed she was in her early thirties.

After introducing himself, he said, 'Before we go any further, can I just check how you are? I'm sure you're fine, but finding something like that, well, it's a bit of a shock.'

'I'm okay,' said Angie. 'Honestly, I am. I didn't even think it was real at first. I mean, why would I? You don't expect to see a foot when you're out running, do you?'

'It's certainly not on any eye-spy list that I know of, no,' said Harry.

'It didn't even register at first,' Angie said. 'I was running at a fair pace, you see, trying to keep my heart rate up, heading across the top of the hill to then head down here. I'd just passed the stone shelter at the top and saw something out of the corner of my eye. I kept on running, but then I was like, hey, that was a foot, wasn't it? But it couldn't have been, so I ran on a bit further, thinking maybe it was just a rock I'd seen wrong, or a lost boot, that kind of thing. But then I stopped. I had to know. Morbid curiosity, I suppose.'

'So you went back?'

'I did,' said Angie. 'And there it was. A foot. Well, not just the foot, most of the calf as well. No knee, though. I could see why I thought it was a boot because the foot was still in a trainer. And the leg was covered in trouser leg, well, the bottom bit, anyway.'

Harry frowned.

'You seem surprisingly calm about all this,' he said.

'I've seen a lot worse in my job,' Angie said. 'I'm a nurse, work over in Northallerton. Once you've survived a few nights in A&E, you can survive anything, trust me.'

Harry found himself warming to Angie immediately. She was no-nonsense, down to earth, and easy to deal with. The kind of person he'd want looking after him if he was ever unfortunate enough to end up in Accident and Emergency.

'I took a photo after I called the police,' Angie said. 'A few photos, actually; thought they might be useful. And I didn't want to stay up on the hill waiting, either, not in weather like this. I'm dressed to run in all weathers, not stand around in it. Get too cold up there and hypothermia sets in. Plus, I had some hot chocolate back in the car and I needed warming up.'

Harry took Angie's proffered phone.

'There you are,' she said, flicking through the images. 'It's just lying there, see? Bit weird, isn't it? Didn't look like it had been dumped there by an animal or anything, or even touched by one, if I'm honest, which means it's probably not been there that long. Oh, and it was really cold, too. The foot, I mean.'

Harry stared at Angie.

'You touched it?'

'Needed to make sure it was real. Didn't fancy calling the police because some idiot had left a prop from a fancy dress shop up on the Pen Hill as a joke. So yes, I touched it. Gave it a good prod. It was very cold, didn't look like what had happened had occurred all that recently either.'

'Why do you say that?'

'Well, you know when you have meat in the fridge?' Angie said. 'A joint or something? A nice leg of lamb? That's what this looked like to me.'

'I've not had lamb in ages,' said Matt.

Harry gave the DS a look to stop him from talking about food.

'Anything else you noticed?' Harry asked.

'The wound itself, it looked cut rather than torn,' Angie said. 'Like something had been used to saw it off, rather than it being pulled or wrenched or yanked off.'

Harry handed the phone back to Angie.

'Matt, we need those photos,' he said. 'Angie, we'll need a proper written statement from you. And we'll possibly need you to pop into the office if we have any more questions.'

'That's fine,' Angie said.

'Jadyn?' Harry said. 'I want you to take a statement, contact details, the usual.'

'I already have,' Jadyn said.

'Well then,' said Harry, turning his eyes up the hill. 'Looks like we're all off on a little walk then, doesn't it?'

CHAPTER TWENTY-NINE

REBECCA SOWERBY WAS IN THE HALL AND PULLING ON an expensive pair of walking boots when she heard the front door open behind her, followed by a cough.

'I know what you're going to say,' she said, not bothering to turn around to face her mum, who had just returned from popping out to see what was happening over in Agglethorpe.

'And what's that?'

'Something about how I need to rest, that there's no point helping me if I won't help myself, that kind of thing.'

'I'm not saying a word.'

'Your silence then is clearly turned up to ten. No, make that eleven.'

Rebecca heard her mum laugh.

'There's little point in me heading out to meet with Harry if you're then going to go out yourself, is there?'

Rebecca said nothing. Boots on, she grabbed a jacket and hat from the hooks on the wall. She turned around then to leave the house. Her mum was standing in the way.

'I'm going, Mum.'

Rebecca was grateful for her mum heading out to check up on things for her, but she'd had enough. Not of her mum, not really, but of the situation. She was fit and well and work needed her. More importantly, she needed work.

She'd argue the point with her boss after the fact, rather than now. And there was no way in hell that she was going to let Bennett continue to infect things the way he was. He was an insidious worm. Clammy, too, she thought. And anyway, she was needed, wasn't she? That man, that supposed pathologist, was already busy with one crime scene and now two more had been called in. There was no way she could let him shove his pudgy little hands into that one as well. She definitely owed her friend back at the office a bottle of wine or two for keeping her so up to date.

'I know you are,' Margaret replied. 'And you know what? I think you need to.'

Rebecca stared at her mum, amazed.

'Hear me out,' Margaret continued. 'For a start, I think Harry needs you. His dislike for Bennett is so thick you could chew on it.'

Rebecca laughed.

'And when you get back, maybe we can have a chat.'

Rebecca's laugh died.

'Really, Mum?'

'Yes, really. But not about anything serious, okay? It's just that after speaking with Harry, I've been having a little think in the car on the way back.'

'About what?'

'About how it's lovely to have you here for so long and how I don't want you to leave.' Margaret sucked in a deep breath, exhaled. 'There, I've said it. It's true. But that doesn't mean I don't want you to leave, even though I don't want you to leave, if that makes any sense? God, it doesn't, does it? You should get going. I'll shut up.'

Rebecca looked at her mum and was overcome with such a sense of warmth and love for the woman that she found herself reaching out and hugging her close. Then, with nothing to say, because so much had just been said without words, she grabbed her bag and dashed out into the rain and down to her car.

When she arrived at the location below Pen Hill, she saw Harry, Jim, and Jadyn just walking away from two vehicles parked off the road in a field. She beeped her horn, whipped the car in through the open gate, and skidded to a halt. Then she grabbed a bag from the passenger seat and was out of the car and jogging over to join them.

'I need to have a word with whoever it is at your office who keeps telling you what's going on,' Harry said, staring down at her from beneath rain-soaked eyebrows.

'You're dealing with numerous crime scenes,' Rebecca said. 'The one Bennett's currently at, the bungalow, and now this. Bennett can't really cover all three at once, can he? He can head over to the bungalow once he's done, and I'll help out here.'

'You've already thought this through, then.'

'I have,' Rebecca said.

'And I'm assuming it's not up for discussion.'

'It is not.'

'Good,' Harry said. 'Then let's crack on, shall we?'

The walk up from where they had parked to the location of the severed foot wasn't too arduous. Rebecca had been up here before and knew that plenty of locals used it as a dog walk when the weather was good. Today, though, it was foul and only an idiot would be out with their dog in this, assuming they could even persuade their best friend to leave the warmth of a house. Across fields they trudged, the footpath already a slippery mire. Sheep were huddled up together against walls out of the worst of the rain and the cloud cover was low and thick.

Instead of heading straight up Pen Hill, they skirted round to the left, the direct route looking somewhat treacherous. Bracken and heather slapped at their legs, soaking them quickly.

The top was navigated through channels worn into the peat, stepping between exposed rocks and fluffy green tufts, until the flat surface of the summit welcomed them.

Looking back, Rebecca saw the view of the Dale below only fleetingly, as the clouds swirled around them, pulled and stretched by the wind like toffee.

'Over there, I think,' Harry said.

They arrived at the small stone shelter, a circular structure of stone with no roof and an entrance on one side, just high enough to crouch behind out of the worst of the weather.

'And there it is,' Rebecca said. 'A foot.'

For a moment, no one said a word.

Matt broke the silence.

'On Pen Hill Crags ...'

Rebecca saw Harry glance over at the DS.

'What was that?' he asked.

Matt shrugged.

'Nothing,' he said. 'Just, you know, standing here on Pen Hill, it reminded me.'

'Of what?'

Matt hesitated.

'Out with it,' said Harry.

'The Burning of the Bartle,' said Matt. 'That's the first line, isn't it, on Pen Hill Crags? Though Bartle tore his rags rather than lost his foot.'

'Well, whoever this foot belongs to, their rags, or their trousers anyway, they've certainly been torn,' Rebecca said.

She stared at the limb, cocking her head to one side in bemusement at the scene before her.

She'd attended numerous crime scenes in her career. Some would possibly haunt her for the rest of her life. But this? A random severed foot and calf, dumped on a hill? It was certainly one of the stranger sites she'd been called to.

'Well, as you're here,' Harry said, catching her attention, 'and assuming we're not due any more poetry from DS Dinsdale here, over to you. We'll cordon the area off, do a search, see if we can find anything, though I doubt we will, with the weather like it is.'

'What about photographs?' Jim asked.

Rebecca pulled a digital SLR out of her bag, along with some PPE.

'This should do,' she said.

'You're not going to bother putting all that on, are you?' Matt asked. 'In this? What's the point?'

'Procedure is the point,' Rebecca said. 'I know it'll make next to no difference, but at least we can say we did everything properly.'

Matt gave her a solid nod of acknowledgement.

Kitted up, Rebecca got on with the job. First, she took a good number of photos of the foot, where it was laid, the surrounding area. With that done, it was time for a closer investigation of what they were dealing with.

'So, what have we got?' Harry asked.

Rebecca waited just long enough for the silence to feel

awkward, then said, 'A foot. I'm fairly certain of that at this point.'

'I'm glad you're here to confirm these things for us.'

'Years of training put to good use,' Rebecca said.

There was very little else she could get from what she was looking at. She had no tent to cover the area, and the rain was really causing a problem, the ground slimy and cut through with thin threads of rainwater cutting its merry way downward. So, she took plenty of samples, filling a lot of little Ziploc bags, and then carefully examined the foot.

Turning the limb over in her rubber-gloved hands, Rebecca guessed from the size of the trainer that this was the foot of a male. It was very cold to the touch, colder than she would have expected. A severed limb exposed to the elements would be cold, yes, but there was a chill to this, she thought, and that made little sense. Neither did how it had ended up here. It was as though it had simply fallen from the sky courtesy of some bizarre airplane accident high above. Where the limb had been severed, it looked like a deliberate cut caused by an instrument of some kind. Not a knife or a surgical saw, but something fast and violent enough to chew its way through with ease.

With a final look, she placed the foot in a larger Ziploc bag, took a few more samples from the ground beneath it, then stood up.

'Done?' Harry asked.

'Let's get out of this,' Rebecca said.

Harry called over the rest of the team and they made their way back down to the parked cars.

'I'll need to get this back to the lab to have a proper look at things,' Rebecca said, dropping her bag into the boot of her car. The foot she placed in a large cool box, something she'd had with her for a good while now and had used more times than she cared to remember, and never for sandwiches and a cheeky can or two of gin and tonic. The weather had eased off for a moment, the rain just a few drops spinning around them in the breeze.

'Of course,' Harry said. 'But you've got some thoughts already, right?'

'As have you.'

'I have.'

'And what are they?'

'The trainer the foot was wearing, I think I recognise it,' Harry said. 'Need to confirm it, but it looks like the pair of one I spotted earlier on.'

'At the bungalow you mean?'

'Exactly,' Harry said. 'And there's more than enough going on there to keep Bennett and the rest of the SOC team busy for a good while, I'm sure.'

'Remind me.'

Harry did.

'So, it sounds to me like we have a possible murder scene at the bungalow,' Rebecca said. 'And for whatever reason, this could well be the lower part of the victim's left leg placed up here on Pen Hill.'

'I'm not so sure,' said Harry, his face creasing with unspoken thoughts. 'What Matt and I saw back at the bungalow, the blood on the wall is black.'

'Old, then?'

Harry gave a nod.

'Very much so. The house has clearly been empty for months, possibly longer. But that foot looks fresh, doesn't it? So, it can't be the same person.'

'And yet the trainer,' Rebecca said. 'Two victims, maybe?'

'Sharing a pair of trainers? That would be weird.'

'Whereas finding a severed foot on the summit of one of Wensleydale's most iconic hills is entirely normal.'

'It's a puzzler, that's for sure,' said Harry. 'But with the week we've been having, it's hardly a surprise.'

'Then let's get over to the bungalow,' Rebecca said.

'Bennett will be heading there soon,' Harry pointed out.

Rebecca, though, didn't really care.

'No he won't,' she said. 'He'll still be busy where he is, I'm sure, seeing as he's turned being thorough into an art form. I'll call the office and have a couple of others sent out to meet us there.'

'You sure?'

'Why wouldn't I be?'

'No, you're right,' Harry said. 'And I don't need to ask if you know where we're going either, do I?'

Rebecca smiled.

'I'll see you there.'

CHAPTER THIRTY

HARRY HADN'T BEEN EXACTLY SURPRISED TO SEE Rebecca Sowerby turn up at Pen Hill. After seeing her the day before in the office, and then having spoken to her mum earlier, her arrival had seemed almost inevitable. And he had welcomed it, too. She had enabled them to get everything done up on Pen Hill nice and quickly and had then done a bloody good job over at the bungalow in Leyburn.

Bennett, on the other hand, had been a royal pain in the neck. Unhappy to have had Margaret Shaw turn up at the first crime scene he had been sent to, his already simmering blood had boiled over upon then being informed that two further crime scenes were now being dealt with by a colleague he clearly had hopes of replacing.

Harry was standing outside the bungalow when Bennett turned up, throwing himself out of the SOC team van with such fervour he hit the ground too hard, stumbled, and landed on his knees. He accepted no help to return to his feet, instead springing up with surprising agility to face Harry down.

'This kind of preferential treatment is, well, it's absolutely unprofessional.'

'Hold on,' Harry said, holding up his hands to warn Bennett to calm down and back off. 'She's here of her own accord. Nothing to do with me.'

'This is my crime scene.'

'Oh, it's yours, is it?'

'Yes.'

'I wasn't aware that was how it worked.'

Harry watched Bennett's sallow face contort.

He asked, 'Has it got your name on it, then?'

'What?'

'Your name,' Harry repeated. 'If it's yours, then—'

'You know damn well what I mean.'

'I'm not sure that I do.'

Harry didn't wait for a response and turned away, only to have Bennett grab his arm to swing him back round. Harry barely moved, Bennett's feeble attempt at something physical almost laughable. Instead, he turned back around so slowly that by the time he was facing Bennett again, he'd gone through at least four different scenarios in his mind where the pathologist ended up more than a little worse for wear.

'I'll be reporting this,' Bennett said as Harry glowered down at him, jaws clenched.

'No, you won't,' Harry said. 'You'll do your job and you'll let Rebecca do hers. Is that understood?'

'You can't talk to me like that.'

Harry leaned in close, his voice the whisper of a bear breathing through its teeth.

'I just did.'

Conversation over or not, Harry left Bennett to fume

alone so heatedly that he was sure he'd seen the rain turn to steam as it ricocheted off his waxy skull.

Inside the bungalow, and with a couple of extra pairs of hands having turned up to help, as well as the photographer, Sowerby was getting on with the job in hand. Wearing PPE, Harry joined her.

'So, what do you think?' he asked.

Sowerby and her team had laid down small, raised wooden platforms, forming a network of short pathways through the house.

'You were right about the trainer,' Sowerby said. 'But we'll need to analyse both to see if the foot in the other one belongs to the actual owner of the one we have here.'

'I know where my money is.'

'And mine,' Sowerby said, and led Harry to the centre of what was laughingly attempting to be the lounge. 'We've plenty of photos and samples from throughout the house, but a quick run-through, if you've time.'

'Nothing pressing that I know of,' Harry said. 'Other than this.'

Sowerby pointed at the wall.

'Blood spatter, clearly,' she said. 'Close range, and judging by the quantity and the spread, I'd say a shotgun. The giveaway, though, is that the walls are peppered with shot.'

Harry thought back to the pick-up truck and trailer.

'It must all be connected,' he said. 'The pick-up's clearly been damaged by a similar weapon.'

'Analysis will maybe give us an idea of the gauge used,' Sowerby said. 'The spread of the shot, that kind of thing. If we get a match, you'll be the first to know.'

'Anything else?'

'We've found marks on the floor. Something heavy was dragged from this room, out into the hall, and out of the building.'

'The body.'

'One would assume so, yes, judging by the traces of blood we've found in the carpet,' Sowerby said. 'And it's not like this place is bursting with things worth stealing, is it?'

'The garage is,' said Harry.

'There's no sign of a struggle. My guess is whoever it is, they were taken by surprise. Plus, there's a good chance they were more than a little high.'

'The mirror in the bedroom,' Harry said.

'Being analysed,' Sowerby said. 'We found traces of other substances in here, too, plus most of what's in that fireplace is the stub ends of joints.'

'When do you think this happened?'

'Months ago,' said Sowerby. 'The smell has faded, the blood is dry, and there's evidence that the fly population has been feeding and breeding in here for a good while. That much is clear just from the sheer quantity of dead ones lying all over the place.'

'You're nearly done, then?'

Sowerby nodded.

'We'll head off soon, get everything back so that we can work on it all immediately. There are a few bags of things to go through from the bedrooms, so something might come out of that. I'll get a report back to you as soon as I can.'

'I'd appreciate that,' Harry said.

'Don't think you want to be held up by anything, after what was found up on Pen Hill.'

'Doesn't make much sense right now, does it?'

Sowerby shook her head.

Wandering back outside, Harry walked over to Liz.

'You look tired,' she said.

'It's been one of those weeks,' Harry replied. 'And it's only Tuesday.'

'Weeks sort of roll into each other with this job, sometimes, don't they?' Liz said.

'They do.'

'Anyway, I've found out a little bit more about the owner, Ian Wray.'

A gust of wind slammed its way down the road, bringing with it a burst of rain which crashed into Harry and Liz like a swarm of wasps.

'Let's do this out of the weather,' Harry said, and they both jumped into his vehicle.

Smudge was now back in Harry's vehicle, returned by Liz, and snuggled up on the backseat, slowly drying off and steaming up the inside of the Rav4. He'd taken her for another quick walk when they'd arrived back at the bungalow, mainly to clear his head and sort through his thoughts.

'What have you got, then?' Harry asked.

'The house definitely belongs to someone called Ian Wray,' Liz said. 'It was originally his mother's, and he lived with her.'

'Where is she now?'

'Died a few years ago,' Liz said. 'Cancer. Left him the house, mortgage-free.'

'And how do you know all this?'

'Chatting with the neighbours,' Liz said. 'Smudge is a great way to start a conversation because everyone wants to say hello, even when you knock at their door on a day like this. Anyway, he's not been seen around for a couple of years.'

'And they never reported it?'

'They don't exactly miss him, ' she said. 'Lots of loud music, parties, the place was a bit of an embarrassment by all accounts. Plus, Ian would drive up and down the road at all times of the night, waking people up.'

'Vehicle description?'

'Red, four-wheel-drive pick-up,' Liz said. 'No vehicle manufacturer given.'

'Sounds like the one we have over at Agglethorpe,' Harry said. 'And it'll be no coincidence either that, like Anthony, Ian's not been seen for two years either.'

'I don't think any of the neighbours liked Ian,' Liz said. 'They all just kept away from him. That's why they never looked into where he was, why he'd not been around for so long. His mum was lovely though, apparently, but he seemed to take after his father.'

'How?'

Liz shrugged.

'Not much to tell there. Left when Ian was a toddler. Reputation for being drunk, fighting, that kind of thing.'

'And you're absolutely sure this Ian hasn't been seen for two years?'

'That's what I've been told.'

'What about friends, regular visitors?'

Liz checked her notebook.

'People were seen going in and out of the property at various times,' she said, 'but no one took much notice. I think it was a case of them all just wanting to steer clear. One was more regular than the others, though.'

'Description?'

'Hooded top, jeans,' Liz said.

'Could be Keith's son, Anthony,' Harry said. 'Could be anyone. Anything else?'

'That's it, I'm afraid,' Liz said. 'No, wait, there was something else.' She flipped over a page. 'That was it ... Someone said they heard something like fireworks being set off.'

'When?'

'That was a couple of years ago as well,' Liz said.

'And they remember it?'

'Yes,' Liz said. 'Their dog isn't a fan of loud noises. Bonfire night they always go away so that it won't get too scared. So, when it heard this one, the poor animal ran off. Took them a couple of days to find it again.'

'Why would someone living in a place like this, living the life they were, have fireworks?' Harry asked.

'The neighbour I spoke to said the sound of it reminded them of the bangers they used to have as kids,' Liz said.

'Bangers? Weren't they banned in the nineties?'

'They were, yes,' Liz said. 'Mainly because kids would throw them at each other.'

A thought struck Harry.

'It wasn't bangers,' he said. 'It was a shotgun.'

'Could be,' Liz said.

Harry glanced through the rain running in rivulets of silver down his windscreen at the smudged view of the bungalow. It was giving up its secrets, whether or not it wanted to, all being carried away by Sowerby and her team.

'I think we're done here,' Harry said.

'Looks that way,' Liz said. 'There's a team coming over from Harrogate tomorrow to sort out the garage, itemise everything, and get on with cross-referencing it all to thefts across the area.'

'I could do with a brew,' Harry said.

Liz smiled.

'You're getting more Yorkshire by the day, you know that don't you?'

Harry nodded at the passenger door.

'I'll see you tomorrow,' he said.

Liz climbed out and Matt climbed in.

'Now what?' the DS asked.

'Tea,' Harry said. 'And lots of it.'

'Let's get back to the office, then,' Matt said.

CHAPTER THIRTY-ONE

THE FOLLOWING DAY, ON THE OUTSKIRTS OF HAWES, AND having arrived at work for eight that morning, Ben was busy under the bonnet of an old Land Rover when his phone buzzed in his pocket. Hands greasy, and already sporting a bleeding knuckle from a knock he'd not noticed, he pulled out his phone and opened the message.

Free tonight?

He had been seeing Liz Coates for a good few months now. She was fun, knew who she was and what she was about, and wasn't one for just lazing around and doing nothing with her time. She'd yet to persuade him to think seriously about buying his own motorbike, but he would never say never. Just not yet. Maybe.

He was free tonight, so that was good. Though what they'd be doing on a Wednesday evening, he hadn't the faintest idea. The nearest cinema was over in Richmond, a good forty-five-minute drive at the best of times, not that there was anything on that he wanted to see. An evening at the pub, then, he thought. Which was no bad thing. A quiet pint or three, a natter, and a board game was a hard thing to beat.

Ben replied in the affirmative. Liz's reply popped up a few seconds later: *Good. Need to have a chat.*

Ben's heart didn't so much stop, as do a suicidal leap up and out of his mouth, quickly followed by his lungs.

A chat? What about? Why not just say? Was something wrong? Had something happened?

Ben did his best to calm down. Deep breaths.

He texted back: *Sounds serious.*

A moment or two later, Liz's reply was staring up at him: *It is, but don't worry xxx*

But that was all Ben could do now, all he would do for the rest of the day. His girlfriend wanted a chat, a serious one, so what else was he going to do?

Walking away from the Land Rover, the open bonnet making it look like the old vehicle was both yawning with tiredness and screaming in pain, Ben stood at the large open door. Beyond it, Yorkshire stared back, the brooding weather of the past few days had been replaced with the slimmest of promises for a brighter day.

Ben's mind jumped back to the message from Liz. Perhaps he was reading too much into it? After all, she'd said not to worry, hadn't she? So, he had to calm down, be sensible about this. He proceeded to type and then delete a dozen or so different replies, but in the end, he shoved his phone back into his pocket and went back to work.

The hum of an engine caught his attention and he looked up to see Mike rolling into the parking area in front of the garage that bore his name. Ben gave a wave as Mike climbed out of a pickup and walked over.

'You look worried,' Mike said.

'What? How?'

'Ah, so you are, then,' Mike said. 'What is it?'

'I'm fine,' Ben said. 'Honestly, there's nothing wrong at all.'

'Said every man ever with that look on their face. Out with it. I'm not going to be spending the day working with that screwed up face and no explanation, I'll tell you that for nowt.'

Ben explained.

'Well, I can see how that would have you all worried,' Mike said.

'Really?'

'Of course not, you daft sod!' Mike sighed. 'Now, pull your head out of your arse and get yourself over to the kettle for a brew. Oh, and here you go, something to cheer you up. Not that you should need it, but anyway ...'

Ben looked down to see a paper bag in Mike's hand.

'Got us a couple of iced buns,' Mike explained as Ben peered inside. 'Was going to keep them for elevenses, but they're still warm, so rude not to, I reckon.'

Ben had to agree. So, he did as he was instructed and made them each a brew, then started on the warm iced bun. And he was really enjoying it, too, when this briefest of respites was disturbed by a throaty growl rolling over a high squeal. Looking outside, Ben saw a leather-clad figure roll across the parking area on an expensive-looking motorbike. A Ducati, by the looks of things, he thought, though he had no idea about what model it was. Despite Liz's enthusiasm for all things two-wheeled with an engine, they kind of all just looked the same to Ben. Not that he'd ever said that out loud.

The figure climbed off the bike. Removing their helmet Ben saw that the rider was a man, dark-haired and tall.

Ben walked over.

'Now then,' he said, a phrase he now used more often than he realised, the Dales seeping into his everyday speech, as well as his love life.

'Needs a quick tune-up I think,' the man said, his accent hard to place, but definitely more south than north. 'Sounds like it's missing a bit when I open her up.'

'Not sure we'll be able to look at it today,' Ben said. 'How soon do you need it?'

'Today,' the man said.

'Oh.'

'Is there nothing you can do? I don't mind paying over the odds if that'll help persuade you.'

Ben rubbed his chin thoughtfully.

'Tell you what,' he said. 'I'll plug it in and see what I can find. If it looks like a quick job, then I'll squeeze it in before lunch. How's that sound?'

The man gave a nod.

'Perfect,' he said. 'Meeting up with a few friends, you see. The roads around here are some of the best in the country.'

'Which is why daft buggers like you end up getting scraped off the roads like meat pancakes,' Mike said, walking over. 'But it's a nice-looking bike, mind, I'll give you that.'

'We're all staying over for a few nights,' the man said. 'Just doing a tour of the area and moving on. Bit of a lads' holiday.'

'Sounds like fun,' Ben said, finishing his iced bun.

Mike added, 'Could've picked a better week for it weather-wise, though.'

The man shrugged.

'It's cleared up a little,' he said, unclipping a couple of panniers from the back of his bike. 'And if it rains, it's just more pub time, isn't it? Anyway, I may as well head off and get myself settled in. Is it alright if I give you a call later this morning, then?'

'Shouldn't be a problem,' Ben said.

With the man gone, Ben noticed Mike was standing there staring after him, shaking his head.

'Something up?'

'Bikers and beer,' Mike said. 'It's never a good mix.'

'Doesn't exactly look like trouble though, does he?' said Ben. 'More like an accountant going through a midlife crisis.'

'Those things aren't mutually exclusive.' Then he turned and headed back into the garage.

Ben lifted the bike off its stand, then rolled it into the garage after Mike.

CHAPTER THIRTY-TWO

HAVING HEADED BACK TO THE OFFICE AFTER THE investigation at the bungalow in Leyburn, Harry had made sure everyone headed home in good time so that they could be in fresh and early the following day, including himself. It was going to be a busy one of that he was sure.

Jim had popped in at Harry's apartment later that evening to drop off Dave's rabbits, and they'd gone straight into the fridge. Nothing had been confirmed with Dave, so, until then, that's where they would stay. Then, with whatever hours had been left to him, Harry spent them asleep, waking up to find Smudge curled up at his feet.

Grace had called and said she would come over the following evening, so that was something to look forward to. As for the properties he wanted to view, he'd cancelled the appointments for now. That could wait. Though a small niggle made him wonder if he was just using a busy week as an excuse to avoid approaching such a huge life change.

The new day had emerged from the storms of the days before like a turtle from its shell, the sun only just daring to peek through the clouds. The wind had calmed to a breeze, the air still damp, and the rivers were throwing themselves down the hills, pausing on the way to flood fields with great mirrors of fresh water. Rivulets cut across them, too, turning the vivid greens into the shattered remnants of a giant stained-glass window.

Woken by Ben heading to work, and not being up early enough to wave him off, Harry had stumbled through his morning routine with all the enthusiasm and energy of a zombie. But Smudge had hauled him out and on into whatever waited for him. Ben had then sent him a text to say he would be out that evening with Liz. Things were certainly going well between them, Harry thought.

Arriving at the office, Harry's phone trilled.

'So, you on for tonight, then?'

It was Dave Calvert.

'It'll be just Grace and me,' Harry said. 'Jim sorted the rabbits and they're in the fridge.'

'Grand,' Dave said. 'I'll be round just after six. Bit early, I know, but then we can all crack on with the cooking together, can't we?'

Dave hung up.

Harry walked into the office thinking how moments of normality sometimes jarred strikingly with what he did during his working life. He'd experienced it in the Paras as well as the police. A normal life outside of the job was vital to stay sane. Whether he was that or not, though, was perhaps best not discussed.

The office was buzzing. No sooner had Harry entered than a mug of tea had been thrust into one hand, a bacon butty in the other, and Smudge had disappeared off to dance around with Fly like an idiot.

'Everyone's here,' said Matt, standing in front of Harry. 'I sent Jim out for supplies, which is why you've got that butty. There's cake for later. Cheese, too. I've a feeling we're all going to need a bit of extra today.'

Harry had to agree. He'd slept, yes, but not well. With so much having happened since Saturday, it was hard to know where to begin. His brain just couldn't rest.

'How's about I start things off?' Gordy suggested.

'I'd appreciate that,' Harry said.

'You sit yourself down, then, and we'll get cracking, shall we?'

Harry did exactly that, slumping into a chair between Jim and Liz. Smudge bounded over to flop down underneath, Fly slipping over to lie at her side, reaching a paw out to rest on her head.

Gordy called everyone together.

'Jadyn?'

The constable stood up and walked over to the board.

'Not sure we're going to have enough space,' he said. 'But I'll do my best.'

'I think it best if we just go through everything one event at a time,' Harry said. 'Starting with Saturday night, all the way through to yesterday with the pick-up truck, Pen Hill and the bungalow.'

'You think it's all connected, then?' asked Liz.

'I don't much believe in coincidences,' said Harry. 'There are a few threads running through all of this, but we need to unpick all of it to make sure we only pull on the right ones. Get it wrong and the whole thing will fall apart. There's something else that's been bothering me as well,' he added, but was then interrupted by the office door opening.

Harry looked over to see Rebecca Sowerby walk in.

'Sorry I'm late,' she said, whisking off her jacket and grabbing a seat to drag over to sit with everyone else.

'You can't be late when you're not actually expected,' said Harry. 'You know that don't you? Helps to phone ahead, just in case.'

'I was in a rush.'

Harry noticed that Sowerby's eyes were somewhat darker than when he'd last seen her yesterday afternoon at the bungalow. She was also holding an energy drink.

'I put in a few extra hours so that I could get everything done,' Sowerby said, finishing her can.

There was an urgency in her voice, a hint of over-tiredness and hyperactivity from the caffeine she was drinking.

With the pathologist now settled, Harry gave a nod to Gordy to continue.

'You were about to say something, though,' Gordy said.

Harry thought for a moment then said, 'I was, yes, but let's go through everything first. I'll think on it a bit more.'

'Right then,' said Gordy, 'like Harry suggested a moment ago, let's start at the beginning.'

Harry heard Jadyn mutter to himself, 'Like once upon a time,' as he turned to the board.

Harry smiled, impressed with how the PC seemed to remember even the smallest of things from months ago, this being a conversation during one of the first big whiteboard sessions they'd had with him on the team.

Harry and Gordy quickly ran through everything from the break-in over at Keith Sunter's place.

'The only DNA from that is from or relating to the victim and his son,' Sowerby said.

'And the sheep,' Jim said.

'Yes, but I don't think we can really go for an arrest there,' said Matt. 'I mean, cuffing a sheep isn't something I've ever tried and I'm not about to volunteer to give it a go, either.'

'Nothing else at all, then?' Harry asked.

Sowerby shook her head.

'Just that white rose in the pot,' she said. 'That's still striking me as more than a little odd.'

'I've checked up on that burglary at Mr Sunter's from two years ago,' Jen said. 'We've a list of items taken, photographs, but nothing stands out to connect the two beyond the fact it happened on the same night.'

Harry remembered what he had been going to say earlier but decided to keep it to himself a little longer.

'Keith refused to press charges at the time,' Jen continued. 'It was his son, Anthony, who did it, so I guess that's understandable.'

'Then why call it in?'

'He didn't, the neighbours did. Paul and Clare. Only things taken were some jewellery and money, not much really. Though could've been more, I suppose. Like I said, he didn't press charges, so I doubt he told us everything that Anthony took.'

Jen handed Jadyn a file.

'These are the details of the break-in from two years ago, plus photos of the crime scene.'

'Leave that for now,' Harry told Jadyn as he started pulling photos out to put on the wall next to the ones from what had happened on Saturday night. 'Let's crack on.'

'Which takes us to the shotgun theft,' said Gordy. 'I can confirm Mr Hill's whereabouts at the time of the burglary; Anna remembers him being at Church. She always makes a point of shaking hands with everyone as they leave.'

'Anything more from the SOC team?' Harry asked, but Jim spoke before Rebecca could answer.

'I'm not sure if it's connected or not,' he said, 'but when I went out to see Mr Black, I found three shotgun cartridges.'

'But I thought you were there because someone had dumped a load of dog shit on his car?' Harry said.

'I was. But while I was there, I found something in the ... well, you know.'

Harry wasn't sure he was hearing correctly.

'You found three shotgun cartridges in the dog shit on Mr Black's car?'

'I did,' Jim nodded. 'In a plastic bag, too. Washed it all off, and I meant to get them over to the SOC team, but with everything that was going on, I—'

'You forgot,' said Harry, his voice a low rumble.

'I did, I'm sorry,' Jim said. 'I'll go get them now. They're twenty-bore ones as well, which is what reminded me.'

'That's the same as Steve Hill's stolen shotgun,' said Jadyn.

'That's what I mean,' said Jim.

'How was Mr Black?' Harry asked.

'Angry,' Jim replied. 'But then, who wouldn't be if someone did that to their car? He was all for arresting Mrs Hodgson, convinced it was her. But he calmed down after he saw the cartridges.'

'Any reason?'

'Maybe the cartridges made him change his mind? Probably gave him a moment to realise he couldn't just go around accusing people of vandalising his vehicle.'

'I can understand why he'd think it was her, though,' said Harry thinking back to the chat he'd had with Agnes on Sunday afternoon.

Jim popped out of the office and when he returned with the bag of cartridges, thankfully sealed inside another evidence bag, Sowerby answered Harry's question about what the SOC team had found.

'The shotgun cabinet was chipped out by power tools, then ripped from the wall,' she explained. 'Most likely by using a kinetic tow rope, as we thought. There are tread marks from the drive as well, but it's a farm, so lots of traffic. We've managed to identify a small section not linked to any of the vehicles belonging to Mr Hill. Very clearly a four-by-four and very much not of the same tread as the pick-up found yesterday.'

'But that could be from anyone,' Harry said. 'This is Wensleydale. I reckon there are more four-by-fours here than anywhere else in the country.'

'Well, that moves us nicely into the next item anyway,' said Gordy. 'The pick-up truck found abandoned at Agglethorpe.'

Sowerby stood up with a file and opened it.

'Here are the photos,' she said, handing them to Jadyn, who started sticking them to the wall. 'We've confirmed that both front tyres were blown out by a shotgun. There's obvious damage to them and the wheels, pitting from the shot, chipped paint. We also believe the vehicle was driven on the flat tyres, so that would have taken place after they were shot out. The damage is consistent with that.'

'You think it was driven there, then?' asked Jen.

Sowerby shook her head.

'There's no evidence at the scene to suggest that.'

'But you just said they were driven on.'

'I didn't say when, though,' said Sowerby. 'My guess, is that it was driven away after the tyres were shot out, then brought back to the location just a few hours before it was found Tuesday morning.'

'This damage didn't all happen Monday night, then?' Liz asked.

Sowerby shook her head.

'The vehicle's tyres show evidence of having been parked for a long period of time, months easily. The trailer, though, that was towed there. Material in the tyres shows us that. We also found traces of yeast in both the pick-up and the trailer.'

'Yeast?' Matt said. 'So, we're now looking for a burglar baker? And no, I won't say that again, no matter how nicely you ask.'

Harry held up a hand to stop anyone else from possibly jumping in.

'I'd be willing to bet that this pick-up was involved in the break-in two years ago at Fred Calvert's, and for some reason has been hidden away until now.'

'My thoughts exactly,' Sowerby said.

'I've not finished ...'

Sowerby folded her arms and Harry saw the impatience in her again. He wasn't sure he'd missed it. But it was better than having Bennett here, that was for sure.

'The pick-up and trailer were used for the break-in at Fred's place and driven away that same night, right? Then, a full two years after that, it was dropped off where Fred found it on Monday morning, the trailer supposedly towed over by a different vehicle before being re-attached to the pick-up.'

'We found glass at the scene as well,' Sowerby said. 'It's clearly been lying in the verge a long time. We've matched it to the headlights, smashed by some of pellets from the shotgun that was used on the wheels.'

'What about the blood?' Jadyn asked.

'I'm glad you're sitting down for this,' Sowerby said. 'We've come up with a DNA match.'

'That was quick,' said Matt.

'Only takes about four hours.'

'And?' said Harry.

'It matches DNA found at the break-in at Mr Sunter's last Saturday.'

Harry was very close to needing something for the growing headache slowly tightening its vice-like grip on his brain.

'It's Keith's blood?'

'No,' said Sowerby. 'The DNA matches his son, Anthony.'

'But there was no blood at that break-in,' said Jim.

'Plenty of other stuff, though,' said Sowerby. 'The team took a lot of samples. Bennett is, in all things, very thorough, including being nauseating. We found a match to some hair from a brush in Anthony's bedroom.'

'What you're suggesting then is that Anthony dropped the pick-up and trailer back at Fred Calvert's farm, a full two years after the original robbery,' Harry said. 'Even though he's not been seen since he broke into his dad's place that very same night. And not only that, he randomly returns the stolen goods and is somehow injured in the process, enough to leave a very clear pool of blood at the scene.'

'I'm just presenting what we found,' Sowerby said. 'But I'll admit, it's very confusing.'

'No shit, Sherlock,' said Jadyn, clearly louder than he'd expected to. Harry narrowed his eyes at him.

'Sorry,' Jadyn said. 'Didn't mean for that to be said out loud.'

'Didn't think so,' said Harry. 'But we all agree with the sentiment.'

'Including me,' Sowerby said.

'Anyway, moving on to Pen Hill,' Harry said. 'Which is where, I hope, everything becomes nice and clear.'

'I wouldn't count on it,' said Matt.

'No, neither would I,' Harry conceded. 'But it does take me to what I was going to say earlier.'

Everyone turned their eyes on Harry, who then looked at Matt.

'It was something you said, when we were up on Pen Hill.'

Matt looked confused.

'I don't remember saying anything important.'

'You said something about Pen Hill Crags.'

'Oh, that,' said Matt. 'On Pen Hill Crags he tore his rags, the first line of the Burning of the Bartle poem.'

'That got me thinking,' said Harry. 'This all started on Saturday night, which was the same night as the Burning of the Bartle. Then we have the burglaries from two years ago, which also took place on the same night as the Bartle. And finally, for some reason I haven't fathomed out yet, we find ourselves picking up a dismembered lower leg up on Pen Hill, which is also where the Bartle poem starts.'

The room was silent.

'It's connected,' Harry said. 'It has to be.'

'Doesn't exactly sound like a coincidence, that's for sure,' said Matt.

Sowerby revealed another file and handed more photos to Jadyn.

'I'm afraid that what I'm about to tell you isn't going to help matters,' she said. 'I'll cover Pen Hill and the bungalow in one go. And I warn you, this is where things get really weird.'

'How can any of this get any more weird than it already is?' Harry asked.

'Oh, you'd be surprised,' said Sowerby.

'I hate surprises.'

'Can't say that surprises anyone,' Gordy said.

Sowerby looked down at her notes. 'Firstly, the foot is absolutely not Anthony Sunter's.'

'I didn't realise we suspected that it might be,' said Matt.

'I'm not saying that we did, just that it's not. But more on that in a moment. We also found various items in the building, which we can link to Anthony Sunter, confirming he was staying in one of the bedrooms at various times.'

'What items?' asked Harry.

'Wallet with a bank card for a start,' she said. 'Plus various DNA samples. I'd probably describe the site as ripe if you know what I mean.'

'That's a pretty accurate description,' said Matt. 'The stink in that place made my eyes water.'

'So, whose foot is it, then?' Harry asked.

'From the rest of the DNA samples we collected from the bungalow, including the solitary trainer found in one of the bedrooms, the pick-up truck and so on, we believe that the most likely owner of the foot is Ian Wray.'

'Who we have footage of over at Hill Farm,' said Jadyn.

'No, I don't think that you do,' Sowerby said.

For a moment, the only sound in the office was that of Fly, who let out a long, satisfied and very asleep huff of contentment.

'Explain,' Harry said. 'And quickly, before my brain starts to short circuit.'

'The foot on Pen Hill shows clear signs of having been frozen for a long period of time.'

Harry held up a hand to stop Sowerby right there.

'Frozen? How?'

'We have frost damage in the cells and various other pointers I don't need to go into. But anyway, yes, the foot, the body it was originally attached to, was frozen. As to how, I'm guessing something very large like a chest freezer.'

Harry rubbed his temples and sighed.

'What you're suggesting, then, is that whoever removed Ian's body from the bungalow, most likely his killer, then took him somewhere and stuffed him into a freezer.'

'Yes.'

'How was it removed?' Liz asked. 'The foot, I mean.'

'Not by a knife or a sharp saw,' said Sowerby. 'Judging by the damage to the flesh, the way it had been chewed almost, our conclusion is that it was cut from the body—'

'With a chainsaw,' Harry said. 'Correct?'

Sowerby nodded.

'It was done while the body was still frozen.'

'A lot easier than using a knife or a hand saw,' Jim said.

'I don't know,' Matt said. 'Butcher's saws will cut through anything.'

'But most people don't have a butcher's saw at home, do they?' said Jen.

'It's probably the chainsaw from Fred Calvert's,' Harry said. 'Obviously we can't confirm that until we find the chainsaw, but this backs up what I said earlier about not believing in coincidences.'

'All I'm saying,' said Sowerby, 'is that it looks likely that a chainsaw was used to remove the foot from the rest of the leg.'

Harry leaned forward, resting his elbows on his knees, his hands clenched together.

'We're missing something here,' he said. 'I know it.'

'What though?' Matt asked.

Harry stood up, walked over to the board. Jadyn had once again done a good job of getting down the details.

'Like I said, everything here is linked,' Harry said. 'Someone is responsible for all of this; from breaking into Keith's place and ripping out the shotgun cabinet at Hill Farm, to that foot turning up on Pen Hill. It all started two years ago, the night Keith and Fred were broken into, the last night Keith saw his son. And we need to figure out not just the who, but the why, because I'm thinking the why will actually lead us to the who.'

Harry noticed then that Matt was staring at him.

'You already have someone in mind, don't you?'

'I have,' said Harry. 'The mysterious, and so far invisible, Anthony Sunter.'

CHAPTER THIRTY-THREE

HARRY WANTED TO CONTINUE THE DISCUSSION, BUT only after a tea break to give everyone a chance to think on what they'd discussed and to look through Jadyn's notes and the photos. However, as he stood up to get the kettle on, there was a knock at the office door.

Jadyn answered it.

'It's you!'

At the door was Fred Calvert.

'I've never seen you before in my life,' Fred said.

'No, I mean, it's you you, not me you,' Jadyn said, and looked from Fred to the very unhappy young man standing at his side. Fred had the young man's arm clamped very firmly in one of his large, strong and scarred hands. 'I thought you were returned to your regiment?'

'Where's that Grimm fellow?' Fred asked, then he spotted Harry. 'Right, there you are. I've someone here I think you should speak to.'

Harry walked over, Gordy with him.

'Well, fancy seeing you again,' Harry said, looking at the young man. 'Hiding in another caravan, were you?'

'Hello, Liam,' Gordy said, then quickly explained who he was.

'But I arranged for someone to come and pick you up and take you back to Catterick,' said Gordy. 'How did you end up back in Wensleydale?'

'Never left, did I?' Liam said. 'Asked to stop for a piss and did a runner.'

'Nearly ran this daft bugger over, I did,' said Fred. 'Sprang over a wall like a spooked deer.'

'You did run over me!'

'I bloody well did not!' said Fred.

'You hit me with the front of your car.'

'You jumped over a wall, I stopped just in time, and you ended up on the bonnet,' said Fred. 'Entirely different if you ask me. Bloody lucky you're not dead.'

Harry held up a hand to calm things down a little.

'What I'm not understanding is why you bought him here, Fred,' he said. 'Liam here's an idiot to do what he did, true, but I'm not sure there's much we can do other than ask him to not go around pretending to be a wild animal jumping out in front of cars.'

'It's what he told me,' Fred said. 'That's why I brought him here. Said he saw someone doing something.'

'They saw me,' said Liam, and Harry saw a flicker of concern in the young soldier's eyes. 'And I saw them, what they were doing, I mean. So I legged it.'

'Who did you see?' Harry asked.

'How the hell should I know?'

'What were they doing?'

The concern in Liam's eyes turned to fear.

'You'd better tell me,' Harry said, narrowing his eyes. 'I don't take too well to being kept in the dark.'

Fred shook Liam's arm.

'Come on, lad,' he said. 'Out with it. You were quick enough to blurt it all out with me, now, weren't you?'

Harry could see that Liam wasn't just on edge, he was knackered, his hair was a mess. He looked like he'd spent the night dossing down in a barn somewhere and there was a smell of sheep and hay on him.

'You look chin-strapped,' he said. 'And I bet you're starving, right?'

Liam narrowed his eyes at Harry.

'Chin-strapped?'

'Ex-Para,' Harry said, pleased that Liam had clocked the army slang for being knackered. 'So, here's what I propose. You tell us what Fred here seems so keen for you to share, and I'll have someone nip out for a pasty. How's that sound?'

'You're taking the piss.'

Harry just glowered at the young soldier.

'Am I, now?'

Liam shrunk a little under Harry's glare.

'Alright,' he said. 'A pasty. Warm, though, yeah? And a coffee. Three sugars, lots of milk.'

Jadyn gave Harry a nod and left the office.

'Over here,' Harry said and guided Liam over to a chair against the wall.

'I'll leave him with you, then,' said Fred. 'And let me know if and when you find my missing chainsaw, won't you?'

Harry didn't want to say that if they did, there was a very good chance he probably wouldn't want it back. He sat down opposite Liam.

'Before you say anything,' Harry explained, 'I'm going to

tell you right now that someone will be taking you back to your regiment today. Is that understood?'

Liam went to say something, but a look from Harry was enough to shut him down.

'Whatever the problem is, running away is only going to make it worse. You know that as well as I do. However, what I'm not saying, is that we're taking you back and leaving you there.'

Liam, Harry noticed, visibly relaxed.

'You'll be taken back, we'll meet with the commanding officer, provide a statement to explain your absence, then get you home, wherever that is. Do you have family who can pick you up?'

Liam nodded.

'Good. After that, there are procedures to follow, as you well know, to deal with whatever it is that's had you buggering off and ending up over here with us. Now, how about you tell me what caused Fred to nearly run you over, then bring you here?'

'You won't believe me,' Liam said.

'I'll be the judge of that.'

Liam hesitated, but only for a second.

'I saw someone,' he said. 'I'd found myself a barn to kip in for the night, right? Just to get out of the wind, and I didn't want a soaking if it started raining again. Built myself a little bed out of some hay bales. Pretty warm, actually.'

'All very interesting, but how about we get to the point?' Harry suggested.

'I am,' said Liam. 'I woke early, but just kept in the warm. Not like I had anywhere to go, if you know what I mean. Lying low. And I heard something outside, someone cough. I thought it was the farmer coming in, so I thought I'd best shift it before I was found. So, I nipped out of this window, and I was just heading off when I saw what they were doing.'

'And what was that, then?'

'They were laying it down on the ground,' Liam said. 'At first, I thought it was a log or something, but then I saw what it actually was, and ...'

'That's when you ran?'

Liam nodded.

'If it wasn't a log, then what was it?' Harry asked.

'A leg,' Liam said. 'He just put it there in the field.'

Harry almost did a double-take.

'A leg?'

'That's what I said, isn't it? I saw it with my own eyes. Blue material covering it, maybe the leg from a pair of jeans or something. No shoe or trainer though. But it was wearing a sock of something I think.'

'You're absolutely sure?'

'Why would I make something like that up?'

It was a fair point, Harry thought.

'Anyway, whoever it was, they were really particular about how it was laid out on the ground,' Liam said. 'They were using binos.'

'Binoculars?' said Harry. 'Why?'

'It looked like they were lining the leg up with something in the distance. Both ways, too, if you know what I mean, from the foot end and the top bit, where it had been cut off.'

'Can you describe the person doing this?'

'They were wearing a black jacket,' said Liam. 'Leather, I reckon. They saw me so I fucked off, sharpish. I mean, some bloke in a field with a leg? I'm not hanging around for a chin-wag, am I? Bollocks to that.'

'Which is when you ran into Fred.'

'He's right, I landed on the bonnet of his car,' Liam admitted. 'When I told him what I'd seen, he brought me here. Not much I could do about it.'

'You didn't try and run from him as well?'

'I tried,' said Liam. 'But that old git is proper strong.'

Jadyn came back into the office.

'Here you go, boss,' he said, handing over a brown paper bag, grease spots already showing from its contents, and a large steaming cup.

Harry passed them over to Liam.

'Get these down you,' he said and stood up. 'Warm you up a bit.' He called Gordy over.

'What've we got then?' asked the DI.

'A witness to more crazy, I think,' Harry said. 'Possible sighting of whoever is behind whatever the hell's been going on these past few days.'

'What do you want me to do?'

'Get a written statement from Liam here,' Harry said. 'And make it quick. Then before you take him back to Catterick, he's going to take us on a little journey.'

'The lucky lad.'

'He is, that.'

CHAPTER THIRTY-FOUR

Just over an hour later, Harry was standing in a field staring at a leg. Matt and Sowerby were by his side. Having guided them to where he'd witnessed the leg being left, Gordy was taking Liam back to Catterick.

'Well, that isn't something you see every day,' said Matt. 'Not unless that day is in this week, and it's the second body part you've seen in as many days, and you're beginning to wonder if you're becoming just a bit desensitised to things.'

While Gordy had taken Liam's statement in the interview room to allow Harry to talk to the team, he'd sent everyone off on what he wanted them to do. With his suspicions currently sitting on Anthony Sunter, albeit precariously, Jen was heading over to Keith's house for another chat. If his son was responsible for what was going on, then perhaps Keith had more information to offer, even if he didn't realise it.

With Jim having revealed the discovery of the shotgun cartridges, Jadyn was tasked with speaking to Mr Steve Hill over at Hill Farm. Harry wanted him to check on Hill's whereabouts around the time of the dog-faeces incident, to ascertain if he had anything to do with what had happened to Mr Black's car. He would also swing by Agnes Hodgson's place as well to do the same.

Liz was over to Leyburn. She would do a fair bit of door-knocking, to see if anyone had seen who they thought was Ian around the place, because if so, then there was a chance that it was actually Anthony in Ian's jacket. Maybe. It wasn't much, Harry had thought, but then they had to work every possible line of enquiry, no matter how thin and fragile.

And Jim was back in the office as a central point of contact, to collate all the information gathered so far, to deal with any of the usual day-to-day enquiries and reports that came in, and to look after Fly and Smudge.

'The team will be here as soon as they can,' Sowerby said, who was now crouching down to examine the leg. They were all in PPE, but she was the only one who was getting in close enough to give the limb a good sniff.

'What do you think, then?' Harry asked.

'I think it's definitely a leg,' Sowerby said. 'I can't confirm that it's from the same body as the foot we found yesterday until I get it back, but the material of the trouser leg it's still wearing looks the same, and the sock could be from the same pair as we found on the foot. And I'm seeing the same kind of damage as the foot suffered, from the way it was cut off.' She rested the back of her hand on the leg then and looked up at Harry and Matt. 'It's cold, too.'

'So, this has been in the freezer as well,' said Harry.

'I'm not going to be accepting an offer for dinner from whoever's doing this, that's for sure,' said Matt.

Harry wasn't listening, he was staring into the distance.

'What is it?' Matt asked.

'Something Liam mentioned,' Harry answered. 'Remember how he said he saw whoever left this here with binos—binoculars—looking in both directions? So I'm assuming that means the way each end of the leg is pointing is important. It's the why, though, that's what's bothering me.'

'Well, that end, the gory bit, is looking up towards Pen Hill,' said Matt.

'And that's why it's bothering me,' Harry said. 'That bloody Bartle again.'

'What about the foot, then?'

They both turned to look along the same line of sight.

'Haven't the foggiest,' said Matt. 'I mean, that's just Agglethorpe down there, isn't it? Why would the leg be pointing that way at all?'

'There's a reason behind every bit of this,' said Harry. 'It's thought out, all of it. I'm sure of it.'

'Why, though?'

'My worry is that this is all leading up to something,' Harry said. 'That foot up on Pen Hill wasn't put there to rot and disappear. Someone was meant to find it and find it they did. Not by chance, but because someone knew—our very helpful runner, Angie Taylor—would be there. And this leg only appeared after that had happened, didn't it? Also, this is Wensleydale, and you can't keep a secret here for love nor money. The discovery of a foot on a hill? Well, that's going to spread like wildfire.'

'So this is a sign, then?'

'Yes,' Harry said. 'You wouldn't do any of this unless you wanted people to know. Maybe someone very specific, I don't know. But it's like we've got different parts of a garbled message and we're missing the secret behind the cypher, if you know what I mean.'

Sowerby was back on her feet.

'To be honest, I don't think there's much to see here,' she said. 'We've a leg, that's obvious, but other than that, this is just a field. There's nothing here that jumps out at me as suspicious or useful.'

'Footprints?' Matt said.

'Thick grass like this, you just won't find any, but we'll look just in case. You never know, might find an imprint somewhere in some mud or maybe a bit of sheep shit.'

'Such a glamourous job,' Harry said.

'It's what attracted me to it in the first place,' said Sowerby. 'Anyway, there's not much for you both to do here. I'll wait for my team, we'll do what we do, then I'll head back. I'll send through anything I find as soon as I can. Plus, there's those shotgun cartridges to look at as well.'

Harry led Matt and Sowerby back to where they'd parked up. Leaving Sowerby to wait in her vehicle for her team to show, Harry and Matt climbed into Harry's Rav4.

'Now what?' Matt asked.

'I haven't the faintest idea,' Harry said. 'But I'm thinking we head back to the office and have another look through everything we've got. You never know, something might jump out at us.'

'Well, I, for one, hope it's not another severed limb,' said Matt.

Harry started the engine and pulled away.

ARRIVING at the Community Centre in Hawes, Matt saw someone that he knew Harry really didn't like. Arguably, the

DCI had quite an extensive list of people he didn't like, and those not on it were a rare breed indeed and included, to his own surprise, everyone on the team in Hawes. Grace and Ben were on there, obviously, and he assumed Harry had a few old friends from his days in the Paras and working down south, not that he ever mentioned them. Somehow, this small group of larger than life, honest, fun, and genuine people, whom Matt himself classed as some of the best friends he'd ever had in his life, had taken Harry to heart, and the same was true of the other way around.

Richard Askew, however, had gone straight to the top of the list of those people Harry didn't like all those months ago when Harry had the misfortune of meeting him. He was a journalist, which was never a good start. He was also someone who clearly spent an awful lot of his life wishing he was some high-flying reporter for one of the nationals, though in reality he was local news through and through and would never amount to anything else. Not that such a minor inconvenience was going to stop him trying, though, Matt thought.

'DCI Grimm,' Askew said, walking up to meet them. 'I have a few questions.'

'I'm sure you do,' said Harry. 'I'm also sure I'm not interested in answering any of them.'

'What can you tell me about reports of a foot being found on Pen Hill yesterday?'

Harry said nothing and kept on walking.

'Is this local justice taking a sick and twisted turn?'

Harry's pace slowed.

Askew spoke again.

'I've heard that people are concerned the local police aren't up to the job and are now taking inspiration from an old tradition called the Burning of the Bartle,' he said. 'Is that true?'

Harry was at the door, his hand already around the handle, heaving it open. Matt was willing him to just keep going.

'Has local policing failed? Are you worried that a wave of violent vigilantism is sweeping through Wensleydale?'

It wasn't at all to Matt's surprise that Harry let go of the door handle and was around and into Askew before he had a chance to put himself between them. Two strides and the DCI wasn't so much in the man's face, as breathing down on him from above, fire in his eyes.

Askew fell back, instinct taking him out of the threat's way.

'These are just questions,' he said. 'The public has—'

'A right to know, yes?' said Harry. 'You bandy that around like a Get Out of Jail Free card.'

'You disagree, then, is that it? You don't think the public should know when the police are failing—'

'We're not.'

'When it's so dangerous out there people are willing to do anything to protect themselves, their homes?'

'Harry,' Matt said, stepping between his boss and Askew, 'you need to remember that Richard here, he's a bit of a special case, isn't he, poor lad? I say special, what I mean is desperate.' He turned to look at the journalist. 'Isn't there a dog show somewhere you should be reporting on? More your level, really, isn't it?'

Matt saw Askew's jaw clench.

'I already have an exclusive with someone who attended a meeting this very week concerning local action. Sounds to me like you've lost the trust of the locals. How does that make you feel? Anything you'd like to say?'

'Oh, there's plenty I'd like to say,' Harry said.

'Now then, boss,' Matt said, stepping just a little bit further in front of Harry, squeezing himself fully in between the two men. 'We've got a lot to do, as Mr Askew here knows. Why don't you just go on into the office and I'll deal with this?'

Harry seemed to swell and Matt wondered if he was about to be trampled as the hunter closed in on his prey. Then Harry turned and pushed his way into the Community Centre.

'Tetchy, that one,' Askew said, stepping back. 'Not going to look good for any of you when I put this out tomorrow.'

Matt turned on his heel to face the reporter, took a few slow, deliberate steps closer, and smiled, close enough to see the veins in the man's bloodshot eyes.

'I've often wondered about you, you know,' he said. 'How you always turn up when things are particularly difficult, where you get your information from, that kind of thing. Other things, too.'

'Like what?'

'Like those eyes of yours,' Matt said, jabbing a pointed finger at Askew's face. He had seen eyes like that before, not just weariness marbling them, but something stronger and illegal, he suspected.

'My eyes? What are you on about?'

'You're a twitchy person,' Matt said. 'There's a nervous energy about you. And is it me, or is that nose of yours a bit red?'

'My nose?'

'Yes, that thing in the middle of your face with nostrils on it like the funnels of the QE2.'

'You can't talk to me like that.'

'I'm thinking I might have to monitor you a little closer in future,' Matt said. 'Just in case.'

'In case of what?'

Matt grinned, but his eyes, for once, were hard and cold. Then he turned back to the Community Centre and left Askew standing alone in the lane.

CHAPTER THIRTY-FIVE

When Jadyn arrived at Hill Farm, he found Steve Hill outside in the yard. He was standing in front of the barn he was having converted and examining a large sheet of paper.

'Mr Hill,' Jadyn said, walking over, his notebook at the ready.

The man turned at the sound of Jadyn's voice and the first thing Jadyn noticed was the black eye the man was sporting. It was an absolute corker, too, he thought, the eye itself nearly completely closed.

'What are you doing here?' Hill said. 'I don't remember calling your office and asking for a visit.'

'You didn't,' said Jadyn.

'Then you won't mind me asking you politely to bugger off. I'm busy, as you can see.'

Jadyn ignored him and closed the distance between them.

'That looks sore,' he said.

'What does?'

'Your eye.'

'Really? You don't say. Nowt gets past you, does it? Proper little detective, you are. Found that shotgun of mine yet?'

'Did you walk into something?'

'You could say that, I suppose.'

Now that he was closer to the man, Jadyn could see that in addition to the black eye, Hill had a few cuts and grazes, not just on his face either, but on his hands, too.

'Just need to ask you a few questions,' Jadyn said. 'Would you be able to spare me five minutes?'

'Like I said, I'm busy,' Hill replied. 'As you can see. So no, I can't.'

Jadyn looked at the sheet of paper in the man's hands; plans for the barn.

'There was an incident yesterday,' Jadyn said. 'Over at Mr Black's farm.'

Mr Hill stopped what he was doing and turned his eyes on Jadyn.

'He called you then, did he? That bastard. Some friend he turned out to be.'

'I'm here at the request of DCI Grimm,' Jadyn said.

'He was round here yesterday, you know?'

'Who was?'

'Chris Black,' said Hill. 'Turned up here all full of fire and bollocks.'

That was a new one on him, Jadyn thought.

'Drove in here like an absolute idiot. Nearly crashed that posh Jag of his into my tractor, would you believe it? Then he was over at my door and half trying to smash it in with his fist. Yelling too, like. Roaring his head off.'

'Where were you?'

'Inside the house, trying to clean up a bit more of the mess under the stairs,' Hill said. 'I went out to see him, no idea what the hell he was on about, and he just launches himself at me! Never seen anything like it!'

'Why did he do that, then?'

'Seemed to think I'd been over his place to put some dog shit on his car. I mean, why the hell would I do that? Agnes Hodgson, she's the one who he should've been round having a go at, shouldn't he? But no, he's here, isn't he? And he's all in my face about it, pushing me around, grabbing me. Never been so angry in my life, and that's saying something.'

'Why did he think it was you?'

'Said something about some cartridges. Apparently, there were three twenty-bore ones in the dog shit on his bonnet. And as I'm the only person he knows with a twenty-bore, he turns up here to have it out with me like that was all the proof he needed. Madness!'

'What did you say?'

'Not enough and too much, I reckon,' said Hill, and pointed at his swollen eye. 'See this? He did it. Whack! Fair knocked me off my feet. But I gave as good as I got, I'll tell you that for nowt. Sent him on his way with my boot planted firmly up his righteous arse. Lobbed a brick at his car as well when he drove off. Nice dint it made in the boot. Serve him right, too, I reckon. And no, I won't be paying for the damage. He can sod right off with that.'

'How did he know about your shotgun?' Jadyn asked.

'How do you mean?'

'You said you're the only person he knows with a twenty-bore,' Jadyn clarified.

'We've shot together,' said Hill. 'Both have farms, don't we? You can't beat an early morning walk with a gun shared with a friend. He's done a few charity clay shoots at his place, too. I'd usually leave my gun there in his cabinet for those, seeing as they could get a bit wild after, if you know what I mean. Lots of port, you see. Lovely stuff. Though I'll not be going back there again, charity or not.' Hill jabbed a finger at his eye. 'Not after this!'

Jadyn glanced down at his notes.

'So, it wasn't you, then?' he said. 'The dog excrement, I mean.'

'Bloody hell, lad, have you not heard a word I've just said? Anyway, I was away that night, wasn't I? No fit state to be heading off anywhere to shovel some dog shit onto that idiot's car.'

'Away?'

'Yes, away,' Hill said. 'You know, as in not here. Despite what people think, us farmers do get away once in a while. Not for long, but it happens.'

'Where did you go?'

'You're nosy, you know that?'

'All part of the job,' Jadyn said.

'I was at the theatre. And before you laugh, there's nowt wrong with a good show. I'm in the amateur dramatics society over in Leyburn, if you must know. A few of us went over to the Hippodrome in Darlington. Treated myself to a hotel room for the night as well, so I could have a few drinks and a good feed. It was worth it just for the breakfast.'

'Sounds fun,' Jadyn said.

'Well, I wouldn't be doing it otherwise, would I? Anyway, I need to get on. I've got Keith coming over later to look things over.'

'Keith Sunter?'

'His son may be about as much use as a glass hammer,

but Keith's a good man. He's done the design for this place. Top job, too, if you ask me.'

Jadyn closed his notebook.

'Thanks for your time, Mr Hill.'

'Is that it, then?'

'Yes.'

'So, you've not found my shotgun yet, then?'

'No.'

'Unbelievable.'

And with that, Jadyn headed back to his car.

BACK AT THE OFFICE, Harry and Matt were with Jim. The afternoon was getting on and Harry was actually rather looking forward to the evening ahead. Rabbit stew, some beer, and the company of Dave Calvert and Grace would serve as a great antidote to the past few days, he was sure. What didn't, was how so many people in the Dales shared surnames. There were the Dinsdales and the Metcalfs—with and without an 'e'—for a start. There were the Blades, the Calverts, the Cocketts. He'd never known anything like it. He doubted Dave was in any way related to Fred, but there was probably a very distant family link somewhere.

Harry and Matt were going over the boards and the photographs. Jadyn had called to say he was on his way and had given a quick summary of his chat with Steve Hill. Harry was now thinking that whoever had taken the man's shotgun was probably the one who had dumped the dog waste on Chris Black's car along with the cartridges. As wind-ups went, it was a little extreme. And whoever had done it was certainly playing a dangerous game. Was all of this to do with the conversations he'd overheard back on Saturday night at the Burning of the Bartle? Was Anthony the one behind everything that had happened since?

'If it's Anthony, then my only thought right now is that something bad happened between him and Ian Wray,' Matt said.

'Pretty bad for him to freeze the body then chop it up a full two years after killing him,' said Harry.

'You'd be surprised what people will do.'

'No, I wouldn't,' Harry said. 'Not in the slightest. Anything from Liz or Jen?'

Matt shook his head.

'Liz will be out for the rest of the day, no doubt,' he said. 'Once Jen's had a chat with Keith, she's going to pop over to see Angie, the lass who found the foot, just to make sure she's okay.'

'Good idea,' Harry said. 'Gordy won't be around till tomorrow now, busy with sorting out that squaddie lad, Liam.'

'Did you ever go AWOL?' Matt asked.

'From the Paras?' Harry asked. 'You're kidding, right?'

Matt shrugged. 'Just asking.'

'No, I didn't,' said Harry. 'I loved it.'

'What about that milling you have to do, or whatever it's called? That sounds bloody awful.'

'Not really,' said Harry with a shrug, casting his mind back. 'You're thrown in a ring with a pair of boxing gloves on to go head-to-head with someone your own size for a full minute.'

'Like I said, sounds bloody awful.'

'We were being trained to fight,' said Harry. 'Front-line troops. If you can't handle a minute in a brawl, how are you going to cope when the bullets are flying?'

'Fair point. Dave round tonight, then?'

'He is,' said Harry with a smile. 'Should be a bit of fun. Think I need it with all this.' Harry stared again at the board, the photos, and thought over what they'd seen and heard and learned. 'Why the leg?' he said, then. 'What's the point of it?'

'Why any of it, I reckon,' Matt said.

Harry's phone buzzed.

'Harry, it's Rebecca, I mean Sowerby ...'

'Everything okay?'

'No,' she said. 'It isn't. Not at all.'

Harry's blood dropped a few degrees.

'Why? What's wrong?'

'The team, we did a wider search of the area, around the leg. And we found something.'

A stone dropped into Harry's stomach and a cold hand reached out and squeezed his heart tight enough for him to almost gasp.

'What did you find?'

'The rest of the body.'

CHAPTER THIRTY-SIX

'JUST WHEN YOU THOUGHT YOU'D SEEN IT ALL ... THIS,' Harry said. He rubbed his eyes, a desperate and futile act to try and erase the images now in his mind. But what he was now staring at—there was no way it would ever be unseen.

'Yeah, it's something special, isn't it?' said Sowerby. 'Sorry I had to call you out, but I couldn't keep it to myself. It needed sharing.'

'You know, I'm not so sure that it did,' Matt said.

With Jim left back at the office with the dogs, Harry and Matt had sped back down the Dale and towards the fields where Liam had led them earlier that day. Only now, they were a few fields closer to Agglethorpe.

'I had the team widen the search of the area, just to be thorough, I suppose,' Sowerby explained. 'We weren't expecting to find anything. And even if we had been, we certainly wouldn't have been expecting this.'

Harry shoved his hands deeper into his pockets.

'I know what I'm looking at,' he said. 'But even so, how

about you give us a rundown of what we have here? I wouldn't want to miss anything.'

'For a start, this piece is the rest of the leg,' Sowerby said, pointing at what was lying in front of them. 'From the foot found at the summit of Pen Hill.'

'You're sure?'

'I wouldn't say it if I wasn't.'

There it was again, Harry noticed, that edge. Sowerby was getting into her stride again.

'No, fair enough.'

Sowerby pointed across the field and on into the fields beyond.

'In the next field, we have a left arm and a right arm. In the field after that, we found the torso. Then, in the next field, about one kilometre away from where that leg was earlier today, which is in this field behind us, we have the head. That's also suffered a little trauma.'

'Why do I think you're understating things there a little?' Harry asked.

'It shows massive damage from a shotgun blast,' Sowerby said. 'The face is mostly intact, enough to get a positive ID, anyway, but the top is missing, from about the bridge of the nose up.'

'The blood spatter in the bungalow,' Harry said.

Sowerby gave a nod.

As yet, Harry and Matt hadn't paraded through all of the fields to examine the other pieces. He was in no real hurry to, either.

'And they were all frozen?' Harry asked.

'Every single piece,' said Sowerby. 'Not by the time we found them, but at the time of being cut away from the rest of the body, yes, definitely.'

'And they were like this when you found them?' Harry asked. 'All in a line, I mean.'

Sowerby nodded.

'Never seen anything like it.'

'I doubt anyone has,' said Harry.

'And we think these were all put out here today,' Sowerby said. 'By which I mean, while we were looking at the first piece, someone came out here and laid these all out.'

'Like a blood trail,' Harry said. 'But leading to what? I mean, what the hell is going on? And just who the hell goes driving around with defrosting body parts in their car to lay out in a field?'

'Someone making a point,' said Sowerby. 'And it's definitely Ian Wray, by the way. Should've said that earlier. We've his whole body, which is a big help, but as I said, we have his head. And despite the damage to it, we were able to check it against a driving licence found at the bungalow. It's definitely him.'

'This is more than someone making a point though, isn't it?' said Harry. 'This is someone making something very damned clear to someone else. You don't do any of this unless there's a very clear reason behind it.'

'Why do you think that?' Matt asked.

'Because of the time and effort that's gone into this,' Harry answered. 'Think about what we know, right? Ian Wray was killed in the bungalow at a date and time we don't know yet. Months ago, though, we can assume. His body was taken from the scene and frozen. Sometime later, that time being now for whatever reason, his body is cut up and laid out in a line, all the way from the top of Pen Hill to here. Not only that, we've got the pick-up and the trailer, two break-ins

... We've even got those sodding shotgun cartridges in that dog shit on Chris Black's car.'

'We've found some fingerprints on those,' Sowerby said. 'Not much, to be honest, and there's nothing in the system to match them.'

'All that means is that whoever touched them doesn't have a criminal record,' said Matt. 'But they'll be getting one soon enough, that's for sure.'

'There are the marks from the firing pins as well, but we need the weapon that fired them to be able to check for a match.'

'Can't see that turning up any time soon,' Matt said.

Harry turned away from what was in front of them and lay across the fields, a scene better suited to a low budget horror movie than the Yorkshire Dales. He needed a moment. No, he needed a lifetime. This kind of crazy was hard to accept.

'You okay, boss?' Matt asked.

'What time is it?' Harry asked.

'Getting on for the end of the day,' Matt replied.

Right now, what Harry needed were a lot of answers to a lot of questions. Yet, all they were being served were more questions.

Taking a few steps across the field, Harry turned his eyes to the fells. Their far-off silence was something he wished he could put in a bottle to drink from at times like this. That pure peace they seemed to exude might have a chance at stilling his mind, but then again, he doubted it.

Whatever was going on here, he and the team needed to figure it out. The horror of it, the raw spectacle of blood and bone, had the capacity to bleed into the land and stay there for decades. However, sometimes, regardless of how impatient you were to solve something, you just had to accept that even though time was never on your side, time was what you needed.

Harry walked back over to Matt and Sowerby.

'There's nowt much we can do here, is there?' he said, his eyes on the pathologist.

'Honestly? No,' she said. 'This is for me and the team to sort out. We're on it, as you can see. It's late in the day, but we'll get things done. If you stick around, you'll probably just get in the way.'

'Thanks for that,' Harry said, a wry smile curling the corner of his mouth. 'We'll head back, then; get out of your hair.'

'And I promise we'll keep you up to date with anything that we find. It'll be tomorrow though before we have anything useful. Assuming, of course, that we do.'

'Come on, Matt,' Harry said. 'Let's get back to the office before the end of the day. Hopefully tomorrow we'll be closer to where we need to be.'

The journey back up the Dale was quiet. Neither Harry nor Matt had much to say, and Harry suspected that they were both trying to work out how best to park what they'd seen somewhere safe in their minds so that it wouldn't spill over. Not easy.

Jim was still in the office when they returned. Jadyn had joined him. Harry asked how things had gone at Hill Farm and Jadyn told him what had happened.

'A black eye?'

'A proper shiner,' Jadyn said. 'I don't think that's a friend-ship that's going to be rekindled anytime soon.'

'Anything more from Askew?' Harry asked.

'Not seen him again,' Jim said.

'Well, that's something,' Matt said. 'Don't want him hanging around stirring things up. He's like a kid with a stick staring at a wasps' nest.'

Harry wandered over to the board, the photos. A few additional points had been added. Jadyn had put something up about the scrap between Hill and Black. Harry read how the two men shot together sometimes, and that during charity shoots on Chris Black's farm, Steve would leave his shotgun there in Chris' cabinet; his shotgun was a twenty-bore, the same bore as the cartridges found at Black's. Jen had put up a little note about Keith Sunter, saying she'd learned nothing extra, and to confirm he was over at Hill's earlier in the day. As to what Harry and Matt had seen over in the fields, that could wait till tomorrow, he thought.

'You'd best head off,' Matt said. 'Dave'll be around in a while, remember? Can't be keeping a man like that waiting. And by can't, I mean you shouldn't attempt to even try.'

Harry called Smudge over, clipped her onto her lead, then headed out of the office. His walk home through Hawes marketplace was lost to the darkness swirling in his mind. He hoped that tomorrow some light would break through.

CHAPTER THIRTY-SEVEN

Harry stared at the huge stewing pot Dave had brought over, which was now centre stage on the table. Grace caught his eye.

'Smells good, doesn't it?' she said.

'Of course it does,' said Dave. 'I cooked it!'

And he had, the whole damned thing. Harry had been expecting them to all muck in, but Dave was having none of it. With a bagful of ingredients, he'd provided them with drinks, then set to work. And now, a couple of hours later, the feast was ready.

'Well, tuck in, then,' Dave said. 'No point waiting on ceremony. I didn't come all the way over here to cook this and have us watch it go cold.'

Harry reached for the large spoon in the pot and piled steaming food onto his plate. He managed to dip a knuckle into the gravy and licked it clean.

Dave passed over a bowl of the creamiest of mashed potatoes and another of greens.

'Where's the recipe from?' Grace asked.

'In here,' Dave said, tapping the side of his head. 'That's where.'

'You should write a cookbook.'

'Wouldn't be very long,' Dave said. 'And the recipes would be a little bit scant on detail. I don't think, *"throw meat in pot, add veg, pour booze on it"* really counts as a recipe.'

Harry tucked in. The food was just on the cusp of being too hot. The meat was sweet, the veg it was nestled in just right, and the gravy was so full of flavour he wanted to tip his plate up and drink it.

'Really appreciate this,' Harry said.

'Then we should do it more,' Dave replied. 'You're not one for socialising, I know, but it'd do you good.'

'I've said the same,' said Grace. 'He really needs to get out a bit more.'

'Not much of a people person, though, that's the trouble,' Harry said.

He reached for the cider Dave had brought, enjoying the taste of the West Country, a change from beer, and an echo of a place he'd once called home.

'Oh, I know that,' said Dave. 'Neither am I. But those I do like, and there aren't many, I like to make the effort. I wouldn't be here if I hadn't, now, would I?'

Harry knew Dave was right; it was a bit of a habit of his.

'So, Grace was telling me you're looking to buy a house.'

'I'm thinking about it,' Harry said. 'Had some viewings scheduled today but had to move them.'

'Work?'

Harry nodded.

'You've rebooked, though?'

'For the weekend, yes,' Harry said.

'Good. Don't want work being the excuse to not get on

with things. Too easy to let that happen.' He looked to Grace. 'You're not getting a place together, then?'

Grace laughed. 'Can you imagine?'

'Yes, I can, actually,' said Dave.

'Early days,' said Grace. 'I think Harry needs to do this for himself, if you know what I mean. No pressure to please someone else. Get himself sorted first.'

'And what about Ben?'

'He's not said much about it, actually,' said Harry. 'He's out with Liz again tonight.'

'That seems to be going well for them.'

'It is,' Harry agreed. 'His probation will be done soon too. Hard to believe how different life is now, for both of us.'

The sound of a motorbike engine roaring at the moon broke into the moment. Dave turned in his seat to look over towards where it had come from, somewhere beyond the walls of the flat and down in the marketplace.

'Bloody idiots,' he said. 'Need to keep it down.'

'Not a fan of motorbikes, then?'

'Oh, I love motorbikes,' Dave said. 'Have one myself. It's bikers I have a problem with.'

Harry and Grace laughed.

'You can't have it both ways,' said Grace.

'Oh, I think that I can. There's no need to go ruining everyone else's day or evening by throwing on some kind of mad racing exhaust or whatever on your bike, then revving it loud enough to burst eardrums.'

Harry was trying to imagine Dave on a motorbike.

'What have you got, then?' he asked.

'The bike? Nothing special. Just an old Triumph Bonneville. Had it for years.'

'Use it much?'

Dave shook his head.

'It's one of those sunny Sunday afternoon things,' he said. 'Nice to head out for a bit of a pootle around the lanes, but that's about it.'

The end of Dave's sentence was punctuated with more noise from outside, this time a few more motorbikes joining in.

'Who's on duty tonight?' Grace asked.

'Jim,' Harry said. 'Then Jen later on, I think. Though with the days as they've been this week, hours get kind of messed up.'

More revving and then the screeching of tyres.

'He's going to have fun with that lot, then,' Grace said.

'He's a good lad,' said Harry. 'He'll handle it, I'm sure.'

With the stew done, the table cleared, Harry, Grace, and Dave settled down in the lounge with another drink and, not exactly to Harry's surprise, a slab of fruit cake from Cockett's and some Wensleydale cheese.

'I'm stuffed, Dave,' Harry said. 'Not sure I can fit anything else in.'

'Of course you can,' said Dave and passed Harry over a plate of cheese and cake. 'Just something to nibble on. Rude not to.'

Harry took the plate as the night was again ripped in two by the sound of screeching tyres and the howl and pop of an exhaust being blasted by an engine revved to the max. Then came a knock at the door.

Harry leaned forward and placed the plate from Dave, and his drink, on the small coffee table in front of him. Smudge was lying beneath it, fast asleep.

'Won't be long,' he said, stood up, and walked to the door.

Opening it, Harry found himself face-to-face with no one at all. Instead, what he heard was a lot of laughing.

Stepping out from his doorway, Harry saw two men in motorbike leathers walking away from his flat, holding each other up, clearly the worse for wear. They were making their way over towards a group of other bikers, all gathered around their bikes, swigging from pint glasses.

Harry wasn't in the mood. With the investigation they were dealing with, a group of idiots making a nuisance of themselves was something he could do without. And where was Jim?

Harry closed the door behind him, pulled out his phone and called Jim.

'Boss?'

'Where are you?'

'Top of Buttertubs Pass,' Jim said. 'Been a bit of a car accident. No one's hurt, but I'm just sorting it out. Why?'

Harry stared at the group of bikers.

'Don't worry about it,' he said. 'You crack on with that and I'll see you in the morning.'

'Something up?'

'Nothing to worry about.'

Harry hung up and made his way over to the bikers.

'Evening, all,' he said, coming to a stop as the two men he'd followed reached the others.

'Sorry, mate,' one of the bikers said. 'It was just a dare, you know? Knock someone's door for a laugh.'

'You see me laughing?'

Harry wasn't in the mood for being polite, though he knew winding the group up wasn't really going to help matters.

His comment was welcomed with more laughs.

Behind the group, Harry saw a few locals stepping out from the nearest pub. Great, he thought, just what he needed, an audience.

'You're disturbing the peace,' he said. 'My advice would be to head back to wherever you're all staying and avoid waking up tomorrow with sore heads.'

A biker broke away from the rest of the group and walked over. He was a big man, Harry noticed. Not in the hairy, Hells Angels kind of way either, but more chiselled and clean-shaven, his leathers stretched over a body built in a gym. The rest of the group were much the same, their bikes all looking to Harry like high-end racing machines, though that was about as far as his bike knowledge went.

'We're only having a bit of fun,' the biker said, coming to stand in front of Harry. 'No harm meant, mate, no harm meant.'

'And so far, there's been none,' said Harry. 'But racing bikes up and down the town, revving engines, that has to stop. Now.'

The crowd from the pub was growing, Harry noticed. Some of them were putting pint glasses down, readying themselves for taking things a step further. A few of them were shouting, dotting their requests for the bikers to leave with some quite exceptionally colourful language. Harry's thoughts tracked back to the meeting on Monday, over in Askrigg.

The biker sneered.

'Does it now?'

'It does.'

'And we're to take notice of you, why? Because you've a face on you like a crushed bucket?'

The biker laughed, turning to his mates for their

approval. And he got it, all of them cheering him on, clapping hands, spilling pints.

'You're right, I have,' Harry said. 'I'm also a police officer.'

'Bollocks you are,' the biker said, taking a sip from the pint glass he was holding. 'Where's your ID, then?'

Harry heard movement behind him. He turned to see Dave; his head crowned in his flat cap.

'Now then, Harry,' Dave said.

'I can handle this,' Harry said.

'You can indeed,' said Dave. 'You left this, though. Thought it might come in useful.'

Dave handed something to Harry, and he smiled as he lifted it to show the biker.

'Here you go,' he said. 'You can read, I assume?'

The biker leaned in.

'Detective, are you?'

Harry slipped his ID into his pocket.

'Now that we've established who and what I am,' he said, 'my advice is to do as you're told and bugger off. Is that understood?'

For a moment, Harry was almost convinced the biker was going to do exactly that. Then, with no warning given, the man lifted his glass and went to pour it over Harry's head.

Harry, though, was too quick. He side-stepped the beer as it sloshed down onto where he'd been standing. Then, before the biker could react, he grabbed a wrist and with an ease that could only come from a lot of practice and a not inconsiderable amount of strength, pinned the arm behind the man's back, right between his shoulder blades. Harry used his other hand to grip the back of the biker's collar.

The marketplace, Harry noticed, was now silent. Around

him, eyes stared, wide and keen, and more than a little surprised.

'What the hell are you doing?'

'Well, I could arrest you,' Harry said, then turned his voice up a notch and stared at the rest of the bikers in turn. 'I could arrest you, impound every bike here, really screw up your holiday.'

'But we were only having a laugh,' the biker said, his voice squeaking a little with the pain of where Harry was holding his arm.

'You were the only ones laughing,' said Harry. 'Remember? So, what's it going to be? Arrest and a fond farewell to those huge penis extensions you ride around on, or an apology and a quiet walk home to bed to sleep it all off. And may I also suggest you have a long, hard think about what happened tonight? My guess is that when you do, you probably won't feel exactly proud of yourself.'

Harry felt the biker relax in his grip. He let go. The biker turned around, went to speak, but Harry shushed him with a raised finger.

'Not a word,' he said. 'You, and the rest of them, you get off now, like I said. And if you do, your bikes will all be here in the morning. However, just to make sure ...' He glanced back at Dave and pointed at his head. 'Mind if I borrow that for a moment?'

Dave pulled off his hat.

Harry took it, flipped it over, held it out in front of the biker.

'Keys,' he said. 'All of you. Now.'

'Oh, come on, mate,' said the biker whose arm he'd just released.

'I'm not your mate,' Harry said.

The hat soon filled with keys.

A few minutes later, and with the situation now calm, Harry made his way back to his flat, Dave's cap heavy with keys. A voice called out and he turned round to see a few of the crowd from the pub facing him.

'Thanks,' one of them said.

'You don't need to thank me,' Harry said. 'It's my job.'

'We were ready for them, though,' said another. 'We'd have helped.'

'No, you wouldn't have,' said Harry. 'What just happened? That's why you leave things to the police. It was dealt with quietly, efficiently, and no one was hurt.'

'But still ...' said another.

'But still nothing,' Harry said. 'I'm here to serve this community. The whole team is. So let us do our job. Now, bugger off back into the pub the lot of you and finish enjoying the rest of your evening. Because I can tell you right now, if you'd joined in, it's the last thing you'd be doing. Any of you.'

CHAPTER THIRTY-EIGHT

HARRY WOKE THE NEXT DAY WITH A SORE HEAD, NOT from too much drinking, but too much thinking. With the bikers sorted, he'd headed back to the flat and the rest of the evening had been more eating and some good old-fashioned conversation. Dave was a man with stories aplenty, so the three of them had spent a good while trading tales. When Dave finally left, having booked himself in at the Herriot, Harry had fallen into bed and into the welcome embrace of Grace and slumber.

Now, though, he rather fancied just staying asleep, because the night hadn't been as restful as he'd hoped, and he'd spent far too much of it awake and staring into the darkness. It had swirled around in front of his eyes, thick with his frustration at not being able to see through to the heart of it all.

A walk around Hawes with Smudge had helped to clear his head a little. He'd followed the same route as earlier in the week, strolling past the flowerbed he'd seen Keith tending to. Today, though, the bed had been dug over,

Harry noticed. Well, some of it had. A closer look revealed a hole dug into the soil, large enough to lie in. Harry was struck then by how much effort gardening seemed to be and had to admire Keith for his dedication. But he understood why.

Arriving at the office early, Harry was able to have a few moments to himself. Kettle on, he poured a brew and stood once again in front of Jadyn's well-laid-out board. In many ways, it was almost a work of art, Harry thought. It reminded him of the map to the London Underground, a thing of such simple beauty it somehow managed to convey all the information you needed in such a clear and concise way, that it was now iconic. He wasn't for a moment suggesting that Jadyn's work had reached that status, but it was certainly something to appreciate.

Having allowed his eyes to wander across the various details and photographs, Harry was now staring at a map of the other end of the Dale. Jadyn had blown up a section, covering Pen Hill and all the way beyond Leyburn. There were pins picking out various locations, each pin attached to one or more threads, which led to numerous clusters of information. A pin on Pen Hill identified the foot found at the summit. A further pin was pushed in where the rest of the leg had been discovered, and so on, casting a line across the various parts of Ian Wray's torso, which had been found over the past few days.

Harry continued to stare at the board as the team arrived. Something was bothering him about the map, and he was scratching his head over it when Gordy came over to stand beside him.

'Been here all night, have you?' she asked.

'Of course,' said Harry. 'It was either this or rabbit stew

with Grace and Dave Calvert. This won out, obviously. How's Liam?'

'Oh, that's all in hand,' Gordy said. 'He's back home and I'm heading over later to have a proper chat with him and find out what's been going on.'

'Bullying?'

'Possibly,' Gordy said.

Gordy was replaced by Matt.

'How were they then, those rabbits?'

'Delicious,' Harry said. 'I'd have brought you some in, except we scoffed the lot.'

'Rightly so, too.'

'How are the two lights of your life?'

'Asleep,' Matt said, and Harry watched him stifle a yawn.

'Long night?'

'You could say that, yes,' Matt replied through a weary smile. 'Wouldn't swap it for the world, though.'

The rest of the team was over at the kettle, thoroughly engrossed in a conversation about the right level of brown required to be considered the perfect brew. Then, as Harry was about to bring everyone together, to inform them about what Sowerby's team had found in the fields by Agglethorpe, there was a knock at the office door. Matt went to answer it, but it was already opening.

'Now then,' said the figure standing in the door.

'Fred?' Harry said. 'Again?'

'It is,' Fred replied. 'Can't seem to keep away, can I? Anyway, I was passing through so just thought I'd pop in and ask about that chainsaw of mine.'

Harry had flashbacks to the day before, overlaid with images created by his imagination of exactly what he suspected Fred's chainsaw had been used for.

'Passing through?' Matt asked.

'Heading over to Sedbergh,' Fred said. 'Farmer I know out that way has some Fell Ponies. Beautiful things, they are. One of the mares has just given birth. So I'm heading over to wet the new foal's head, as it were. Good excuse for a bit of a natter as well, isn't it?'

Harry told Fred they had no news on the chainsaw yet.

'Well, not to worry,' he said. 'It's probably gone the way of all that stuff from over the way at Chris Black's place.'

Harry glanced at Matt, then at Fred.

'What stuff?'

'The stuff that he had nicked,' said Fred. 'That stuff. What else do you think I'm on about?'

Harry looked back at the team.

'Anyone know what Fred here is talking about?'

'Not a clue,' said Liz, as the others shook their heads.

'So no one knows of Chris Black being broken into?'

'I'm not making it up, if that's what you think,' Fred said.

'Didn't say that you were,' said Harry. 'It's just that this is the first any of us heard of it.'

'Maybe he never reported it, then,' Fred said. 'Sometimes, it's hard to see the point, seeing as we never get it back, do we? I've been lucky this time round, besides that chainsaw, obviously. It's because I go to chapel regular, no doubt.'

Harry glanced over at Jen.

'When you were looking through the files about the break-in over at Keith Sunter's—'

'I didn't find any mention of anything over at Chris Black's,' Jen said. 'It's not like there's been so many thefts in the area that any of us would forget, either.'

'I'm just telling you what I know,' Fred said. 'That's all.

It's a long time ago, mind. I might be wrong. Anyway, I'll be off.'

Fred made to close the door.

'When exactly was this?' Harry asked, catching Fred before he left. 'When Chris's stuff was taken?'

'Funny you should ask,' said Fred.

'Why?'

'It was the same night, as it happens. Whoever it was that did it, they went off with all that stuff from mine and a few things from his, too. I can't remember what. I don't think he ever actually told me. I wasn't about to pry, either.'

Harry's mind was in free-fall.

'So, you're saying that Chris Black was broken into two years ago on the same night as you and he never reported it?'

'That's what it sounds like to me,' said Fred.

And with that, he was gone.

The room was silent for a moment until Matt said, 'Well, that's a bit odd, isn't it?'

Harry wasn't listening. He was over at the board, staring, willing it to reveal something. Anything.

'What I don't get,' said Jim, 'is why it was only Fred who had his stuff returned?'

That was the question which was bothering Harry as well. Three break-ins on the same night; Keith's, Fred's and now Chris Black's, too. Then, two years after the fact, one of the victims—Keith Sunter—suffers the same, but he thwarts the burglar. The items taken from another of the victims—Fred Calvert—are returned a couple of days later. So, what about Chris Black? Why didn't he report the break-in? And why was his farm the only place not yet somehow part of this inves—

Harry's thoughts rammed into a brick wall in his mind so hard he nearly stumbled into Jadyn's board.

Matt's hand grabbed him.

'Boss? Something up?'

Harry stared at the map, at the line drawn from the severed foot found on the summit of Pen Hill belonging to Ian Wray—the thoroughly disliked friend of Keith Sunter's son, Anthony—a line which traced its way through the carefully laid out pieces of Ian's body, all the way to—

'Bloody hell ...'

Harry dropped his index finger onto the map.

'What is it?' Matt said, leaning in to see what Harry was pointing at.

'It goes right through it,' Harry said. 'Right through the middle of the bloody place!'

'What does?'

'The line!' Harry said. 'The bloody line!'

And before anyone could do anything, he'd snatched a set of keys from a table and was out of the door.

CHAPTER THIRTY-NINE

HARRY TORE OPEN THE DOOR OF ONE OF THE INCIDENT response vehicles parked in the marketplace, and leapt in, stabbing the key into the ignition. Matt threw himself in next to him, clipping himself in as he spoke.

'What the hell's going on, Harry? What is it?'

'Everything is going on!' Harry said, ignoring that Matt had just used his first name at work, something he rarely did, maybe had never done before. 'It's all been leading up to something, hasn't it? Absolutely everything! Bloody hell! Bloody shitting hell!'

Harry crunched the gear shaft into first and slammed his foot down on the accelerator, lights and sirens blaring.

'Where are we heading?' Matt asked. 'Come on, boss, tell me what you're thinking, what you saw on the map.'

'Something happened that night two years ago,' Harry said as they sped out of Hawes.

'We know that,' Matt said. 'Three break-ins on the same night as the Burning of the Bartle.'

'No, something else,' Harry said. 'And all of this is payback, someone getting revenge.'

'For what?' Matt asked.

Harry dropped a gear for a corner, took it fast enough to have Matt hold on white-knuckle tight.

'Right now, I'm still betting the house on it being Anthony,' Harry said. 'At least, I think it is. His blood was at the scene, wasn't it?'

'But no one's seen him, not since he burgled his own dad two years ago.'

'Exactly,' Harry said.

'I'm not seeing it,' Matt said.

Harry was pushing the car hard now along the straight before the hill up to Bainbridge. The fields and fells were a blur.

'It doesn't all quite make sense yet,' Harry said, 'but we need to get over to Chris Black's place as soon as we can.'

'Alive as well if that's possible,' Matt said.

Harry ignored Matt and kept his foot down.

'My guess right now is that Anthony and Ian were out together that night,' he said. 'They were doing a few jobs together; Keith's place, Fred Calvert's and Chris Black's, and something went wrong.'

Bainbridge zipped by, the Roman Fort at the other side gone in a moment.

'What, though?'

'One of the places they broke into, they disturbed the owner, or the owner disturbed them. Either way, that's when the shotgun came into play.'

'But we've got blood from Anthony and Ian's dead.'

'I think Ian was killed that night,' said Harry. 'Anthony, though, was only wounded.'

Aysgarth was soon racing down to meet them, the hill leading up to it falling behind them like water from a sluice.

'The only shotgun we know of is the one taken from Steve Hill's place,' Matt said.

'My money's on it being the same shotgun,' Harry said. 'We know Steve would go shooting with Chris, don't we? And he'd leave his gun over there in Chris' cabinet for those charity ones, right?'

'Makes sense,' Matt said as they hammered out the other side of Aysgarth and down the hill.

'Maybe Chris heard something or saw something or both, I don't know. But he grabbed the first gun in the cabinet, which was Steve's, a handful of cartridges, and headed out to scare the hell out of whoever it was trying to take his stuff. Only, he more than scared them.'

'He shot them, you mean?'

'Exactly that,' Harry said. 'He took the tyres out on the pick-up truck, then things went sideways.'

They raced across the river at the bottom of the hill, Harry dropping a gear to sweep them quickly up the hill on the other side and on towards West Witton.

'I think Anthony was wounded,' Harry continued. 'I also think Chris didn't realise he'd injured him. He fired that shotgun in the dark, and it's easy to make a mistake like that, particularly with a shotgun and when someone is running away from you. So, he sees who he thinks is Ian getting away with the stuff he's had stolen, sees red, shoots the tyres out, shoots at who he sees running away, can't find him, but he knows where he lives, right? That's the only way this makes any sense.'

'And he heads over there and blows the top of Ian's head off? Really?'

'You'd be amazed at what someone will do when rage takes hold,' Harry said. 'And Chris strikes me as someone who has plenty of it bubbling just beneath the surface. He's not like Steve, who seems to always be angry, is he? There's something held back within him. Something dangerous.'

At the top of the hill, a strange building peered at Harry and Matt from behind a tall wall on their left. Partially obscured by trees, the Temple Folly sat quietly on the Hawes side of West Witton, a building so odd and out of place, it was impossible to not notice. Harry had no idea as to its history, but the way it loomed was unnervingly ominous. And that seemed to fit all too well with the moment and what they were now racing towards.

'None of that explains the pick-up truck and trailer,' Matt said. 'Or Fred's stuff getting returned. Or Ian's body being cut up into pieces.'

'Anthony arrives back at the bungalow and finds Ian dead,' Harry said. 'He knows who's responsible. At this point, and I'm not too sure what happens or why, but something flips in Anthony's mind. As things can when a situation goes from bad to batshit crazy.'

They were racing through West Witton now, the village a smear of grey stone and a multi-coloured wash of cars.

'He can't go to the police because he'll be arrested, plus he'll have that injury I mentioned. And he can't have it looked at because more questions will be asked, but a few pellets he could probably deal with himself. Maybe there's some guilt, too, for doing something that ended up getting Ian killed. He wants Chris to know that he's coming for him, but it takes a while for the plan to come together.'

Harry took a right and Matt shook his head.

'Some of this hangs together,' the DS said, 'but only up to the bungalow. After that, it's a mess.'

'I know,' Harry said. 'But these things always are when you're trying to figure them out. The pick-up truck, Ian's body, all of that I can't explain, but the rest of it? Well, it's enough to have me more than spooked. And whatever this turns out to be in the end, I still think it's all been leading up to Chris Black. He wounded Anthony and killed Ian for doing his place over, and now someone not only wants to kill him, but for him to know that they're coming for him.'

'And you think that this someone is likely to be Anthony,' Matt said. 'Sounds like it, too, when you look at it all, doesn't it?'

A few minutes later, Agglethorpe filled the windscreen and Harry bounced the car along a track towards Chris Black's farm. It was the first time he'd been out to the place and he could hear dogs barking as he skidded to a stop, grit kicking up into the air.

'What's the plan?' Matt asked as he unclipped his seat belt.

'Plan? I don't have a bloody plan! We just need to find Chris and now!'

Matt was out of the car and off, legging it over to the house to hammer his fist into the door. As the sound of it mingled with Matt's shouts for Chris Black, Harry dashed past the house and on into the yard behind, the sound of dogs barking growing louder with each step.

'Chris? It's DCI Grimm,' Harry shouted. 'I need you to come with me. Now!'

Harry gave a moment for a reply, but none came.

He repeated the call, this time on the hoof, running across the yard, checking buildings.

Still nothing.

'Boss!'

Harry turned to see Matt jogging out of the back door of the house.

'Not there?'

Matt shook his head.

'Checked the whole place. Nice, it is, too. But he's not there. No sign of him at all. No, that's not true. Someone's had breakfast, I think, judging by what was in the kitchen sink.'

'And he lives alone, right?'

'I think that's why him and Steve got on,' said Matt. 'They had that in common, anyway.'

'Fred as well,' said Harry.

'No, Fred's one of a kind,' said Matt. 'For him, it's a choice. For Steve and Chris, not so much. Neither would be a catch to be proud of, would they?'

Harry cast his eyes around the yard.

'All I can hear are those dogs,' he said. 'I've been shouting, but there's been no response. Maybe Chris isn't here.'

Matt pointed at one of the outbuildings on the edge of the yard, darkness and shadows resting on what was inside.

'If that's here, then he's here,' Matt said.

'The Jag?'

'It is.'

'He could be out in the fields,' Harry suggested. 'Taken one of the tractors.'

'Looks to me like everything's here that should be,' said Matt looking around the yard. Harry did the same, saw no signs to suggest that anything was missing, or an empty space where a tractor would be parked. And with the place laid out as it was, it didn't look as though Chris Black was the kind of person to leave a vehicle just parked out in the yard for no reason; everything had a place and everything was in it, exactly where it should be.

The dogs were driving Harry to distraction, and he was clenching his fists tight as the barks and howls stabbed their talons into his nerves. He remembered then the visit he'd had from Agnes Hodgson.

'They don't bark like that all the time, do they?' he asked. 'It would drive me mad.'

'I'll go and shut them up,' said Matt. 'Might help us think.'

Matt walked off towards where the sound was coming from. Harry stood there, trying to think, to reason everything out, make sense of it, when Matt's voice cut into the moment.

'Harry!'

There was urgency in his tone, and Harry sprinted to where Matt had left the yard to enter one of the buildings.

'You've found him? Where is he? Is he okay?'

Inside, the noise from the dogs was even worse, crashing and clattering around the place, trying to escape.

Harry saw Matt. Then he saw the reason the DS had shouted his name.

CHAPTER FORTY

At the far end of what looked to Harry like a building which had, many years ago, been stables, he saw a thick shadow on the ground, the unmoving and unmistakable shape of a human body.

'It's Chris,' Matt said, but then his voice fell silent, choked by the sharp sting of a cocktail of sorrow, anger, and shock.

Harry walked over to stand beside the DS and rested a hand on his shoulder.

'This looks fresh,' he said.

Steam was in the cool air of the building, twisting up from the body and the catastrophic wounds it had suffered. The chest had been blown apart, its shattered form an open cage of exposed ribs and flesh like ground mince.

Stepping away from Matt, Harry examined the scene, detaching himself from the horror of it, forcing himself to be calm and collected. As he did so, Matt walked over to a pen where Chris' two, large chocolate brown Labradors were carrying on. The barking stopped as he reached in to let them lick his hands. He scratched their heads, talked to them, calmed them down enough for the barking to give way to snuffles.

Chris was lying on his back. Beside him lay a shotgun, his left hand still clasped around the stock and barrels.

'That's a twelve-bore,' Matt said. 'I can tell you that just by looking at it.'

'Not the weapon that killed him, then,' Harry said. 'Because this isn't self-inflicted.'

This end of the barn had no exit, Harry realised. So, Chris had been caught here, unable to get away. He'd armed himself, too, probably chased in here by his killer. It was impossible to know what had happened, but the result was the same; a man lying dead in a pool of his own blood, his chest blown apart, a messy tale told by shredded clothes, ruined flesh, and still-warm blood. The battlefield smell of it all Harry remembered of old and would probably never forget.

Around Chris, various items had been thrown, none of them the kind found or stored in an old, though well-maintained, stable.

Harry's eyes flitted from one object to the next. A roll of cash and a wallet, a gold bracelet and a couple of watches, a phone, other electronic devices including an expensive-looking food mixer and a digital radio, shoes and boots, and even a couple of paintings. And on top of it all, more than a little incongruously, sat a single white rose.

'He was chased in here,' Harry said, staring at the rose. 'Trapped. He knew what was going on, armed himself with that shotgun.'

'What little good it did him,' Matt said.

'Explains why the sight of those cartridges hit him like

they did when Jim went to see him. Why it sent him over to have words with Steve Hill. He suspected Steve knew something about what happened that night two years ago. He didn't, though. Couldn't have.'

Harry turned from the body to look around the stable. He saw marks scored into the wall just behind him, smashed brick and shattered wood.

'He got a couple of shots off,' he said, pointing at the damage. 'Probably fired from the hip, terrified, no aim, just desperation.'

'And with good reason, too,' Matt said.

'He would've been dead before he hit the ground, a wound like that,' Harry said. 'No doubt killed as he tried to reload.'

'And I'm guessing all that stuff around him, that's what was taken from his house the same night Fred's place was broken into.'

'And Keith's,' Harry said as he looked again at Chris' body. His eyes were open, staring blindly into the darkness of death and whatever lay beyond it.

Matt pointed at the white rose.

'That's a bit of an odd touch,' he said.

'I think they were Anthony's mum's favourite flower,' Harry explained, remembering seeing Keith tending to the same flowers on the traffic island in Hawes. The words on the plaque came back to him then: *You hold my heart still, and I will tend to your white rose.*

Harry's phone buzzed. He answered it.

'Harry? It's Rebecca.'

What was it with today and people using his first name? Harry thought.

'Good job you called,' he said. 'We've another crime

scene for you. It's a bit bloody as well, I'm afraid. If you can get over here as soon as you can, we can secure the scene. We need to find—'

'It's blood I'm calling you about, actually,' said the pathologist.

'How do you mean?'

'Well, I'll be firing someone later today because of it, that's for sure, but that's not your concern right now.'

'What is, then?'

A pause.

'The blood you found at the pick-up truck and covered with your jacket.'

'What about it? You matched it to Anthony and that's who we need to find considering what we're staring at right now.'

'Turns out it shows the same damage as the body parts.'

Harry's world swam.

'What?'

'The technical explanation has to do with the concentration of electrolytes found both inside and outside the cells, which I'll include in the report when I send it.'

'The technical explanation about what?'

'About the fact that the blood was frozen as well, Harry. Just like Ian's body.'

Harry stared at Matt and saw a frown growing on the DS's face, his brow the relief of a ploughed field.

'What are you saying?'

'I'm saying,' Sowerby explained, 'that just like Ian Wray's body, someone froze Anthony Sunter's blood at some point in the past, defrosted it, then left it at the crime scene for us to find.'

Harry went to say something, but his voice caught in his throat. Then a whisper escaped, his words barely audible.

'... *and I will tend to your white rose ...*'

'What was that, boss?' Matt asked.

'Rebecca, call the office,' Harry said down the phone. 'They'll tell you where Chris Black's farm is. I need you here right now.'

'What? Why? Where are you going?'

'To catch a killer,' Harry said, then looked over to Matt as he hung up. He pointed at Chris's body. 'Anthony didn't do this.'

'What?'

'Anthony, Keith's son, this wasn't him. None of it was.'

'But everything that you just said, your explanation for us driving over here in the first place,' said Matt. 'It was all about Anthony.'

'It was then, but it isn't now.'

Harry then told Matt what he'd learned from the call with Sowerby.

'Well, that makes no sense at all,' said Matt. 'Frozen blood? What the hell is going on?'

'Your white rose,' Harry said. 'That's what's going on.'

'That's the second time you've said that.'

'Why would he say it, though? Why would he call him a white rose?'

'Why would who call who a white rose?' Matt asked.

Harry was on his phone again and Jen answered.

'Boss?'

'Jen, I need you to find something out for me.'

'What's happened? Where are you?'

'Sowerby's going to call you,' Harry said. 'Give her the

address to Chris Black's farm. We're here now. Chris is dead.'

'What?'

'I'm heading over to Thoralby and I need you to do a quick bit of research.'

'Chris is dead? How? What happened?'

'Listen,' Harry said, turning from the body on the floor to head back out of the stables. 'Can you check if there's a connection between the name Anthony and white rose, or rose, or something like that? I know it doesn't make sense what I'm asking, but can you do that for me?'

'Yes, of course I can, but why?'

'A hunch,' Harry said. 'I'm leaving Matt here to secure the site and wait for Sowerby. Like I said, I'm heading over to Thoralby right now. I need to find Keith.'

'Keith Sunter?' Jen said. 'But he's here.'

Harry stopped in his tracks.

'What do you mean Keith's there? At the office? What are you talking about?'

'No, not at the office, he's in town,' Jen said. 'Well, at the bottom of town, anyway. The traffic island. You want me to go talk to him about this rose thing you're asking about?'

Harry shook his head.

'No, I bloody well don't,' he said, his voice stern and sharp. 'I want every road, every access to where he is right now, shut off. You understand?'

'Of course. But w—'

Harry wasn't listening.

'Pull the team in, get everyone down to that end of town, but don't spook him. Work quietly, work quickly, and make sure the only thing surrounding him is fresh air. But whatever you do, you all stay the hell away from him, you hear? Leave him alone. Leave him to me. I'm on my way.'

'Harry? You're not making any sense!'

'I'll be there as soon as I can.'

Harry hung up, and turned to face Matt.

'Sowerby's heading over,' he said. 'Shouldn't think she'll be too long, either.'

'And you're off to Hawes, I heard,' said Matt. 'So, what's all this about a rose, then?'

'It was there from the beginning, wasn't it?' Harry said, his frustration ripping up the edges of his words. 'That first break-in, right through to now.'

He broke into a run. Matt followed.

At the car, Harry yanked open the driver's door, dropping himself down into the driver's seat.

'I know you're going to drive like an idiot,' Matt said, 'but I tell you now, if I have to come out there in a few minutes and scrape what's left of you off the road, I'm not going to be happy.'

'I'll be careful,' Harry said.

'No,' Matt replied. 'Of course you won't. Just don't end up dead, that's all I ask. There's enough work to be done as it is without having to deal with that.'

Harry clipped in, started the engine, and floored it, spinning the vehicle around and then out of the yard to race back up the Dale to Hawes. In the rearview mirror he saw Matt offer a casual salute then head back into the stables.

CHAPTER FORTY-ONE

HARRY HAD THOUGHT THAT HE'D FIGURED EVERYTHING out; the bloody trail of body parts, the shotgun, everything that had been happening, but he'd been wrong. Not about all of it, true, but about enough of it to not prevent the death of Chris Black. Not that the man hadn't had it coming, after what Harry suspected had happened, resulting in the deaths of both Keith's son, Anthony, and Ian Wray, but it was no excuse, no reason enough for any of this. Two years in the planning, that's what this was. By a heart-broken man with nothing to lose.

Flying back up the Dale, he tried to get everything into order, but it all just kept on jiggling around, switching places. He hammered the palm of his hand into the steering wheel, teeth clenched, a roar managing to break through.

The temple zipped past once more, a blur of stone born from a creative and perhaps bizarre mind. Harry wondered about the state of Keith's own mind, the actual course of events which had flicked that switch in his head, sending him from the deepest grief to somewhere far beyond it, reaching into a place filled with endless darkness and no way out. And there the man had stayed, his focus no doubt clear on the course of events, their timing, everything. It always amazed Harry how, in the darkest, most despairing of times, the human mind could sometimes see the clearest. And be the most dangerous weapon of all.

Speeding down the hill, which tumbled out of Aysgarth like a waterfall, Harry felt almost weightless, not so much like he was driving, but flying, the tyres barely touching the road. He was willing himself on, faster and faster, reading the road far ahead, falling back on every single bit of driver training he had ever had, in the Paras and the police. Everything was smooth; his gear changes, his steering, his breaking, the car threading its way along the lane with nothing slowing it down.

When Hawes raced up to greet him, Harry didn't hold back, the blues and twos telling everyone to get the hell out of his way. The auction mart zipped past on his left, the Methodist Manse on his right, and there, at the bottom of the hill, he saw the traffic island, between him and it, Jadyn standing in the road, a small number of cars backed up in front of him.

Harry slowed just enough to avoid slamming into the car at the back of the queue, hooked himself onto the wrong side of the road, rolled down past the stationary traffic, saw Jadyn's eyes follow him, then brought the car to a dead stop, just in front of the old Rope Maker's shop. Keith Sunter was just visible in the traffic island.

Harry switched off the engine, climbed out of the car. He looked around, saw that his team had worked well to clear the area quickly; no pedestrians, no cars, everything was quiet, still, just the squeak of a swing moving in the breeze, a crow on the wind, the far-off call of a buzzard circling for food.

Walking round the front of his car, Harry made his way down the road, closing the short distance between himself and Keith. A break in the clouds sent shafts of sunlight to cut a line of gold across the road in front of him. He stepped through it and saw that Keith was kneeling in the hole he'd noticed earlier that day, dug into the flower bed. The man's head was bowed as though in prayer.

His phone buzzed. Harry took it from his pocket, glanced at the screen, and read a message from Jen. Then he called the man's name and Keith lifted his head. When he turned to face Harry, he gave a gentle nod and a sad smile, hung beneath dark eyes raw from tears.

'Whatever it is that you're thinking of doing, Keith,' Harry said, 'I think you've done enough, already, don't you? So, come on, let's have you out of there, okay? No more, now. It's over. Whatever all of this is or has been, you're done. Let's go somewhere and talk.'

Another shaft of sunlight broke through, throwing itself across the traffic island. Keith leaned his head back into it, basking in the golden heat.

'And I think it's only fair that I tell you I'm here to arrest you on suspicion of the murder of Christopher Black. You do not have to say anything, but it may harm your defence if you do not mention, when questioned, something which you later rely on in court. Anything you say may be given in evidence.'

'You delivered that well,' said Keith.

'Thank you,' Harry replied. 'I've had a bit of practice over the years.'

For a moment or two, neither man spoke, and Harry hoped that maybe Keith was going to give himself up. But then Keith started talking and Harry knew it wasn't going to be that easy. But then it never was, was it?

'The day we lost Helen, our lives ended,' Keith said, and he lifted his right hand to click his fingers. 'She was gone, just like that. One second, she was there and the next she wasn't. And Anthony, he saw it all, you know? Saw his mum die in front of him, her life smashed out of her by an idiot in a car right in front of his eyes.'

'I know,' Harry said. 'And it doesn't bear thinking about, what you both went through, how scarred Anthony was by it.' He then added, 'It might be worth my reminding you, Keith, that you're entitled to legal representation. Saying anything without it isn't advisable.'

'He was never the same,' Keith said, ignoring Harry. 'I tried, you know? I really tried to be there for him, to be both of the parents he needed, but I wasn't even able to be half the father I was, never mind both. I loved that kid. With every beat of my heart. I still do.'

Harry took the smallest of steps closer to Keith, trying in his mind to just allow the events to untangle themselves and fall into place.

'The break-in at the weekend,' he said. 'There wasn't one, was there, Keith? At your house, I mean? It was you. You did it yourself.'

'I knew the police would get involved as soon as everything started.' Keith sighed, as though the words themselves were lifting the weight of everything from his shoulders. 'It was a way of distracting you from the start, I suppose. Made me look like a victim, I think.'

'There was more to it than that, though. The rose in the pot.'

'That was a way of having Anthony there, from the

beginning, looking over it all, maybe. I'm not sure. I'm not sure of anything now. But what's done is done. Not everything has to make sense, does it?'

'No, it doesn't and it can't either,' Harry said. 'Helen's accident was exactly that, an accident. We can't control everything, make sense of it all. Life's not like that, Keith. Never has been, never will be, either.'

'And we try and make the best of it, I know,' Keith replied. 'But it makes you wonder why, doesn't it? What the bloody hell is the point of it all?'

Another step ...

'Not really, no,' Harry said. 'We can't wrap ourselves, the people we love, in cotton wool, can we? What kind of life would that be like for anyone?'

'A safe one.'

'I'm sure you did your best with Anthony,' Harry continued. 'I doubt anyone could've done any better. He has to take some responsibility for his own life. Not much, maybe, but enough to not have you bear responsibility for everything. And you can't go through life shouldering all of that blame. You didn't kill Helen.'

Keith laughed, but what warmth there was in it, went out quicker than a match's flame in a hurricane.

'No, you're right, I didn't, but I failed him anyway.'

'So, you faked your break-in and then took Steve's shotgun,' Harry said.

He knew now that he needed to keep Keith talking. The man was planning something, though what, he wasn't sure. And the longer he kept him speaking, the better chance he had of either talking him out of it or getting close enough to stop him.

'I knew when he'd be at church,' Keith said. 'And I'd

taken his keys a while back, when I was around at his surveying that barn for the conversion. I put them back, he never knew.'

'You knew Chris had used it on Anthony.'

Keith gave a nod.

'I found those cartridges when I drove over to Anthony. They were just lying there on the verge. Steve was always over at Chris' shooting, and I knew he used a twenty-bore. I shoot a bit myself, you see? Most folk around here do.'

'But why the dog shit?'

At this Keith really laughed.

'Couldn't resist it,' he said. 'I took the opportunity to mess with him a bit more.'

Harry tracked back to the break-in at Steve Hill's farm.

'It was you that Steve Hill recorded on his camera, wasn't it? You were wearing Ian's jacket. You let yourself in.'

'And ripped the cabinet out with a tow rope attached to my Defender,' said Keith. 'Nice and simple. The cabinet itself wasn't exactly easy to break into, but I managed it in the end. Went through a few drill bits, though.'

So, that's three events down, Harry thought. What was next? And why was Keith just kneeling there in the hole? What was he planning?

'Two years ago, then,' Harry said, taking another step closer to Keith, hoping not to spook him. 'Anthony and Ian, they broke into your house, then I guess they went over to Chris' place and then onto Fred's.'

'Anthony was actually alone that night,' said Keith, 'when he broke in, I mean. I didn't stop him. It just made me so sad, all of it. And to have him there, to confront him in my own house—*his* house—it crushed me. If he'd needed money, all he had to do was ask. What the hell had I done to get everything so wrong that he didn't think he could come to me? He did the other two places that same night. Chris saw him and took the law into his own hands.'

'And you're sure it was Chris?' Harry asked.

'I know it was.'

'How do you know?'

At this, Keith looked at Harry and tears were streaming down his cheeks, shining rivulets of water flowing with ease.

'I know because Anthony called me,' he said. 'But by then it was already too late.'

CHAPTER FORTY-TWO

'YOU DON'T HAVE TO TELL ME WHAT HAPPENED,' HARRY said. 'I'm not here for a confession, and like I said, legal advice is sensible, no matter the circumstances. I just need you to climb out of that hole and come over here, Keith. That's all. You can do that for me, can't you?'

Keith didn't move.

'I knew something was up as soon as I heard him on the phone,' he said, Harry's words dying before they'd even reached him. 'It was in his voice, you know? The fear of what was happening to him, that he was ... That he was dying.'

Keith's voice broke on his words, smashed to pieces by the harsh finality of them and the weight of the memory they were forcing him to relive.

'But he called me,' he continued. 'Right then, at the end. He called me, his father. And he asked me to come and take him home.'

'You went to him, then?'

And this was the part of the events Harry wasn't clear on, that night two years ago.

'Of course I went to him,' Keith said, his voice cracking with emotion, the events of that night clearly still raw in his mind. 'I drove like an idiot, not that it made any difference. I found him huddled under a bush, hiding from Chris.'

'How did he know that's who it was?' Harry asked. 'It would've been dark, he'd been shot, in shock.'

'He'd seen him,' Keith said. 'That's how. Anthony told me that someone shot the pick-up's tyres out first and then, when he tried to run, shot him in the back. He saw who it was as he crawled away in the dark, already dying. He saw that it was Chris.'

'Bloody hell,' Harry said. 'That poor kid.'

'Chris came after him, couldn't find him. I think he thought the person he'd shot had got away from him. And he wouldn't have liked that, not Chris. Which is why he then drove over to the bungalow.'

'To finish the job.'

'I'm pretty sure he didn't realise it was Anthony he'd shot,' Keith said. 'Maybe he didn't even realise he'd actually shot anyone at all. Regardless, he thought it was Ian that he'd seen. Told me as much himself today when I finally confronted him. They looked the same with their short hair. And it was dark. He'd have recognised the vehicle. And Ian has, or had, a reputation.'

'Why did no one ever report him, then?'

'They did,' said Keith. 'But Ian always had an alibi: Anthony.'

'Clever.'

'No, not clever,' Keith hissed, venom spitting from his lips. 'That shitty little bastard used my son! And he deserved what happened to him, what Chris did. The world's a better place without him in it.'

Harry was close enough now to jump over the small fence and grab Keith. But as the thought crossed his mind, he spotted something lying in the dirt; a shotgun. Steve's, he guessed. He had no idea if it was loaded. And he wasn't about to take any chances. Not yet.

Keith was still talking.

'I held Anthony as he died. My own son, breathing his last, in my arms. I was covered in his blood. But I didn't cry. There was nothing left in me then, I realised. Nothing at all. I was empty. I still am. Helen was gone and now my son. And for what? A watch, some money ... Was that really all his life was worth?'

'No,' Harry said. 'It wasn't. Everyone knows that, Keith. And so do you, I'm sure.'

'And I'm supposed to just go on with it, am I? Just deal with it all, accept what happened, learn to live with my grief? How? How am I supposed to do that? You can't tell me can you, Detective? No one can.'

Harry said nothing.

'I drove him home like he asked. It was where he wanted to be. Then I went back to where Chris had shot him.'

'You didn't think to call the police?'

'I'd promised Helen, hadn't I, to look after him? I'd failed. But I wouldn't fail again. It was for me to sort out, my responsibility. I had to do what I did.'

'No, you didn't,' Harry said, but Keith didn't act like he heard him.

'I took the quad bike off the trailer, then switched the trailer from the pick-up to my Defender,' Keith explained, as though everything he had done was normal, the kind of thing anyone would do on any given day. 'Then I drove the pick-up onto the trailer and took it back to my place like that, hid it in the garage. Then I just headed back out with the trailer again to grab the quad. By the time Chris came home, the scene was clean. Easy, really.'

'The demijohns back at yours,' Harry said, remembering another detail. 'You make your own wine, don't you?'

'Actually yes, I do,' said Keith. 'It's good stuff, too. You can have a few bottles if you want. Can't see that I'll be having any myself, now.'

'There was yeast found in the treads of the pick-up. Brewing yeast, I should think. But why take everything?'

'I wanted everything from those last moments. I didn't want anyone to touch them. They were a part of Anthony, paid for with his blood. And I wanted Chris to think that maybe Anthony had taken everything anyway, you see? That after what he'd done, he had still lost.'

Keith laughed then, but the sound came out as cold as an arctic winter.

'Can you imagine how angry he would have been? Coming back home, thinking he'd dealt out a bit of proper justice, ready to collect his stuff, only to find that it was all gone anyway, that he'd killed someone for nothing? Keeping Fred's stuff added to it. And there was no way that Chris could report the theft, was there? Not after what he'd done. So, I made him live with it all. For two whole years. Can you imagine that? Two years thinking he'd got away with murder.'

'Why wait so long?' Harry asked.

'Revenge is a dish best served cold,' Keith said. 'And I wanted it to chill him to the fucking bone.'

Harry heard ice shatter in Keith's voice.

'He'd have blamed Anthony for everything being gone

when he arrived home,' Keith continued. 'Probably thought Ian had called him that night or something. I don't know. It was a fun game to play. For me, anyway.'

'So you went to the bungalow,' said Harry, realising now how twisted Keith's mind had become that night. 'Took Ian's body away.'

'I drove over there to collect anything that had belonged to Anthony, anything that would remind me of him. I hadn't expected to find Ian dead.'

'I'm sure,' said Harry.

'Chris had always been so vocal at the Burning of the Bartle. Him and Steve, every year, they'd go on and on about how what was needed was a bit of local old-fashioned justice. Well, I wanted him to know that was exactly what was coming for him and that there was no escaping it.'

There was a wildness in Keith's eyes now, and Harry knew he'd have to make a move soon.

'On Pen Hill Crags he tore his rags,' Keith said. 'The Bartle poem starts there, so that's where I laid the first piece of Ian, the rest leading all the way to Chris' door. I knew Angie would be up there the following day. I used to run a lot myself, too, so I knew she would be there. She runs that route regular as clockwork. And Ian's foot would be impossible to miss.'

Harry noticed Keith's trainers, remembering them from when he'd first met him over at Clare and Paul's.

'I had to empty my chest freezer to store him,' Keith said, then he laughed and added, 'Ate a lot of fish fingers for a day or two, I can tell you.'

Another detail surfaced in Harry's mind.

'You used Fred's chainsaw to cut up the body.'

'Didn't have my own,' Keith said. 'It wasn't a pleasant task, but by the time I got round to it, he was just frozen meat, really.'

That was quite the statement, Harry thought, *frozen meat*.

'You returned Fred's things,' he said.

'When I put the pick-up back, yes,' Keith replied. 'I had no need of them. They were his. And it would mess with Chris' head even more, wouldn't it? Can you imagine what he must have been feeling these last few days? Knowing that someone knew what had happened?'

'I can, yes,' Harry said. 'But you still had one final thing to do.'

Keith smiled.

'I drove over to Chris' place with everything Anthony had taken from him. Chris had heard about Ian's body being found—news travels fast in the Dales—and was screaming at me when I arrived.'

Harry could well imagine the terror Chris had felt when Keith had turned up at his house.

'What did he say?'

'Not enough for me to spare him from me doing to him what he'd done to Anthony,' said Keith. 'He had his own gun with him. He'd been expecting Anthony. When he realised it was me, I don't think he could believe it.'

'What happened?' Harry asked, remembering the scene he'd found at Chris' farm.

'He shot first,' Keith said. 'Raised his gun and took a shot at me in the yard. He missed, then ran off into the stables in a panic.'

'You followed him.'

'He wasn't thinking straight. The building was a dead end. He tried again, both barrels this time. While he was reloading, his fingers fumbling with trying to get a couple of cartridges into his gun, that's when I looked him in the eyes and told him exactly what he'd done.'

Harry was readying himself for something now. He just wasn't sure what.

'He didn't believe me. Like I said, he thought Anthony was behind it all because he'd killed Ian, that he'd come back for some revenge or something. Can you believe that?'

'Yes,' Harry said. 'I thought it was Anthony as well.'

'Laughable really,' Keith said. 'How could he do anything when he's here?'

At this, Harry was confused and immediately looked around where they were both positioned, half expecting Anthony to walk out from behind a bush. But that was impossible.

'What do you mean, he's here?' He asked. 'Where? He's dead, Keith. You've just told me that yourself.'

Keith patted the soil gently.

Harry dropped his eyes to the flower bed, the hole Keith was kneeling in. *No ...*

'I've tended to this place since we lost Helen,' Keith explained, his voice calm and collected. 'I talk to her when I'm here. I couldn't bury Anthony at home and I couldn't bury him at church; both those options would have meant everyone knowing. So, he's here, where he lost his mum, where I lost my wife.'

Harry shook his head.

'Anthony is buried here?'

'I just came over late one night, when Hawes was asleep.

They're together now, you see? We all are. I took some of his blood, just in case. Froze that, too. Used it when I dropped off the pick-up. Another little detail I suppose. Maybe that was too much. Still, there we are and here we are.'

The message Harry had received from Jen a few minutes ago now made sense.

'Anthony,' he said, his voice quiet. 'The name, it's from the Ancient Greek word Anthos, isn't it?'

'To describe a rose or a flower,' said Keith.

'And you buried him here, beneath them.'

'I did,' said Keith. 'And it's over now, it's done.'

Keith turned and looked up at Harry who saw pain in the man's eyes, a pain he doubted would ever ease, the wounds he'd not only taken but caused himself, and so deep that healing would be impossible. He also saw a calm acceptance.

Then Keith picked up the shotgun.

Without a thought for his own safety, Harry threw himself over the fence, his body slamming into Keith like a freight train. The shotgun was knocked from Keith's hands and landed in the dirt. Keith roared in shock and anger and desperation.

'No, please, you can't! I have to be with them! I have to! Please!'

Harry had a serious weight and strength advantage, but Keith was wriggly and slight. He squirmed in Harry's grip, reaching for the shotgun, fingers clawing in the dirt for purchase.

Harry didn't want to hurt Keith, but neither was he about to let the man finish this the way that he wanted to, by ending his own life. He pinned Keith's arms to the ground, his own muscles burning as he struggled to stay on top.

One of Keith's arms wriggled free. It shot forward, fingers touching the shotgun, but Harry yanked it back.

'Jadyn!' Harry shouted, but the constable was already there, and Harry saw him reach over to quickly take the shotgun. Then he jumped over the fence to join Harry, and Keith, at last, struggled no more.

'You okay, boss?' Jadyn asked as he placed cuffs on Keith's wrists.

Harry could think of no immediate reply as Keith's body was racked with sobs, his sorrow falling onto the white roses as tears.

He stood up and with Jadyn's help pulled Keith to his feet.

'Come on, Keith,' he said. 'It's over.'

'I know,' Keith said, and Harry guided him gently away from the grave of his son.

WHEN THE WEEKEND CAME AROUND, Harry really wasn't in the mood for viewing properties or for that matter talking to an estate agent who would no doubt be wearing a bad suit and too much aftershave. The events of the past week had been traumatic for the whole team, the whole Dale in fact.

Keith was in custody, the body of his son, Anthony, had been recovered from the traffic island at the bottom of town, and now there would be an awful lot of paperwork. Harry hoped that anyone still thinking that taking the law into their own hands was a good idea, would now be thinking twice about doing so.

He was standing in the hallway of his flat, busying himself with putting on his jacket. It was taking a lot longer than usual and Harry knew that he was stalling. Grace was ready at the door, Smudge at her side.

'You okay?' Grace asked.

'I am,' Harry said, at long last finishing doing up his jacket, but then checking each of his pockets, though for what exactly he had no idea.

'No, you're not.'

'No, you're right, I'm not,' Harry said. 'But I will be.'

'You're not buying anything today, you know that, don't you?'

'I might do,' Harry said. 'You never know.'

'That would be very impulsive.'

'I can be impulsive.'

Grace laughed.

'Yes, you can, when a life is on the line or whatever, but that's work and this is, well, it's your life, isn't it? And that's a little different. It's not really life and death.'

Harry hadn't told Grace all of the details about what had been going on, he never would do, either. It was confidential for a start, plus he didn't want to go putting stuff on her to think about when he was more than capable of dealing with it himself. Probably not the best for his mental health, he knew that, but right now, that was the choice he was making. He had told her enough though, he realised, for her to put two and two together. Plus, everyone knew what had happened in Hawes with Keith. An event like that was difficult to keep a lid on.

Grace came over to stand in front of Harry.

'All you're doing is viewing a few houses. That's it. It'll hopefully give you an idea of what you want, that kind of thing. There's no pressure. It'll be fun. I promise.'

'That's quite a promise,' Harry smiled, drawn to Grace's

enthusiasm for the day ahead, the warmth in her eyes helping him to relax a little.

'You've had a tough week. Let it go for a few hours. Enjoy a bit of normality.'

Harry was momentarily back at the traffic island, struggling with Keith, the shotgun right there, the smell of the dirt, Anthony buried somewhere beneath them. A tough week didn't come anywhere close to describing what it had actually been like.

'This feels strange without Ben, though,' he said.

'He's living his own life now,' Grace said, reaching out a hand to rest gently on Harry's arm.

'Moving in with Liz, I know,' Harry said. 'It's a big step for him. Hard to believe where he was a year ago.'

Harry thought back to when Ben had told him. His brother had been out with Liz the night Dave had been around with the rabbits. Apparently, it had been Liz's idea and they'd had a long chat about it over a bottle of wine and a takeaway. And he'd told Harry the following day, after the events with Keith.

'I'm proud of him,' Harry said, remembering the bright lights of happiness in Ben's eyes, the excitement in his voice, the words tumbling out of him.

'He knows that.'

'I hope so,' Harry said.

Something tapped against Harry's leg. He glanced down to see Smudge. She stared back up at him with her huge brown eyes, her tail thumping gently on the floor.

'I see you're ready then,' he said, and the dog's tail thumped a little harder.

Harry led the way along the hall and pushed open the door. Outside, the day was turning itself from grey to gold,

Hawes was busy and alive. The storm which had played its merry hellish dance in the skies over the last few days had finally been swept away by something brighter. The air was rich with scents rolling in from the fells, of moorland and grass and stream. God, this place is beautiful, Harry thought.

Grace's hand slipped into his.

'Come on,' she said, and with a gentle tug, pulled him forward into something new.

If you enjoyed the grisly goings-on in *Blood Trial*, you'll love Harry's next chilling case. Grab your copy of Fair Game today!

JOIN THE VIP CLUB!

SIGN up for my newsletter today and be first to hear about the next DCI Harry Grimm crime thriller. You'll receive regular updates on the series, plus VIP access to a photo gallery of locations from the books and the chance to win amazing free stuff in some fantastic competitions.

You can also connect with other fans of DCI Grimm and his team by joining The Official DCI Harry Grimm Reader Group.

Enjoyed this book? Then please tell others!

The best thing about reviews is they help people like you: other readers. So, if you can spare a few seconds and leave a review, that would be fantastic. I love hearing what readers think about my books, so you can also email me the link to your review at dciharrygrimm@hotmail.com.

AUTHOR'S NOTE

The Burning of Old Bartle is an annual ceremony and takes place in West Witton on the evening of the Saturday closest to St Bartholomew's Day in August. An effigy of Old Bartle is carried through the village, stopping at various houses along the way, to recite the poem you read at the start of this book, and to also allow those carrying him to have a couple of drinks. At the end of the night, Old Bartle is thrown against a wall, stabbed and burned. One theory as to the origin of this tradition is that Old Bartle was a sheep rustler who was chased around the area by the locals until they caught him outside the village and finished him off. It's a wonderfully gruesome tale and I couldn't resist using it as the background for *Blood Trail*. 'Shout lads, shout!'

ABOUT DAVID J. GATWARD

David had his first book published when he was 18 and has written extensively for children and young adults. *Blood Trail* is his tenth DCI Harry Grimm crime thriller. For more information:

www.davidjgatward.com

Dave love's to hear from readers so drop him a line at:

dciharrygrimm@hotmail.com

 facebook.com/davidjgatwardauthor

ALSO BY DAVID J. GATWARD

THE DCI HARRY GRIMM SERIES

Made in United States
North Haven, CT
29 June 2022

20759006R00198

BLOOD TRAIL

A gruesome tradition, a blood-spattered crime scene, and a killer hiding in plain sight.

Detective Harry Grimm is a worried man. When a group of vigilante locals start patrolling the Dales in response to a recent spate of crimes, he is forced to warn them off. Things only get more complicated when he is called out to multiple crime scenes—each with plenty of blood but no bodies.

Very soon, though, body parts start turning up. Delivered in a way that echoes a local poem and an old-but-grisly village ceremony. Faced with the bloody evidence in front of him, Grimm soon realises that his worst fears have come true: someone has already taken the law into their own hands.

With an ancient tradition being used to commit modern-day murder, can this battle-scarred detective stop the lanes of the Dales running red with blood?

Blood Trail is the tenth book in the riveting Harry Grimm police procedural series. If you like compelling characters, twisting plots, and beautiful British countryside settings, then you'll love David J. Gatward's nail-biting mystery.